RECIPE
FOR
A
WITCH

Recipe For A Witch

Bea Alexander

ISBN 978-0-939613-67-0

Cover Design by Caroline Murphy
Edited by Ross Edwards

Chapter 1
I Make a Fateful Decision

I never knew I had a special destiny. Maybe, as a child, there were clues, but no one ever said anything that even remotely suggested I was different or special or endowed with gifts beyond imagining. I realize now that was because they didn't know, either. By the time I left home, all I knew was I liked to cook and I was pretty good at it. Not that I thought there was any magic in my talent. It was rather by default that I had even started cooking.

My mother never set foot in the kitchen unless it was to open the back door for a delivery. Her idea of cooking a wholesome meal was calling Hang Wu's on nineteenth street and ordering lo mein. Every other night. Or pizza from Al's around the corner. Al's cardboard boxes spent more time in our kitchen than she ever did. So I took up cooking as a simple survival skill.

I guess that's what led to my decision, how it changed my life forever, and how I discovered that there are such things as witches who cast spells and have magic in their fingertips. If you think about it, cooking is a kind of magic. I mean, you take a bunch of things like flour and butter and eggs and mix them together and pop them into a hot box and out comes something puffy and delicious that impels you to eat it. Those ingredients are like a seed you plant in the earth. That tiny seed, that you could just as easily ignore as a speck of nothingness, contains all the knowledge to reach for the sun and grow into something beautiful—even enormous. We take such everyday miracles for granted and never really think about the magic behind them.

❋

I had always thought of myself as completely ordinary. I mean, everyone is an individual and all that, but I always felt like I blended in, that nothing about me stood out. Not like my ex-beauty-queen, gorgeous mom, Foxy. Real name Roxanne. Roxanne Anders. From Pete Anders, pro football star turned sportscaster and all-around (you'll excuse the expression) D-bag. He's not my father, at least not my bio father who died before I was born—or so I had been told. I never truly bought that story. I'm not sure why. Maybe wishful thinking.

You couldn't even say Pete Anders was the man who raised me, because he was never really interested in me, so we never hung out or anything. He was just the guy whose shoes were in my mom's bedroom until the day they—and he—were gone. It was ugly for a lot of reasons, mostly because he left us absolutely, abjectly broke.

That same year Nick and I started dating and my class was assigned *The Diary of Anne Frank*. That book inspired me to start a journal. I still keep a running commentary on my life and everything that happens around me. Also that year I was heavily into the goth thing. Black everything and silver jewelry, what little I could afford.

Foxy used to say, "Amanda Anders, don't you realize the world is full of color? Black is for funerals and the odd cocktail party when you wear a little black dress with some dangly earrings to add some sparkle."

"I know, Foxy," I stopped calling her "mom" the day I realized Pete Anders would be our downfall. It was also when I realized my drop-dead gorgeous mother had packing peanuts for brains. "And I wish you wouldn't call me 'Anders.' He is not, and never will be, my dad."

At that point Foxy would waft out of the room with a final sigh, leaving behind the scent of Chanel Number Five (purchased at an outlet mall for half price). Everything about our situation was embarrassing and I was in no mood to try to fit in at school or anywhere else. I mean, like, I just wanted to crawl into a cave and hide until I was at least twenty-five. Nick was the only thing keeping me sane. After he graduated, we promised to stay together, but then he went off to Cal Tech in Pasadena. It might as well have been Jupiter's moon Europa.

That left me plenty of time to pester Foxy about my bio dad. But whenever I asked about him, I got a stone wall. Something—I had no idea what—propelled me to find out anything I could about him. It's like I was obsessed, especially after Nick was gone. Where were the wedding pictures? Where were all the relics of the past? There were plenty of framed pictures of Foxy the beauty queen scattered around our house. Of my grandmomma. Of garden parties and college dances and sorority sisters. But where was HE?

Then, one day, after I found a battered banker's box at the bottom of Foxy's closet, I pulled out one old photo. On the back of it in a neat script in blue ink was written, "Jack, Pasadena" and that was all. The faded color picture was no more than three inches high, of a man staring out from in front of a nondescript building. He had sandy-colored hair and wore a tweed jacket and green tie. He was holding what looked like some sort of bridle and he had on tall black boots—tight, like the kind equestrians wear—and his pants were a light beige. He was smiling broadly. And he was handsome, elegant even, and when I found the picture, I felt an unfamiliar tingling in my fingertips. It was almost like an electric current had somehow reached me, but I was nowhere near any outlet or fixture.

From the moment I found that picture, I decided I had to get to Pasadena, even though, at the time, I had no idea where that was. It was right after we'd moved from our big house in a fancy neighborhood to a rowhouse where Foxy had to rent out the top floor and the basement as apartments to pay the mortgage after she sold our other house and paid off all the debts Anders had left behind. All he left me was a last name. Thanks a lot, muscle for brains.

So here I was, having ignored Foxy's demand that I go to cooking school somewhere close and live at home for free. By then I knew Pasadena was in California and, by some miracle, I got myself a partial scholarship to Napa Culinary College (AKA NCC) and, by working about a thousand odd jobs after school, during vacations and in the summer, I had at least enough cash to get myself from Virginia to San Francisco. What I would do after that was a huge blank space—except Nick was in Pasadena at Cal Tech and I figured that's where I was meant to be.

I was desperate to be with Nick again. We'd started dating my junior year, much to everyone's astonishment, especially mine. Nick was a really sweet guy a year ahead of me at school. When he took a liking to me, it was such a mystery that I thought there must have been something basically wrong with him that no one could see. But he wasn't any kind of outcast or anything. He was a senior and popular in a quiet sort of way. Lots of girls wanted to date him. He was like the most boy-next-door guy you'd ever want to meet.

I did find out that Nick had his troubles, though. One day, while we were both avoiding going home after school, we ended up on a trail in Rock Creek Park and sat down just to enjoy the trees and the sound of the creek burbling along.

"My mom left a few years ago," Nick said without any warning so I could at least prepare what to say to that startling news.

"My dad thinks she ran off with some guru who started a cult in California. My dad says there's a lot of that 'out there,' which is the main reason I applied to Cal Tech instead of MIT. Maybe if I'm there—you know, in California—I can find her."

He stopped talking and I was kind of dumbfounded. At least Foxy didn't walk out on me. Of course, there were plenty of times that I had thought about walking out on her.

"I'm sorry, Nick." It was all I could think of to say. It felt to me like we were in a lifeboat together. And then, for some reason I added, "I've always thought my real father was in California, too. That's weird."

We just sat there, listening to the creek, and didn't say anything else.

After his senior year, when he went off to Cal Tech, I missed him like mad, as if I'd had an arm severed, and I had to endure my senior year alone. He promised to keep in touch and made me promise to come out to see him if he couldn't get home for the holidays. That seemed like a fantasy because where was I going to get the money to fly all the way to California? From Foxy? Get real.

That summer, right after Nick graduated, his dad passed away from a really aggressive cancer, leaving him with all the stuff you have to do when a parent dies. He was really busy and sad and kept saying I was the only thing that he cared about now and, if it wasn't for me, he'd never come back east. His dad had willed everything to him, so he sold the house they'd lived in—Nick said there was no way he could take care of it while he was in school, and, anyway, he didn't want to remember his dad dying there. He did keep his battered BMW.

With the money he'd gotten from the house and his dad's life insurance, Nick could pay for any school that would accept him. He was one of the smartest guys at our high school, and a lot of colleges were recruiting him his senior year. He could have gotten a scholarship, too, but he said he didn't want to owe anything to anybody.

Even though I hadn't yet told Foxy, we'd talked about me going to culinary school on the West Coast so I could help him look for his mom. It seemed as if we might make a go of it. But long-distance relationships are pretty tough to maintain, and ours kind of lagged and then sagged in the middle. We didn't have so much in common anymore, and the things that had kept us together—like problems at home—were no longer there. I was a senior stuck in high school in Virginia and he was out in exotic, new California. In the background was the thought that, one day, we'd be back together and closer than before because we'd be focused on the same thing: finding his mother. For now, he was with a bunch of brainiacs studying things like nuclear engineering.

What is that, anyway? I looked it up because he started texting me about it and I was completely and utterly lost. Like in a total mental wasteland. So, in case you want to know, my good friend, Mr. Wikipedia, explained to me that it's the branch of engineering concerned with the application of the breakdown of fission as well as the fusion of atomic nuclei and/or the application of other sub-atomic physics, based on the principles of nuclear physics.

Well, obviously, his new fission-rich life had no place in it for me. Or so I thought.

Chapter Two
I Say Hello to California (and Emilio)

I arrived in San Francisco with a few pieces of clothes, very little money, and no place to live. My scholarship covered half my tuition for the first year of culinary school, but that's all. I'd worked three jobs that summer, so maybe I could afford to rent a furnished room in someone's basement while I learned the craft of cooking. Besides, this decision put me in the same state as Nick. We hadn't seen each other in eight months and, finally (finally!) we could get together. Although I had no extra money—even for bus fare to get from northern California way down to Pasadena—I figured somehow we'd manage.

The el-cheapo flight from Washington D.C. to San Francisco must have touched down at every airport across the whole country so that, by the time we got there, I was red-eye tired and grumpy.

It was Monday, and disoriented as I was, still dragging my rollaway behind me like a reluctant dachshund, I went straight to the student help office to find a place to live. Mrs. Mendosa, a pleasant enough woman sitting at a desk in front of a computer, asked my name and other pertinent data and then clicked away for a few minutes.

"This takes a little time," she nodded at her computer. "They keep promising new faster ones, but ..." she shrugged. I could see a screen appear, looking like some kind of list. "Ah, finally. Let's see now. I did this for quite a few other students who arrived earlier than you did, so I'm afraid this list has been picked over, especially for housing near school and reasonably priced." She squinted at the screen and leaned in for a closer look. "Well, this is odd. It wasn't here earlier today. A guard's cottage on the grounds of The Manor. Well, well. Fancy. The Manor is just over there."

She pointed vaguely, as though we could actually see anything outside her windowless cubicle.

"And look at the price. A steal. Aren't you the lucky girl? It's only one room, but most of the students rent studio apartments or a room in someone's house, so that's not a drawback." She shrugged and tapped the print button, then handed me the paper listing.

"I would get myself right over there if I were you. Wouldn't want anyone else to snap it up. The instructions are all there on the printout."

I thanked her and headed for the street while reading the listing. It said the key would be hanging on a hook next to the door and to go ahead in and bring my things. When I saw the cottage and where it was situated just inside the perimeter of a gated estate, I was so thrilled I didn't question my luck or the fact that I wasn't required to give a damage deposit or two months' rent or anything up front. I took down the key—a huge old iron thing that looked like it could have been used for a prison cell during the French Revolution—and unlocked the door to the cutest one-room cottage imaginable. Old, with a beamed ceiling and an uneven floor, it had four small windows and you could see the original stone walls both outside and inside. It was cozy and had the feeling that maybe an elf might have lived there once a long time ago. It felt almost as if I'd been expected.

My very first assignment at culinary school not only came out of the oven as flat as it had gone in, but it was stuck so tight to the bottom of the pan that it simply would not release. With everyone in the class snickering at me, it was all I could do not to start bawling right there over my school-supplied Sunbeam Mixmaster 2371.

At that moment, even taking into account all my reasons for being there, I was sure that coming out to San Francisco to get a culinary degree—rather than going to college back East like the rest of my senior class—had to be the worst decision of my life. What was I thinking?

With me standing at my cooking station and that contemptuous cow-patty of a cake staring up at me, in walked the most gorgeous man I'd ever seen. He stood just inside the door, surveying the class, his gaze moving leisurely from student to student. Even though I'd come all the way to San Francsico to at least be in the same state as Nick, I admit I was absolutely riveted when this elegant older man's gaze landed on me at workstation number eight. It was like I'd been bewitched or something, and suddenly I understood why men were always falling all over themselves when Foxy showed up.

If, in the moment, I could have managed to think clearly, I might have noticed a certain electric feeling at my fingertips, like a faint shock. It passed quickly but later I would remember it as the exact same feeling I'd had when I touched the photo of Pasadena man.

"Class," announced Ms. McCracken, the dean of NCC, "I want you to meet the renowned Chef Emilio, this semester's visiting professor of culinology, who's come all the way from Tuscany to teach first-year students. You have no idea how lucky you are, class. It's not often an important chef takes time out of his busy schedule to teach novice student chefs. We're just thrilled to have him here," she gushed like a broken water main. "I want you to give him your warmest welcome," she added after chest-heaving in a reserve gulp of oxygen.

Warmest welcome? Absolutely no problem, I thought, while trying desperately to figure out how to deep-six this underperforming Bundt. But there it was, sitting right on top of my work counter with me standing over it so that no one, especially not this Tuscan hunk-'o-chef, could possibly mistake my tortilla-look-alike for anyone else's abject failure. No, that crown belonged right on my head. So I decided to own it.

"Ah," breathed Tuscan Chef hunk with a decidedly magnetic Italian accent. "I see you are making Bundts today."

He slowly surveyed the room, counting heads, no doubt—sizing us up, figuring out where to expend his energies on the most promising of us neophyte spatula wielders.

As he ambled around the room from table to table, making comments on various cakes, connecting with students, he nodded approval. Until he arrived at mine. Which is when I almost lost it. Not only because my cake was such a piece of misery, but also because the man had eyes that could pierce right through the kitchen's stainless steel oven doors.

Let me explain. When he walked into our classroom, the first thing I noticed was his height. Our regular instructor, Clive Batchelder, also a chef, was about five foot three. And bald with a slight lisp. Not that there's anything wrong with that. It just didn't add anything to his sex appeal

11

quotient, which was about as high on the allure chart as a hangnail. But no girl enters culinary school looking for the man of her dreams. Anyway, I loved Nick, so who cared?

Certainly not me. Until Chef Emilio had walked through that door. He must have been at least six-three, with curly black hair that covered his head in a halo of short ringlets that made you just want to wind each one around your finger until your hands got lost in that mass of curls. I had always thought boys outgrew their curly baby hair, but not this Tuscan god-chef. Then there were his eyes. Yes, piercing, but also black and sparkly like a star-filled night, with thick lashes and dark brows, arched in a way that gave the impression of interest and surprise, as if you'd just told him something he'd never heard before and he was totally intrigued by it—and you.

But I also had this vague feeling that there was something else about him. Something I couldn't nail down right away. Just a slight sense that made me tingle at the back of my neck. I didn't have time to think about any other signs because, as he walked by each station to look at the Bundt cakes, girls tittered and cooed all over the room. The guys seemed taken with him, too, as he made we're-all-males-in-this-together type comments that showed he was a guy's guy. I watched him work his way from station to station until he came to number eight. Mine. Last, of course.

"Hi," I said. "I'm Amanda. My specialty is flat cakes." That was owning it, all right.

He didn't say anything for a few seconds. But he stared at me in a way that made my knees wobble. The class was giggling audibly by now and I was sure he was going to make some smart crack at my expense. Instead, he reached out and took hold of my Bundt pan and deftly tapped it until out slid a perfect cake, round, firm, golden, with a wonderful aroma that filled the air and made my mouth water.

"You only tried to release it before it had set enough," he told me in a voice as smooth as caramel.

The class went silent. I could only stare at my master-baker cake while Chef Emilio smiled broadly, catching my eye to suggest he had more to say to me. But right then, he gazed around the class and clapped his hands once.

"Now, class, we will study the elements of a great cake. Unless you are making a flourless cake, it begins with the flour. Your ingredients must be the freshest, the most pure, and absolutely unsullied by chemical additives. We will learn why fresh, natural ingredients make for better recipes." That Italian accent had us all under his spell.

I listened as intently as I could, but somehow that cake kept beckoning to me, and I couldn't help sneaking surreptitious glances at it—half expecting it to fall flat or crumble before my eyes. I couldn't rid myself of the feeling that something really bizarre had happened.

But Chef Emilio was explaining that culinology merges culinary arts and food science, so I had no time to reflect on why I had a feeling he might not be what he seemed. He explained that he would be teaching us the nuances of this new field while giving us recipes that showed how the two—science and cooking—merge to form the new wave in food. And here I thought spaghetti was just pasta. Oh well, this was what I had come all the way out to the West Coast for, so I cleared my head, turned my attention to the master, and found him staring intently back at me.

I didn't really know what happened with that pathetic attempt at a Bundt cake, because I'm usually a pretty good cook. I mean, hello, that's why I went to culinary school.

There is something wonderfully satisfying about taking a bunch of inanimate things that used to be growing somewhere and combining them so they come out smelling and tasting good. And when people like what you've made, it's a total kick. After I had developed a few recipes I could whip up after school, even Foxy noticed—which is saying something, because Foxy was always pretty self-absorbed. I mean, don't get me wrong, she never mistreated me or anything. It's just that she grew up in the deep South, where being ultra-beautiful meant things got handed to her. I think that's detrimental to a person's development in some really basic way. If you never have to struggle, you really can't cope when things get tough. On the other hand, Foxy knew one thing well: men. Gay or straight, she attracted them like a moth to light. So she'll never starve. And she'll never be anything but green-eyed, long-legged, auburn-haired, gorgeous Foxy.

Anyway, I'm glad I'm far away and can become my own person and not worry about her anymore.

I just wonder what's going to happen now that I'm practically completely on my own. I'll credit Foxy with one thing: my change from goth to cute. It was Foxy who kept after me to cut my hair and toss all my black clothes and, when I finally did, it made a diff in my attitude. And I started having fun. So, thanks for that, Foxy, even though you really make me crazy sometimes. And one other thing: She absolutely loved Nick. That's the one thing we agreed on a hundred percent.

So let me ask you something: Is it possible to love your high school boyfriend and then get horribly attracted to someone else—especially if that someone is older and, well, kind of irresistible?

It was that very first day after class, and we'd gotten to make a second Bundt cake. This time, mine came out just fine. First, we reviewed that a recipe has two parts, which of course we all knew, but anyway—the ingredient list and the method of preparation. I followed the Bundt recipe for my first Gugelhupf. It comes from Austria and also Germany. It's a perfect brunch cake, if you're ever having one.

We all sampled each other's, and mine got the second highest rating from our regular teacher, Mr. Batchelder. A guy named Armand got the highest for his cake. He was quite a bit older than the rest of us, I noted, and he was already working as a chef somewhere in France. He'd been sent to the States to learn California cuisine, he'd told us. Well, lah-dee-dah on him. He did congratulate me in sort of a snotty way, by leaning over and saying in a low voice so only I could hear him, "Fairly good for a novice."

I decided right then and there to beat him out every chance I could.

Right after Bundt class, as I walked back to my incredibly teensy one-room cottage, there was Chef Emilio leaning against a live oak tree looking absolutely dashing and tempting. Which I fought hard—not to be tempted, that is— because it was obvious he was staring at me approaching him and his tree trunk, if you'll pardon the not-too-veiled reference, and I didn't want our first private meeting to include me lying on my back in a dead faint.

My mouth went cotton-dry while the telltale heart in my chest thumped faster than normally comfortable because, really, your heart is always beating—and the only time you notice it is when you're scared or excited. I didn't know which one I was at that moment. Maybe both, since something was certainly about to happen.

"Hello there," he pushed away from the tree with an elegant ease and fell into step beside me. "Going my way?" He grinned down at me. I'm five foot five but that was not nearly tall enough to see eye-to-eye with him.

"I don't know." I was muttering and stuttering, having not the faintest idea how to converse with a very-likely-noble European. Oh, I knew I was going his way from the first second I laid eyes on him, but couldn't get my throat to cooperate with my vocal chords and, just as I was thinking how mesmerizingly handsome he was, that nagging wariness or doubt or whatever it was crept into my mind again and told me to wise up and hang onto the guard rail.

"Where are you going?" Finally, I got out a normal sound. I was so relieved that I could still talk that I actually smiled at him. I have very good teeth and, when I smile, my blue eyes crinkle cutely. Anyway, that's what Nick told me once.

"I know where you live," he said.

Okay, now that was getting iffy.

"And why would you know that?" I asked.

"Because we live at the same place. At least I live there temporarily, as I suppose you do as well."

We were walking along a path that leads past the common building where the school holds assemblies and special events. Because it's in California—and this is one of the things that I came to love about being there—events were usually held outdoors next to the building at a natural amphitheater. I'd been told this was where they held graduation every year. It was a big, flat, grassy area with a raised grass stage at one end which you accessed from the side by wide stone steps. Over the stage area towered huge, old, live oaks with branches that twined and twirled as if reaching to the sky. It was breathtakingly lovely, and he took my arm lightly and veered us off to the path that led to those stone steps.

Something about the way he took command squelched any objection I would have normally made, and I allowed myself to be led behind one of the towering trees and straight to the steps. There was a long stone bench just to the side of them—I guess for anyone waiting to go up on the grass stage—and he led me to it and plunked me down while he stood in front of me, a quizzical look on his face. I finally found my voice, and my courage.

"What is this? Did I do something wrong in class?"

"No, no. Nothing is wrong. At least nothing with you."

So, if nothing was wrong, was this some very upfront come-on from a teacher to a first-year student? That I had to find out. Because I was not into that kind of thing. Or at least I had never had the chance to be into it. And none of the teachers I'd had in high school would have been in the remotest way worth thinking about in that way. But Chef Emilio? Any girl would have to consider that an opportunity to seriously consider.

"What is it then?" It was not the most seductive moment of other memorable stumbles I would rather forget. Matter of fact, I don't have a real fix on the whole seduction game. Nick was my one and only and we never actually got past kissing, which I know is rare these days and it wasn't because I didn't want to. It was Nick who held back. Sweet, thoughtful, careful Nick, who had so much going on during senior year that he just couldn't add one more responsibility. I told him he didn't have to feel responsible for me at all, but he said he would anyway, and we could afford to wait. Well, I'd been waiting long enough.

Emilio looked around to see if anyone was nearby or could hear us. The amphitheater and grass lawn were empty. The sky was blue. Puffy white clouds floated lazily above. And the trees rustled when a vague wind wafted by. It was a beautiful day to be seduced, and I found myself rather more than a little intrigued. In fact, as the moments passed, I was almost drooling with delight to be singled out by this gorgeous sophisticate from Italy, which could have been another planet as far as I was concerned.

"This is a little bit—how shall I say—unusual," he began.

"No, it's not," I broke in before he could continue. "I've heard about this happening lots of times. Especially with first-year students, but I've only heard about it from girls who've come back after their first year at college. I mean, I've never known anyone who went to culinary school before, but I guess it's no different. I mean, why would it be? After all, there are young women students and teachers just like at college so ..." I didn't finish because, by that time, I was feeling kind of lame for babbling on and on like some bobble-headed baby. I didn't know what it was like to be seduced and maybe I thought I was supposed to tell him it was okay with me. Trouble is I didn't really think about whether it would be okay, just that he was so gorgeous and I was so flabbergasted that he would be interested in me. Anyway, thankfully, I shut up.

Emilio smiled down at me. It was a gentle, bemused smile that didn't tell me much.

"You have a wonderful, feisty way about you," he said softly.

I fully expected him to drop down to the stone bench and kiss me passionately. When he didn't, I was a little annoyed. And "feisty" was not the endearment I would have preferred. Slowly, it entered the dull-witted chasm masquerading as my brain that maybe he had never intended to make a pass at me and that my "feisty" speech about how this happens all the time (and how would I know that for a fact, anyway?) was utterly out of line. The color that spread instantly from my neck to my hairline must have been blood red, bordering on purple. I'm glad I couldn't see it.

"Ah," he said, in what seemed to be a slow dawning of what I'd been getting at. "You American girls are so straightforward. I forgot. Forgive me. I am not suggesting any—how do you call it over here—"hunky dory." He flashed that bemused smile again and I was beginning to understand that he might actually be a little embarrassed. His misuse of the phrase "hunky dory" made him seem a bit less intimidating, and I almost giggled.

I wasn't sure whether to correct him but, as an afterthought, I blurted out, "I think you mean 'hanky-panky.'"

"Ahh, yes. American idioms are so confusing." He smiled at me.

"Look," I said. "I really better get going. I guess I'll see you in class tomorrow."

I started to get up but he held out a hand as if to stop me.

"Oh, no. You'll see me much sooner than that. You see, I specifically talked my Aunt Augusta into inviting me to stay at The Manor during my time here."

Now this was getting really confusing. If he hadn't been so devastatingly good-looking, I probably would have bolted by now. But who his Aunt Augusta was and why he should be telling me about her was way past confusing—what with our little misunderstanding about his interest in me and all. Then I put two and two together and came up with something resembling four but not quite. Maybe three and a half.

"Does this have something to do with where I'm living? Are you saying you want to sublet my little one-room cottage?"

He shook his head and took a step back from the stone bench and turned away from me for a moment. Again, I was about to stand up but then he whirled around and sat down beside me, took my hand and opened it, palm up. I was too flabbergasted to pull it away, and I think I was hoping this was about to become his second attempt at seducing me, hand first, then who knew where it might lead. I felt kind of fluttery in the stomach.

"Do you see this line?" He traced one of the lines in my hand. Then he took the other one and opened it, also palm up. "And this one?" Again, he traced the same line which has always been much shorter on my left palm than on my right one.

"Of course I see them. I mean, I've *seen* them. They are my hands and I've been attached to them for eighteen years now." No, no. That was all wrong. I shouldn't be so flippant. I tried to get back on track. I didn't know much about this sort of thing, but I had seen plenty of movies. I couldn't stop myself and asked, "What are you getting at?"

He was holding my hands, was all I could think. So he *was* interested. I blushed again but ignored it this time because I'd started to get excited again and it was nice having him hold my hands. I felt kind of electric at that moment, as if I might light up like a pinball machine.

"These lines … the fact that they are not the same length … this means something. And this small symbol—has no one ever told you about this?"

He traced the lines in my palm, and the electric feeling almost crackled. I pulled back and stared at him. That little thing he was pointing to in my palm was nothing but a birthmark. Foxy had told me that when I was very little.

He stared right back, and it felt to me like his stare could have pierced body armor. I pulled my hands away and shook my head. My throat had gone dry again. I couldn't figure out why. Then a wind came up from out of nowhere and blew like crazy all around us. It was kind of creepy and kind of exciting. He leaned close to my ear so I would be able to hear him above the wind.

"I'm living in my Aunt Augusta's house, which is The Manor, where you are staying in the little gardener's cottage. I'm here because you are here. I'm here to teach you."

Well, this was no information. Except of course that he was living on the same grounds that I was. Which meant we were very close neighbors. That had an intriguing angle to it. I'd seen the sign on the gate—The Manor—but hadn't really thought about it. Some houses have names, even at the beach. Like Gull Haven and Sea Dunes. So what?

"I know. I was in class this morning, remember?" I didn't mean to sound smart-alecky again. It just popped out. "And by the way, how did you make my Bundt cake come back to life?"

The minute I said it, a chill ran down my legs right to my toes. I clapped a hand over my mouth and I think I must have gasped.

"Ahhh," he said. "The light begins to shine."

He meant it was beginning to dawn on me, but I still had no idea what was dawning.

"Okay," I managed to blurt out. "What do you want?"

"I'm here on a delicate and very important mission," he said slowly. The wind had disappeared as suddenly as it had arrived. "To teach you cooking, yes. But also to teach you spells. All the spells you can learn in—let me see—twelve days. Before it's too late."

"Too late for what? What spells? What are you talking about? And why are we sitting here away from everyone?" I couldn't think of any more questions right then, so I stopped talking and just stared at him. Staring at him was a good way to pass the time anyway. I thought again about how men fell over themselves when they met Foxy. There's something about extreme beauty that is kind of mesmerizing and full of power. I'd totally forgotten what he'd said already and then he started to explain, so I tried to snap back to the here-and-now.

"Look at your hands," he told me. "See those irregular lines? They mean something. Something very special. See?" And he opened his palms in front of me. "I have the same lines. This means you are capable. You can be taught. As I was taught by my Aunt Augusta."

Taught? Hands? Lines? Aunt Augusta? What was he saying? Why couldn't he just spit it out and get it over with?

"I don't understand," I said, and I must have sounded like a complete idiot, because he sighed deeply. Still, he was supposed to be teaching us culinology, so he should have been able to explain whatever he was trying to say a little better. I mean a teacher has to be a good communicator, right? Of course, there were only two high school teachers I'd had who fit that bill, but that was then. And this was now. I expected more.

"Perhaps we should go back to The Manor and let my aunt explain everything to you. You've met her, yes?" He had such an intense look on his face that I couldn't look away.

"No. I haven't met anyone there but the woman at school who told me about the cottage, and all I know about the place came from the instructions inside that told me where I could and couldn't go on the property. I've never been anywhere near the big house."

"The Manor," he repeated for what seemed the umpteenth time.

"Okay, The Manor," I agreed.

"We'll go there now. You can drop your things at the cottage and we'll go straight to meet Aunt Augusta." He pointed at my book bag, which was a leftover from high school, battered and bulging with cookbooks and recipes, my laptop, phone, and anything else I felt like cramming into it every morning, just in case, because you never knew what you'd need. Or at least I never did.

He stood and reached out to take my hand. Of course I was intrigued. Who wouldn't be? I still didn't know for sure if this was a gesture of friendship, teacherly bonding with a student, or something more. Whatever it was, when his fingers touched mine there was a definite tiny shock that went from the tips of my fingers up my arm to the top of my right ear. It turned out I was totally wrong about what that electric current meant.

Chapter Three
I Learn My First Spell

As we walked back toward my cottage and The Manor, he let go of my hand and kept pace with my walking gait. He didn't talk again, which gave me time to think. My thoughts were disorganized but kept coming back to the year Foxy had moved us out of our big house—the year step-daddy Pete Anders got caught in the fountain of the Bellagio hotel in Vegas, naked with a showgirl or stripper or newscaster or something. I did my best to avoid all the salacious news stories the media pumped out about him for weeks—and by reference about Foxy, who was painted as the poor, wronged wife. Which of course she was, but I didn't feel in the least sorry for her. I had long ago stopped trying to figure out why she had ever married that hunk of muscle between the ears. She could have done so much better.

But that year was tough for both of us. I almost felt sorry for Foxy, but I was too busy feeling sorry for myself to worry much about her. A lot of the time, it seemed like our roles were reversed anyway. I tried to get her to curb her shopping addiction. With little success. And I pointed out on numerous occasions that she was not exactly the best judge of men and should swear off for at least a year. Well, that didn't last long.

I thought about these things as we walked back to my rented cottage. What if this was just a ruse to get me alone and ... what? I was thinking of veering off suddenly and running back to school, but what would I say? I was worrying myself into a real sweat about what was going to happen when we got to my cottage, and then there we were—at the gate. The gardener was trimming some vines with tiny pink flowers that grew along a tall stone wall, and he looked perfectly normal and said hello to us and smiled so sweetly that I thought, well, I was just being silly. When I looked back at him, he was watching us intently, and the way he held that trimmer—it had a long, thin blade with tiny barracuda-like teeth—made me nervous again, but just for a second or two. I dismissed whatever cloud had gathered in my mind and forged ahead with Chef Emilio until we reached my cottage door.

The grounds around the cottage were vast and lush, with tall trees that must have been a hundred years old or more. They crowned at the top, giving the place a feeling of being beneath a series of giant green umbrellas. Sunlight streaked through the branches, creating an intricate pattern of light and dark on the grass and flowers and shrubs elegantly planted to give a sense that nature had left her footprint here without the help of humans.

The first day, after I'd moved in—which didn't take long, with my few paltry bits of clothes and two pairs of shoes—I'd noticed the gardener working on the grounds, trimming, weeding, digging, clipping. There was such a variety of plants that I could imagine how he'd never get finished. It was the gardener who made it all look so natural, I concluded.

All those plants were new to me. West Coast vegetation was certainly different. Everything was different—at least different enough that I'd felt slightly out of sync ever since I'd arrived. I realized that I hadn't seen much of the world and that this was a really great opportunity, but it was also disconcerting to be away from all the daily life I had taken for granted. I wanted to call Nick and tell him all about it, but we'd had orientation, paperwork, buying supplies, and learning the basics of food preparation and how our cooking stations functioned. We had been told it would be a waste of class time if we didn't know from the start how to peel and cut an onion, sauté mushrooms, make a stock for sauces, and a bunch of other stuff. I already knew some of it but was glad they didn't expect us to know everything before we got there, so I wouldn't feel like a total loser stacked up against people who'd been cooking professionally for years and were just getting around to a degree.

So there hadn't been any extra time for calling anyone, and I still felt jet-lagged. I knew I should have at least texted Foxy that I'd arrived, but somehow that didn't happen either. And now I was fixated on Emilio and whoever Aunt Augusta was.

We arrived at my cottage—even calling it that was giving it more importance than it had—and I went to unlock the door, but Emilio held my hand back. With two fingers raised, he gestured in an odd way toward the door and, bang, it unlocked and opened all in one fluid motion as if it was on some sort of automatic electric opener.

Okay, I was dumbfounded and all I could do was gape at the door and then at him. He made a slight bow and waved his arm aside so I could enter. I just stood there like some dumb pigeon stuck on a piece of gum.

"How'd you do that?" I asked finally. I peeked inside the door. Everything looked the same as when I'd left that morning.

"Would you like to learn how?"

That was an odd question, I thought. "I'm not into breaking and entering, but if I were it could sure come in useful."

"One day you may need to use it."

"Is that what you meant by learning spells? Like magic? Some kind of trick?"

"Go in," he said and beckoned me into the cottage.

So this is the seducing part, I thought, where he invites me into my own place and then kisses me and tells me how wonderful I am. Wait a second, that's just a dumb fantasy. I'm in love with Nick. So stop it, I told myself. By that time, we were inside and he'd shut the door. I dropped my book bag. What a relief, I thought. I have to stop carrying so much junk around. At the same time I had that thought, I also told myself I was being really freaky for thinking about my book bag with this demigod now inside my little cottage. It was then I realized how small it really was, because he seemed to take up all the room, even though he was just standing there inside the door. He didn't seem to feel awkward or anything, and I thought I should offer him a seat, so I pulled out one of the two chairs that flanked a tiny table.

"Would you like to sit down?" God, I could sound so lame, it was frightening.

"Thank you." He sat.

And I noticed the faint scent of gardenia in the cottage but had no idea why or where it could possibly be coming from.

"I'll teach you one right now, if you like. I'll teach you the most basic spell of all. How to move a small object. Put your hand out like this. Your right hand, palm up."

He showed me and I did the same.

"Now wink your right eye and touch your left index finger to that spot on your palm that you call a birthmark and say these words: 'I command.'" And when you say the words, look at the small object you want to move."

I was ready to bust out laughing. This was the oddest way to get a girl into a compromising position I'd ever heard of but, just to see what else he was going to try—and because he was still the most gorgeous man I'd ever seen, much less had in my bedroom/living room/kitchen—I opened my palm, touched my finger to my birthmark, looked at a small flowerpot on the window sill, winked, and said, "I command."

Chapter Four
I Meet Aunt Augusta

When the little pot flew off the shelf where it had been sitting perfectly still and solid a second before, I nearly passed out. My jaw must have dropped about a half mile and all I could do was stare at the broken pieces on the floor.

"I'll show you how to make it land in a safe place later. But, for now, I hope you're convinced that I'm serious. And now we must visit Aunt Augusta. She's waiting for us at The Manor."

He held out his hand and led me to the door. I wanted to go over and sweep up the broken shards, and then I thought he was going to open the door with another piece of magic—which I didn't want to miss—but, before he put his hand on the ancient brass doorknob, he leaned down and looked me straight in the eyes and said, "You must keep an open mind, Amanda." Then he opened the door and stepped out into the sunlight.

I forgot about the pot and the shards and what I might miss, and started to wonder what he meant because now I was getting a definite uncle vibe from him. And then he was outside and I was following him like a puppy. I closed the door but forgot to lock it with that ancient lock that matched the cottage.

One thing about the cottage ... it felt sturdy. I'd been a little worried about California earthquakes but soon found everyone who lived there was really nonchalant about them.

Little tremors on and off didn't seem to bother anyone, so I figured I'd adjust, too.

Everything was happening in such a jumble there was no time to digest what I'd just done. Moved a freaking planter. With my hand. I tried to make sense of it but, with Emilio pushing me along, there was no time to think. Even if I'd wanted to stop, I couldn't have, at least not without making a huge scene like a big baby.

We walked along a stone path with some carefully trimmed herb separating the stones. I think it was thyme. The blooms gave off a sweetly pungent aroma and, when my feet crushed the edges, it really set off the scent—reminding me of spaghetti and pizza. To the right side there was a hedge, and beyond that the high wall with vines cascading all over it. I had not walked this way since I'd read this part of the property was off limits and private. I was drinking in all the beauty when we turned a corner and there was the front door of the house with a sweeping drive that made a huge circle in front of the entrance.

The gardener was pruning some huge yellow roses, cutting away the old blooms. He looked sideways at us and made eye contact with me. I thought he smiled but it was hard to tell, so I gave him a little wave and he nodded and went back to his roses. As we walked up to the front door, and Emilio let the large brass knocker fall against its strike plate, I looked back at the gardener and saw he was making a weird sign with his free hand. It looked like he was batting at a fly or something, but he did it three times very quickly and then spun around on one foot. It was too creepy, so I looked away and, at that moment, the door of The Manor opened with a creaking of its well-worn hinges.

"Your aunt has been expecting you, Master Emilio. She's waiting in the music room."

That sounded a bit off-putting, like maybe we were late or something. And whoever this woman was who'd opened the door looked about a hundred years old. She was bent over like a question mark and her hair—it looked more like a bird's nest than hair—perched at an odd angle on the top of her head. I wanted to reach out and adjust it so it wouldn't slide off. She was wearing a pale blue dress and a starched apron that looked like it might have been a maid's outfit from an old movie, when people still wore uniforms—which maybe they still do, but how would I know because I was, like, never invited to places that have maids and butlers and stuff like that.

She closed the door behind us and somehow got the hem of her dress stuck in the door jamb, so she had to open it again. Then, when she turned around, the other side of the hem got caught. It was like watching a comedy routine from a silent movie I'd once seen. So Emilio opened the door, released her hem, and then closed the door for her.

"Tessa, you really should wear your glasses all the time," he told her.

"Well, at least I know where I'm going," she said and motioned for us to follow her through the football-field-length front hall, past the equally huge staircase that curved around as it went up, past a couple of other rooms that I didn't have time to scope out, and finally she opened a set of double doors to a room that had one wall of glass from floor to ceiling. The ceiling was, I would guess, about twenty feet high. I felt dwarfed by the glass wall, the huge, long red velvet couches, the tall, tall lamps, the enormous grand piano, and a landscape painting of some people in red coats hunting, on horseback, with dogs running around beside the horses and hills in the background. The painting looked to be ten feet tall. It took up one whole wall.

In front of us, seated in a ginormous wing-back chair, was a woman in a dark green dress with pointed, matching green shoes, her feet propped on a tufted leather ottoman. She had white hair pulled up in a braid wound around her head like a halo, and around her neck was an intricate necklace of some shiny metal. I couldn't tell what kind, but it glittered in the afternoon sunlight that was pouring through the glass wall. It had an ornament suspended from it. The ornament hung almost down to her waist, which was as far as I could see because of the way she was sitting. Beyond the wall, outside, were more roses and trees and shrubs and another well-tended lawn. Boy, I thought, that gardener could really use some help.

"Aunt," Emilio moved forward and took her right hand and kissed it. "So glad to see you looking well."

"Of course I'm looking well. What did you expect?" She looked past him at me. "Is this the one?"

"Yes, Aunt. This is Amanda Anders. My Aunt Augusta." He motioned to me and then to the seated aunt as a way of introducing us.

I didn't know what to do. It occurred to me in a flash (that I quickly dismissed) that maybe she expected me to curtsy. I'd seen that's what women did when they met the queen of England. But that seemed a bit much. "How do you do," I said, a bit tentatively. I kind of smiled and must have looked really lame.

"Come here. Let us have a look at you."

She motioned for me to come forward. I wasn't sure who the "us" was until I noticed a tiny dog on her lap. I'd never seen a dog that small. Or that fluffy. It was a creamy white color, dressed up with a velvet bow around its tiny neck, and it looked so soft that, without thinking, I stepped forward and said, "Oh, what a cute little doggie." I extended my hand to let it sniff me and it immediately leapt out of her lap and ran away. It looked like a little fluffed-up bug hopping out of the room. It must have had a little bell attached to the ribbon because a tinkling sound followed it out of the room.

"Bauble's quite flighty with new people," Aunt Augusta said as she looked me up and down. "He'll be back."

She crooked a finger at me, so I inched forward toward that overwhelmingly huge chair. As I got closer to her, Emilio moved to her side and rested his hand on the back of the chair. She smiled at me in a way that seemed, to me, triumphant. That confused me for some reason. I mean, what was I doing there anyway? I remembered the flying clay pot and the lines in my hand, and I was about to ask why she wanted to see me, when she called to the dog.

"Bauble, come here at once."

I heard faint tinkling, and in sped the tiny bug-dog from somewhere in the house; but, instead of jumping back into her lap, he plunked himself down at my feet and let out a little yip. Then he sniffed at my shoes and looked up at me with bulging eyes that were way too big for his little face. And the odd thing was, it looked to me like he had the same triumphant smile on his face that Aunt Augusta had on hers. He looked really cute, but I had the urge to rip that ribbon off him, now that I knew he was a boy doggie. He looked from Aunt Augusta to me and back at her.

"You know why you're here?" She looked at Emilio.

"Oh, I've tried to tell her, but it's been a bit difficult. She doesn't seem to ... "—he couldn't find the right words— "get it, as they say here."

He looked rather lost. I wanted to tell Aunt Augusta, "But he did kiss me and that was totally confusing." But I kept my big mouth shut for once. Which is saying a lot.

"But she must be told. We can't teach her everything she needs to know until she's been told. Why haven't you done it yet? I can't believe you've let practically the whole day slip away. We don't have much time left, you know."

Not much time left? What was she talking about, and what did it have to do with me?

She slid her feet off the ottoman and pushed herself out of the chair. Standing in front of me, once she was out of that behemoth of a chair, she was really quite small. And for the first time I noticed that her hair was not really white but a glistening silver as if it was made from Christmas tree tinsel. Her green shoes caught the light and also glittered. She was like some ornament.

"I suppose I'll have to do it then."

"I am sorry, Aunt. There's been so much to do, what with the first day of class and then trying to get her alone. I won't fall behind again. I promise. We'll spend as much time together as needed, whatever, whenever."

Hmm, that sounded intriguing. I was warming up to this visit, as it was definitely going in a good direction.

"Oh, all right," she nodded at him. "Let's begin. Amanda Anders, you are going to learn the craft. Spells. Incantations. Potions. Brews. Transportations. Levitations."

She looked at me again, rather sternly, and reached out to take my arm. "We'll begin in the kitchen. I do love to cook. And you'll be doing so much cooking anyway, no one will be the wiser. Better to learn the basics here, and then the rest you can practice during class and after. Feel free to come over anytime you want to borrow a cup of this or a spoonful of that. My kitchen is fully stocked, I assure you."

What she'd said about spells and incantations and all was confusing, and I wanted to ask questions. I was about to utter an astonished thank you, but she led me so decisively by the arm toward the kitchen that there didn't seem an appropriate time to say much of anything. Along with her firm grip, she smelled of some spice—cinnamon, I thought. We walked through another long hallway, this one narrower, and I peeked into the rooms we passed. Each was large, laid out beautifully, and looked as if it was never used. Finally, we came to the kitchen. Bauble stayed right at my feet the whole time, his little bell tinkling every time he moved his head. I wondered what it sounded like to him. It would have annoyed hell out of me. If only Foxy could see me in this big house, walking with gorgeous Emilio and his obviously rich-as-it's-possible-to-be Aunt Augusta.

"Well, here we are, all ready for you."

When Aunt Augusta let go of my arm, I surveyed the large room, which was really weird for a kitchen. First of all, right in the middle was a fire pit with a crackling fire going, and above it—suspended from the ceiling and attached to a wide, black stovepipe—was a circular hood to direct the smoke out through the roof. Hanging from two andiron-type gadgets was a huge black iron pot. It reminded me of the kind of kitchen equipment we saw on a learn-all-about-colonial-times school trip to Williamsburg, Virginia, in fourth grade.

But the fire pit and the huge pot were nothing compared with what seemed to be inside the pot—steaming or boiling or whatever it was doing. I realized the scent was coming not from Aunt Augusta but from the mass of goo in

35

that pot. Fat bubbles rose to the surface and popped, making weird squishy sounds; and each time one popped, it let out a puff of what looked like very fine powder that smelled sort of like cinnamon but with a stale after-scent—like, first you smelled the cinnamon but then you smelled something kind of dank, like rotted leaves in the woods.

I was about to ask what it was when Emilio strode over to the pot and clamped a heavy lid on it with a loud clang. He looked over at Aunt Augusta admonishingly and said, "I really wish you'd be more careful with them. When they get loose it's always such a nightmare to corral them again."

He gave her a stern look and, once again, I was confused about who was the boss here. The phrase "You're not the boss of me" came to mind, but I stifled myself and just kept it quiet while thinking I should check the room for an exit, because it seemed to me I might have entered a place I'd want to escape quickly and forever. I mean, like, Emilio was gorgeous and everything but ... what—or who—was he referring to when he said "them?"

Chapter Five
I Discover Who (or What) I Am

I suppose I would have beat it out of there except I was hugely intrigued. I mean, I had a boatload of questions, for sure. Who wouldn't? I had no idea what I was getting into. I hadn't thought of Nick in literally hours, and he had been pretty neglectful over the previous few months—hardly texting or emailing, and never calling me. There's nothing like a boyfriend ignoring you to make you look for new opportunities, even if they turn out to have less seduction vibes and more kindly uncle ones. This new opportunity seemed to hold so much promise right there in that room, that I guess I let my guard down, for there I stood surveying this scene with me smack in the middle of it, and I completely and unwaveringly forgot about checking for an exit.

Bauble was still at my feet, his tiny tail knocking against the floor like a little shoemaker elf's hammer. At that moment, in wandered the door-opening maid, Tessa. I still thought of her as the maid, although I personally had never had a maid, since Foxy couldn't afford one and I was usually the person vacuuming and dusting and all that stuff.

She walked right over to that big boiling pot of goo and lifted the lid. I wanted to jump in and tell her to use a pot-holder, but the handle didn't faze her one bit. She leaned over, and it looked to me like she took a big whiff of the steam—the way you do when you're making a stew, to see if it smells delicious yet and ready for tasting. When she lifted her head back up, it was covered in blue slimy stuff and she announced, quite happily, "They're ready for the oven."

She clamped the lid back down and lifted that huge pot off its supports. How she did that, I could never say. It looked like it must have weighed about a million pounds. But she hauled it over to a door in the wall and blinked twice and sort of spat some of the blue goo on her face at the door and it popped open, revealing a cavernous oven where she slid the pot toward the back.

She turned back around to face us, grinning all the time, and backed into the oven door to close it. At that point a look of total dismay came over her and she looked at me and asked, "Do you know the spell? I seem to have forgotten it. I do remember the first part. 'Oh, come to us, you tater tots, and with you we will make some ...'"

She stopped and shrugged. "What is it?" she asked. "Spots? Dots? Lots? Plots? Oh, dear me. It's so difficult." She sat down on the floor, and Bauble hopped over and licked her hand.

"Oh, Tessa, if you can't remember the spell, you mustn't disturb the pot. How many times do I have to remind you?" Aunt Augusta asked her.

Then she walked over and pointed at the oven door. "I command you, pot, to remove the spell and change the tots to a harmless stew." She clapped and blinked and opened the oven door. Inside was a normal-looking baking dish with what smelled like a fabulous concoction. She took two pot-holders and pulled it out.

"All right, Tessa," she said. "Get up now and serve us dinner. Everything will be fine. You see, my dear," she turned to me as she handed the pot-holders to Tessa. "You will learn the spells right here. And soon you will be the one we turn to." She leaned over and helped Tessa up off the floor.

Tessa looked totally confused. "I used to be so very good at this," she sighed and pushed the top of her hair over to the other side of her head. "It all just rattles around now." She poked at her head as if she could rearrange the insides, too. Then she stared straight at me and asked, "Who are you? I haven't seen you here before, have I?"

"She's the new one. We told you yesterday," Aunt Augusta said while giving Tessa a little shove toward what looked like a pantry. "Now be a good soul and set the table. We'll do some lessons while we're waiting."

Tessa wobbled off, her hair moving from side to side on top of her head. She carried the baking dish to a side table and began gathering plates and silverware and glasses, walking in and out of the kitchen through a large swinging door that made a whooshing sound behind her each time she went through it. The odd thing was, it never really opened. She simply was on our side of it and then she wasn't and then she was again. I was beginning to get really freaked out, when Emilio took my arm and led me back to the stove.

"No need to worry, Amanda," he said. "You're going to do very well. I am absolutely sure of it."

"What is going on here, anyway?" I finally got to ask the main question of the afternoon. I mean, honestly, I was ready to burst by then. "Who are you, really? Not a chef from Tuscany, am I right?"

At that moment, with Tessa coming and going and me waiting on some answers from the god-chef, Aunt Augusta breezed over and took me by the hand and not very gently hauled me over to the stove, upon which she had placed a rather large, uncovered pot.

"Look in there and tell me what you see," she commanded.

I have to say, I was pretty cowed by her tone and manner, so I leaned over and looked. "Looks like water to me," I said and stepped back because, by now, I'd realized you never knew what was coming next.

She took my hand and opened the palm—the one with the birthmark and shorter line.

"What would you like it to be?" she asked.

"Oh, I don't know. Maybe a huge chocolate mousse."

"Ask and you shall have it. Just point and touch this spot on your palm and say these words: 'With this wish I do command, a chocolate mousse to fill that pan.'"

I giggled because it sounded so ridiculous, but just to show her up, I did it. Touched my birthmark and said the words and, holy molies, there it was! A huge pan filled with chocolate mousse that smelled really, really good. She dipped a long iced-tea spoon into it and offered me a taste. Which I took because, first of all, it looked soooo good, but second, I was famished. Astounded but famished.

"Wow," I said. "This could be really useful." I was thinking about all the times I'd spent doing homework and housework and cooking and all the stuff that takes so much time, and here was, well, I didn't know what I was being offered. Yet.

"Come. We'll sit down to lunch now."

"But I have a lot of questions, and I haven't gotten any real answers."

Emilio took my arm and, leading me from the kitchen, he said, "Soon you'll know everything. Be patient."

Poor old Tessa. I wanted to get up from the table and help her, but one warning look from Aunt Augusta and I stayed put. When she was finished making her serving rounds—and dripping and spilling and breaking stuff in the process—and she was finally out of the room, Emilio turned to me with a smile that could have melted the polar ice cap and said, "She's so old. We've given up trying to improve her performance."

"And besides," Aunt Augusta elaborated for my benefit, "she's family. And when someone is family, you have to make allowances. Don't you agree?"

I thought about Foxy, and how many times I'd been disappointed with her, but also about the times when there was a crisis: how she tried to be there for me. Then I thought about Nick and, when his father was dying, how he'd stayed and taken care of him. So, yeah, I knew what she meant, and I nodded.

"What is she, your grandmother or something?" I looked at Emilio.

He waved his right index finger at the spilled food and it magically disappeared. He then pointed to the broken dishes lying around on the floor and the table and whispered something I couldn't hear, and they instantly stacked themselves on a side table against the wall. He laughed. He'd started eating, so I did, too. The food was amazing. Little rolled pancake-like things stuffed with some kind of cheese and ham and spinach. They were light and tasty and kind of melted in my mouth. And then there was the stew that had started as some blue mess that smelled like rotten leaves and cinnamon. It tasted wonderfully rich and mellow. I couldn't wait to get the recipe. If, in fact, there was one.

"Grandmother? You could say sort of, I suppose," he said. "She has been around for … let's see, about three hundred and fifty years now, I expect. Not exactly a close blood relation but, nonetheless, within the blood line." He smiled and finished his little rolls and rang a tiny glass bell.

I assumed he was being facetious. I mean, c'mon. Three hundred fifty years? He must have a sense of humor although, so far, he'd kept it well under wraps. I was torn between trying to be polite and wanting to know what in God's name I was doing there and what they wanted from me. But just as I was about to demand answers, something else happened and I was forced to wait.

In waltzed Tessa again, this time carrying a long silver tray. I expected her to trip and spill it all but, this time, she was more stable as she delivered plates with a salad for each of us, along with a clear glass bottle of something dark red. I assumed it was wine, but it didn't look like any wine bottle I'd ever seen. It was very slender, with a long neck that curved, ending at the top with what looked like the open flute of some exotic flower.

"The good stuff," she said to Aunt Augusta. "As you requested." She placed the bottle on the table. "I admit, I took a small sample for myself." She patted her wayward hair and wandered out of the room with a whoosh of that mysterious kitchen door.

It was turning out to be a really weird lunch—although the salad Tessa had laid out was as good as the other courses had been—and I had about a million questions and was just waiting for my chance to ask them. Meanwhile, I ate what was put in front of me and wondered if we were going to get some of that vat of chocolate mousse for dessert.

"She forgot the glasses," Aunt Augusta said. "Oh, bother. I don't want to call her back now."

With one point of her finger, three goblets appeared—
one in front of each of us. I was like, whoa, could this get
any cooler? For a moment I wished Nick could be there with
me to see this because, when I told him about it, he would
never believe me. I hoped he hadn't changed much now that
he was at college and, since I still hadn't felt my phone buzz
with any texts, maybe he *had* changed. But Aunt Augusta
was saying something.

"I toast to you, Amanda." She picked up her goblet and
poured some red liquid from the weird bottle into her glass,
my glass, and then Emilio's glass. Then we all raised our
glasses in a toast and drank.

Whatever it was tasted really good. So I had another
drink. And then another, and I noticed Emilio was smiling
at me, so I smiled back and lifted my glass in a mini toast to
him, at which point I giggled and realized I was a little
drunk. Or something. Not exactly drunk. But definitely not
normal. Just a bit off kilter.

"I don't understand," I heard myself saying. Obviously,
my inhibitions had been loosened. "I mean, why am I here
anyway? And what does all the pointing and poofing and
whooshing and rhyming mean?" I clapped my hand over my
mouth to try to shut myself up, but I went on anyway.
"What do you want with me?" I asked and finally did
manage to shut up, although I had the urge to pick up my
glass and drain it dry. I didn't fight the urge too hard but,
when I picked up the glass, it was already empty and there
was Emilio smiling at me again.

Oh, I thought. Maybe they've brought me here to do
some really weird *Rosemary's Baby* thing and they've gotten
me all drunk to do it. I had the urge to push myself up from
the chair, but then Emilio said, "Not to worry, Amanda.
You're perfectly safe here with us. We're family, after all."

Huh? I was thinking: You're not my family. Then I remembered, in a vague way, about that line in my palm and the same line in his. So I looked down at my open palm. Yep, there was that short line, and I opened the other palm and there was the longer line and the birthmark. I must have looked confused (and maybe a little shaky) because Emilio was standing next to me by then, although I hadn't seen him get up or anything. He was holding a huge magnifying glass in his hand. Or maybe it was that drink and I was like Alice in Wonderland seeing the big me in the mirror. But no, it wasn't, because he took my left hand and held the glass over it.

"That's right," Aunt Augusta was saying. "Show her the mark."

"My birthmark, you mean?" I think I looked up at her but, to this day, it's still all foggy, so maybe I only imagined I did. Or I wanted to or tried to but didn't really. Anyway, it didn't matter because I did look through the giant magnifying glass and that's the first time in my life I really got a close-up view of my birthmark. I mean, come on, whoever really looks up close at their moles and freckles. But wow. I mean, when I saw what it was, it just knocked me out.

"Now do you begin to understand?" Emilio asked. "You are special, Amanda. And that means you must learn how to use the gifts you've been given."

I stared at that birthmark for what seemed like a week. It was not just a dot; no way. It looked like a cat curled up in a ball with its tail tucked around its body. But it was the eyes of the cat that truly amazed. When I looked at it, it was looking at me. And when I looked to the side, it did the same thing. And then the oddest thing happened when I looked back. Its tail twitched. I know. Really unbelievable. I mean, what kind of a birthmark moves around, right? So this didn't totally throw me. I mean, okay, I was pretty surprised—everything being revealed all of a sudden from what seemed out of nowhere. But Emilio had started to talk again, so I shifted my attention back to him.

Chapter Six
I Hear from Nick

Oh man, why do things always happen at the absolute worst time? Just when I desperately wanted to hear Emilio's explanation of what was going on, my phone started buzzing like mad, and I just knew it was Nick texting me. I don't know how I knew it, but I did. Probably because he was, like, overdue by maybe a week or three months or whatever. He was going to get it, no doubt. But first I had to hear Emilio out—and he was already talking.

"You see," he was saying, and I was sure he could hear my phone buzzing, too, "Amanda, you're the last in a long line of spell casters that descend from your father's side."

I was trying to pay attention, but I also had to know what Nick was texting, so I'd pulled my phone out of my pocket and was trying to sneak a look at it and also get it to shut off. All I could see at one glance was ...

call me miss u

I slipped the phone back into my pocket for later and hoped he wouldn't text me again while I was still at Aunt Augusta's house. And that was weird, too, because I had begun to actually think of her as Aunt Augusta. Like maybe she was my great aunt or something, which I had never been told I had an aunt anywhere. Just a grandma living in Georgia somewhere, who Foxy never spoke to because she blamed grandma for ruining her life by making her enter beauty pageants from the age of three. Anyway, that was

Foxy's story. It was probably true. At least true enough to explain some things about Foxy and why she didn't know squat about being a mother.

But Emilio was talking about my father. My father? I couldn't believe what I was hearing.

"Wait a sec," I suddenly came to life. "Are you saying my father was a ... ?"

"A spell caster," Aunt Augusta said and raised her goblet in a sort of toast as if my father might have been somewhere unseen in our midst. "He was a practitioner of the first order of the realm. And a damn fine polo player." She emptied her goblet and set it down and I saw a little smile at the corners of her mouth, like she was pleased with her little joke. Or maybe I was misreading her, which was possible, given the weird way the day was going.

"Polo player? What are you talking about? Foxy told me my father was dead. She said he died in a plane crash and that's why she had to marry the football player to support us. She would have married my father, but ..."

I was thoroughly confused. The way kids are when they find out that what they've been told is a pack of lies. Or a half pack. Like Foxy's semi-truths about my grandma. I'd heard stories at high school from kids about finding out one of their parents had been married before and they had half brothers or sisters somewhere who they'd never even known about. So much for blood being thick and all that.

"Sadly, that part is true. Or at least true as far as we know. There was a plane. It did disappear—or it may as well have, for he disappeared without a trace and was presumed dead. Until very recently. Which is why we had to contact you."

"Okay, this is getting too weird for me. You mean my father just went poof, like over the Bermuda Triangle or something? And you contacted me? That's not what happened. I came out here to go to culinary school instead of college. That's why I'm here."

"Quite true," Emilio broke in. "But what seems like your own choice was actually engineered. I know it's a bit of a shock to find out like this, but there was really no other way."

I pushed back my chair. This was not what I had expected, and I sure wasn't going to stay to hear anything else. "I think I need to go now."

"Where will you go, Amanda?" Emilio spoke softly. "Now that we've told you the beginning, you're not free to go until you hear the whole story about your legacy and your destiny. I'm sorry, but that's just how it is. That mark in your hand is a symbol, and you can't deny it or run away from it. It will either destroy you—like it almost has your father—or save you."

I think it was at that point I began to tremble. It started with my hands and moved to my face, at which point my teeth started chattering. Then my whole body felt as if it was made of rubber bands. I thought maybe I was going to keel over and die from a stroke or something. I'd heard of that happening—usually (but not always) to really old people—so I stood up and sort of teetered across the room. I only got as far as the side table. And then Tessa came in again and, when she saw me kind of skittering around, she went right to the bottle and poured me out a big slug of whatever was in there and came over and said, "Here, Dearie, I always find this helps lift my spirits when they're down. Of course, it happens to me quite a lot but, at my age, it's expected."

I couldn't think of anything to say, so I took the goblet and drank it and felt better right away and then asked her, "How old *are* you?"

"Three hundred and twenty-seven of your years, as of two o'clock this afternoon." She smiled at me and put her hand to her face and looked a little confused. "At least I think that's right. I never was good at figuring the difference between years here and years out there." She waved at some vague "out there."

"Well, happy birthday, then" I said, but I was so confused by that time I had no idea what to do or how to even ask any questions. That's when Emilio came over and put his arm around me in a reassuring way and, even though I could barely breathe, I let him lead me to a small couch over by the wall. He sat me down and settled in beside me. I felt better by then, so I looked at him, inhaled a big gulp of air, and said, "Tell me everything. Please. I'll be quiet and just listen."

"What do you say?" he looked over to Aunt Augusta, who shrugged and downed the rest of whatever red liquid remained in her glass.

"Might as well get it all out in the open now as wait for later. The sooner we get her started, the better for everyone. We've already wasted years waiting for her to get here."

They'd been waiting for me? That was more news. I didn't think anyone was much aware that I was around anywhere. Except for Foxy and Nick, I'd pretty much kept to myself and not made any good friends. I didn't miss anyone back home and hadn't been at NCC long enough to meet anyone I couldn't live without seeing again. I always figured I was just a loner type. Nick wasn't like that, although he said he was. He was one of the most popular with boys and girls. Which was why, when we started dating, it was such a shock. But these people had been waiting for me? All I could think was ... why?

Chapter Seven
I Learn About My Mission

They walked me out to the garden. No chocolate mousse for dessert. Maybe Tessa was polishing the silver with it. Who knew, in that house? The gardener was there, still clipping hedges. He seemed to go from one side of the enormous yard to the other without ever finishing, like those bridge painters who are always starting at one end just to start again when they finish at the other. There was something about the gardener, though. Something I couldn't quite identify. He just gave me the willies. So I stopped looking at him as Emilio and Aunt Augusta led me to a painted iron bench by some roses and sat me down. Aunt Augusta plunked herself into a matching chair and, from out of nowhere, Bauble bounded over and jumped into her lap, from which he stared at me unwaveringly while Aunt Augusta rubbed his fluffy, little head.

"Where should we begin?" Emilio directed the question to Aunt Augusta and then turned to me.

"Are you asking me?" It was certainly confusing. "I have a few questions, if you want to know. Like what is going on here? Are you part of some magic troupe on your way to Vegas and you want me to join up? I mean, I can't figure out why you want anything from me. It seems like you both have everything anyone could want."

"Start with the father," Aunt Augusta was very firm on that point, ignoring my outburst.

I waited to hear the story but wondered about how Foxy had gotten herself entangled in this and if she knew anything much about my bio father. Did she love him? That was the real question. And did he love her? I mean, I'd always wondered about what happened with them.

"It's never a good idea for one of us to mix in a—how shall I put this—in anything more than a carnal way with non-practitioners."

Well, if Emilio thought that was a satisfactory start of the story of how I came to be, he was so totally wrong that I wanted to smack him one. But I didn't have time, because he seemed to catch on and added to the beginning.

"What I mean is," he corrected himself, "Your father had deep feelings about your mother. From what I heard at the time, she was most beautiful and charming, and he was simply swept away by her. And for us practitioners, that is eminently dangerous."

I had to break in. "What do you mean by 'practitioners'? You're not, you know, like doctors or anything, right? Are you talking about making my Bundt cake rise and turning a pot of water into a mousse and all that other stuff? I mean, what is that? I guess magic tricks, but they're pretty involved."

I had a sinking feeling I knew what it was, but I must have been in some sort of massive denial about it because, really, who would believe it? I was right there and I didn't believe it. Some things just don't add up, no matter what kind of calculator you use. So I kept focusing on "some kind of tricks" as the explanation to everything, because I desperately wanted some practical, easy-to-explain-away reason for all this weirdness.

"Practitioners of the magic arts, Amanda. Witches. Not the kind of witches children dress up as on Halloween. We live in a world all our own and we practice the magic arts. We do not decide on it. We are chosen at birth. As you were. As we all were. As your father was."

Okay, there it was. He'd said it. But it still seemed ridiculous and unbelievable. Except for what I'd already seen. He'd shown magic. Aunt Augusta had too. And even Tessa, in her incompetent way.

"But not my mother, right? Not Foxy." The minute I spoke, it seemed like a dumb way to get at the whole truth.

"No, not her."

So I tried to get the whole story, but it was hard to digest even this amount.

"But did she know about my father? I mean, was he like poofing stuff and getting her things? I mean, like, can you just poof and get yourself some fancy jewelry or a car? I could really use a car out here, by the way."

I was thinking there might be a really huge upside to this thing, and I was starting to get kind of excited about learning how to zap myself some neat stuff. Not that I was ever into having lots of stuff. But maybe part of that was because I couldn't afford it—and the other part was having watched Foxy shop 'til she dropped through most of my childhood and adolescence. You get pretty turned off when you see your mother unable to lay off her credit card even when it's so maxed out it's practically gasping.

"That's not the way it works, Amanda. Everyone lives by rules. Ours are just a little different from other people's." Aunt Augusta's voice had taken on a soothing tone, and she was still rubbing Bauble. I could hear him almost purring like a cat.

"Your father got into trouble because he broke the rules. Not that breaking the rules killed him; it simply weakened him and, when it came time to use his powers at their fullest—when he was up against another great power—his own powers were too weak, and he's suffering for it now. In the beginning, he did it for a good cause. Because you're here today. And then, what we understand is, he didn't release himself in order to save someone else. Of course, he should never have done that if he had any hope of regaining his full complement of magic. You must learn from his mistake. Don't misuse your magic or you risk depleting it."

At this point Bauble stood up and leaped out of her lap. He bounded across the wide lawn right up to the gardener's feet and yapped wildly at him. The gardener bent down and picked him up, said something to him that I couldn't hear, and then put Bauble on the ground. He bent down and held out his hand for Bauble to take something. The dog stood there for a moment like he was making up his mind, and then he walked quietly back across the lawn and sat at my feet. I could see he had something in his mouth. I thought maybe he had a stick for me to throw, so I leaned down and he dropped whatever it was into my palm. It was a tiny pine cone.

Well, I didn't know what to make of this. Who would? Why would some gardener I didn't know give a little dog a pine cone for me?

"Close your hand around it," Emilio said.

So I did.

"Open it now," he said.

Wow. It was all I could think. Like, just wow. The pine cone was gone. And in its place I held a beautiful gold necklace with a gold locket hanging from it. And just so you know, it wasn't just some standard gold chain with a locket.

This was an intricate gold interlocking mesh chain that looked to me like it was really old. Like great-great-grandmother old from a totally different time. It even felt old to me. Heavier than your normal gold chain. And the locket had a carved pattern on both sides. And where it opened, it had a little latch, not just some indentation you push with your fingernail.

"Open it," Emilio said.

I popped the little latch and it sprang open. Inside was a picture of a man. Young, sandy-haired, with wide eyes and a really sweet smile. Handsome and kind of boyish, he looked familiar. I looked up at Emilio and then at Aunt Augusta, expecting an explanation. Something, anyway, because I was sure this was not just some random thing happening. And then it occurred to me—all of a sudden, like getting caught in a wind tunnel and whirled around. That's how I felt. Twirled in my head. Just too much to comprehend until I connected the man in this picture to Pasadena man from home.

"Is this ..." I started to ask.

"Yes," said Emilio. "Your father."

I had so many questions I didn't know where to start. So I blurted out, "What was his name?"

"Jack Wiltshire. He was born near Stonehenge and named for Wiltshire County."

Aunt Augusta answered that time, and she seemed to have more to say, because a dreamy expression came over her face and she leaned back and closed her eyes.

"That was some three hundred years ago, long before he came to this land, long before he realized his powers. He had such promise. A lad who began to practice spells as a young boy and, by the time he was your age, had grown to be a master of the art. As you soon will," she said quietly.

"Everyone in the caste agreed. He was the most powerful, the most gifted."

"How did he—?" I was almost afraid to ask, but I wanted to know everything about him. Whatever they could tell me, anyway. I didn't even know how my father had met Foxy. Only that she was in college and then he disappeared and she was pregnant.

"You're wondering about how they met, aren't you?" she asked and didn't wait for an answer, like she was reading my mind.

"She was in a parade. On a float. One of those decorated things they drag around a town to celebrate a game or spring or what you call 'homecoming.' I don't know what exactly the occasion was. But there she was, on the float. All dressed up and looking like an angel and he fell in love. Which is not impossible for us, you know. Even though some will say it is. No, love is not impossible, although it is unlikely. We prefer the more ..." and here she opened her eyes suddenly and glared at me, " ... earthy pursuits."

She finished the sentence and I definitely caught her drift. I mean, maybe I was earthy like they were. It was me who wanted Nick to—ahem—cement our relationship. He was the one who wanted to wait. For what, I always wondered. He'd said the time wasn't right, that he didn't want me to get in trouble with Foxy, that his life was a mess with his dad sick and his mother abandoning them the way she had. He'd said he couldn't be responsible in the way he wanted to be if we'd had sex. Blah blah blah, I thought at the time. I guess I could have had sex with some other guy, but there was no one else I really liked in high school. Even after Nick left, I felt attached to him. I still did. In fact, I was aching to text him back.

"You want to know how he disappeared. More important is how he lived."

"Yes," I said. "I know that's important. But how could he have been born three hundred years ago? How is that possible? I mean, do you live forever? That sounds really creepy, to be honest."

"No, we don't live forever. We all have what you might call a 'shelf life.' Your father's was—I mean is—longer than most. And he could have gone on. That's how gifted he was. But love weakened him in certain ways. Weakened his magic. He said it was worth it because it made his life force stronger. But I argued that. I've seen no evidence that our magic deters our life force."

"Did you know him?" Now I was really intrigued.

"Yes, of course. In a way, he was what you might call my godson. I like to think of our relationship as more guide or mentor. But it is really quite immaterial what term you use. We are all of the same magic caste."

"So, you're like my grand-godmother or something?"

Aunt Augusta smiled at me and raised her hands in a gesture of resignation. "If you like," she said. "But let's get down to the business at hand, and that is the business of spells. And your role from now on. Before we can reveal to you any more than you've already seen—because, at this point, we can wipe out whatever you've seen or experienced and you'll not remember any of it. But if that does not happen, we must be sure, and you must be sure, that this is the road for you to travel. Because to enter into our caste is to unleash the power of magic and knowledge that is life altering and always—with notable exceptions—to be guarded from general view."

Okay, so she was asking me to take, like, a blood oath or something, and that was creepy sounding, even though she hadn't used the word "blood." So I decided to just come out and ask, because by then the whole thing sounded beyond suspicious. I mean, how can your life just change a hundred and eighty degrees in one day? You've known yourself to be who you are for eighteen years and then—whammo—you're, like, totally different.

"What would I have to do, and how would it change me?" I asked them.

"The rules are simple." This time Emilio spoke. "You must learn the basic forms of magic. All the forms. From them, you can improvise at your own discretion. The basic forms are simple. You are allowed to tell a few other people about your powers, but only once you are certain they will not do anything with this knowledge for their own gain. If they are ever about to reveal your magic for their own gain, the knowledge will be wiped from their memory and they will forget they know anything about the powers. You must use your gift wisely to realize the greater good. Granted that is sometimes difficult to determine but if that benefits you also, it is acceptable."

He looked at me—I guess to see if I understood or had any questions. But at that moment I was too dumbfounded to think up any questions.

"Now, as to the basic forms of magic. There are three: You can move things, you can change things, you can create things."

He looked at me again but didn't say anything else.

"Is that it?" I asked.

This cracked Aunt Augusta up. She laughed and laughed until tears rolled down her old cheeks and Bauble ran over and whirled like a tiny tornado at her feet.

"That's quite a lot," Emilio explained. "Do you have any idea how much that covers?"

"Yeah. Vaguely," I said. "The Bundt cake. The flower pot. This necklace. So is the gardener a—I mean, like—one of you, too?" I realized I had slipped the necklace into the pocket of my jeans. I took it out then and held it in my open palm.

"He is," Emilio nodded. "You'd be surprised by who is and who isn't. You never know, until you've been inducted, just who has the magic. And even then, another practitioner might not want to reveal to you."

He got up and came over to me and held out his hand for the locket.

"Let me put it on you. It is a talisman. By wearing it, you bring good fortune to yourself and also protect yourself and the ones you love from mortal danger."

When he slipped it around my neck and fastened it, I felt a warm glow surround me—that and a feeling of safety I'd never felt before. It was all so much to absorb that my normal BS detection system had gone totally silent. Maybe that was a good thing.

"What about him?" I pointed to Bauble, whose tiny ears perked up.

"Bauble is a messenger. We use animals in this way, to carry things for us—things that have the power to transform—and sometimes to carry out our magic or what we call 'spells.' You might even say they are more than messengers; they are transitional spirits who cannot act on their own but can be powerful when we use them in conjunction with magic."

"And do I get an animal, too? Because I've never had one, except a goldfish when I was nine. But it died. I think Foxy poured gin into its bowl."

"You can have an animal if you choose to. It's up to you."

"So let me be sure I understand this. I can have this magic because of this little mark in my hand, which I always assumed (and was told) was a birthmark. And you're going to teach me the three basics. And then I'll be able to make cakes rise and cause flower pots to fly across the room and turn pine cones into jewelry. Right?"

"Sort of. That's at the most basic of levels. In fact, we expect you to do much more."

"How much more?" So here it was. Coming at me like a comet on fire. Overthrow the government or something like that. Turn the Earth into a wasteland and colonize Mars or some planet I'd never heard of in some other galaxy. I wasn't at all sure I was ready to hear what they wanted with me. But I'd come this far. And there was that basic information about my father. I began to wake up then, to sense some sort of danger ahead. Maybe this spell stuff was not going to be like going down a waterslide into a warm pool. Maybe what they wanted from me—or for me—would be like a waterslide into a pool of crocodiles, and would turn out to be more than I could (or even wanted to) handle. After all, I had come out to NCC just to get a culinary degree. With that, I could make my own way. What did I need with magic and spells and mysterious messenger animals?

I touched the locket around my neck and, once again, a feeling of warmth and safety enveloped me. I swear, it was like nothing I'd ever felt, and it made me want more. More of what was a question mark, but I could feel myself slipping toward whatever this was. So I was prepared to go along with them. And hopefully it would all turn out for the best.

My phone, which had been silent all this time, buzzed again and, except for the part about my first impressions of Emilio, I was dying to tell Nick all about this and vaguely wondered if he would be on the list of people I could let in on this secret life I had decided I wanted to have. But I couldn't look at my phone at that moment, so I let it buzz until it stopped. I knew I would look at it later and text Nick back. And, all of a sudden, I wanted nothing more than to see a friendly face. Which was odd since I was about to make the biggest decision of my life and then be handed the secrets of a mysterious, wondrous kingdom.

Chapter Eight
I Learn Spells

I'm not even sure what happened next. I mean, I was like some defendant on the witness stand in a murder trial who remembers every little detail leading up to the crime, months and months of events, of he said this and then I said that and we went there and then these guys joined us at the bar—but then how the gun ended up in my hand and went off ... shrug ... I just can't remember. But yes, I shot him, your honor. But I wasn't in my right mind when it happened, and now it's a total amnesiac black hole.

So maybe I wasn't in my right mind, either, because the period of time after I agreed to let them do whatever they had to do to transform me is almost a complete blank. But not totally blank. That would not be accurate, either. And I want to be accurate because that time changed my life forever. So I feel like I should remember it clearly.

Except that it's like a patchy fog I remembered from one early morning when Nick was driving us to school, the year Foxy had moved me from the big house in the burbs. I hated that year: my junior year in high school. I didn't have any friends. Not because no one would have anything to do with me. More like I wouldn't have anything to do with them. I was like some bulb in the ground waiting for spring. Okay, some goth bulb all cloaked in black. I just wasn't ready to pop my head up and declare myself present. Or burst into bloom. Until I met Nick.

That morning, we could see the road ahead sometimes, see trees outlined against the misty sky, follow the white line in the middle of the road. And then we'd go down a hill or around a curve and it would be all foggy, like smoke had settled in, and everything was a blur. We'd slow down and crawl forward—hoping no one was stopped in front of us. Then, in a little while, it would be almost clear again. It went on like that the whole ride to school. It was scary and romantic, and I wanted us to drive in that fog forever. But then I had History first period and the feeling of being in the middle of that fog evaporated and I was listening to Mr. Evans drone on about The Louisiana Purchase and why Jefferson decided to buy it from the French. Okay, it was a good deal for the country after all but, by that time, I was already thinking about culinary school and wondering why I was studying this and not spending my time learning how to make sauce reductions. So, in a way, what happened that day at Aunt Augusta's mansion was kind of an extension of my education, even though I never did need to know that much about The Louisiana Purchase, which by the way cost fifteen million dollars in 1804 or about three cents an acre. A fairly good deal for a third of the entire country.

And I don't want to make it seem something like, oh these aliens abducted me and turned me into a witch. That would not be accurate, either. I was willing, all right. At the end, even eager. Yes, that would be accurate. Because I could see the potential. I mean, think about it. Without being, like, greedy or anything, I now had a really gorgeous gold locket that I didn't have before. I had seen my Bundt cake resurrected. Being able to send an object flying across the room could prove useful someday. Maybe I'd find all sorts of magic at my fingertips that I could use on who knew what occasions. I mean, it was really heady to think about, but I tried not to go into imagination overdrive until I had all the lessons down.

And then there was my father. My real father. A family I'd never thought I had. Even being a member of this caste was like having an extended family all of a sudden. An uncle and a grandmother and Tessa, like a crazy aunt to amuse you at special occasions.

So when Emilio walked me back to my cabin after it was all over and I couldn't remember what had happened, I wasn't really sure much of anything *had* happened. As we were following the path between a row of some kind of flowering shrub, there was the gardener again. This time, when we passed him, he raised his cap to me and nodded as if we knew each other. And then he did something I'll never forget. He picked one of the pink flowers off the shrub and held it in his hand, then opened his palm and blew on it softly. Right there, in front of me, standing on that path, the pink flower turned into a parrot and flew right out of his hand like some Las Vegas magic act.

I'm sure my jaw dropped about a half mile and I stumbled, because that parrot—it was a smallish green one with pretty tail feathers in bright colors—circled above us and then came right back toward me and landed on my shoulder as if I had trained it from a baby bird. It sat there and I looked at it; it looked at me and blinked.

"What?" it asked, in a voice higher than my own, just only different enough to make me feel as if the bird was making fun of me. And it sounded as if it thought I looked like I wanted to ask it a question.

"I don't know," I answered. Stupidly, I admit. I mean parrots just mimic what you teach them back at you. They can't come up with stuff on their own.

"What are you lookin' at, girl?"

What? This bird was actually talking on its own.

"Um," I think I stammered.

I know I had not the faintest clue what to say. And then the gardener showed up on the path and held out his hand. The bird jumped from my shoulder to his finger and took a peanut that he held out.

"Mmmm," said the bird, "love peanuts. And cashews."

When he asked how I'd like a bird as a companion, I kind of nodded vaguely because I was too confused to make what you could call an informed decision.

"Her name is Quetzal," he said. "Say hello to Amanda."

Quetzal mashed up the peanut in her beak and swallowed it. "Amanda," she repeated. "Amanda. That's an okay name. How long have you been one?"

"One what?" I was carrying on a conversation with a bird. It was silly. But the whole day had been weird, so just add that to the rest of it.

"One of the magic makers. Boy, you're slow. This is going to be a hard gig." Quetzal jumped to the gardener's shoulder and said, "Thanks, Bolivar."

Was the gardener's name really Bolivar? The bird's tone sounded ironic. As if he could tell what I was thinking, the gardener told me that Quetzal was just teasing and then he told me his name was Ramos, which to me sounded just as foreign. But to me, California was still pretty much like a foreign country.

"Go to Amanda now," he told Quetzal. "And behave yourself."

I swear the bird rolled her eyes.

"So what do I do with this bird, now that I have her?" I asked as we continued walking back to my cottage.

"She will be your companion," Emilio said in an eerily calm voice, like before a storm when the atmosphere feels jellied, all heavy with something about to happen.

"I saw an old movie once about a witch. She had a cat. And in the movie they called it a 'familiar' who did her bidding. Is that what Quetzal is?" She was perched on my shoulder and I was aware of her head bobbing up and down as I walked. But she was quiet now.

"That is fantasy." He sounded a bit impatient. "Movies are not real. This is real. Yes, that term has been used, but we prefer 'companion.' It's clearer. Quetzal is your companion now and will be available like any companion. And while we're on the subject of movies, the way we're portrayed in those Hollywood fabrications full of half-truths and fictions of all sorts is quite a crime, leading people to think of us in ways that do us more harm than they can imagine. Someday I would like it if one of our kind went to Hollywood and did ..."

He stopped short of saying what he wanted done to Hollywood, and I wondered if there weren't some of Emilio's "kind" already there. It would make sense, I thought, but right now I needed to know about Quetzal.

"But will she do my bidding? I mean, if I asked her to like hex someone, would she?"

"You're thinking about this all wrong. Do you remember what happened in The Manor today?"

I tried to remember as we walked. Tried very hard. I could see the meal, and Tessa dropping stuff, and Aunt Augusta whisking everything away as if it had never happened. I remembered her telling me how Tessa was very old and, anyway, had never been good at spells, so they had never expected much from her. But she was family and they forgave her. I could see myself as if I was looking through the wrong end of a telescope, very tiny and far away, going through some sort of chant and following a recipe with bits of sugar and flour and some sort of thick liquid. There I was, pouring a kind of batter into a bowl and mixing it and repeating certain words—or were they rhymes?—and then strange things happened.

Like a butterfly flew past my head, and a cat leapt onto the stove, and a window flew open. There was Emilio encouraging me, looking deep into my eyes and I felt that I wanted to run my fingers through his curls and Aunt Augusta said something to him so he looked away. We were at that big table and I remembered after we finished eating and then ...

"We didn't get any of that chocolate mousse for dessert," I was almost shouting, glad that I remembered that much.

"That's correct," Emilio said. "And then?"

"Then things get misty again. I do remember some poems. No, they weren't poems. Just phrases. Like, 'I do thee bid' and 'At my will, it shall be as I say it.' Stuff like that. Is that all there is to it?"

"Not all of it. It's a beginning. You can practice back in the cottage."

"Will you be there? I mean, in case I mess up? What if I turn a chair into a horse or something?" I was imagining all the ways this could go horribly wrong. I was getting nervous again as we reached the cottage door.

The cell phone in my pocket buzzed with another text and I said, "Oh man, I forgot all about answering these texts." I pulled it out and it was Nick. He sounded upset so I texted him back right away.

Nthng rong. Text u ltr
But bam, he hit me right back with: *y not now*
So I texted him: *busy w stuf*
And he answered right back again: *come down this weekend?*

Well, that stumped me. I looked at Emilio who was smiling down at me.

"Boyfriend?" he asked.

"From home," I said. "He wants me to come down to Pasadena this weekend. He's at Cal Tech. I haven't seen him in six weeks. Not since he went back to school early. I haven't even talked to him since I got out here last week. It's been so busy."

"Why not go, then?"

"Could I?"

"I'm not your father," he said. Without turning the doorknob or anything, but just pointing at the door, it unlocked and opened.

"I wanted to ask about that, too. I mean, about my father. Anyway, I might as well stay here because I have no money and no car to get down there."

I must have looked altogether pathetic because he said, "I'll drive you down. I had my car sent over from Italy. It's my favorite. I'm sure you'll like it."

Quetzal chose that moment to fly from my shoulder into the cottage.

"Where's my perch?" she asked. "I need a perch. And a cage for sleeping. And I'm hungry. And I need a water dish and a swing, and I like fresh flowers nearby." She circled the small room and finally landed on a lamp. "This," she said in a strident voice full of attitude, "will not do."

"Here's a very good opportunity for you to test what you've learned so far. Why not give her what she needs?"

Emilio said as he walked into the cottage, once again seeming to fill the space with his presence.

My cell was buzzing again and there I was, trying to remember the spell for making things. I was just feeling overwhelmed and pressured, so I just spun around and pointed at a chair and said, "On my command, you will become what the bird requested to be well nested."

Shazam, there it was! A beautiful bird cage with an attached perch, a bowl of water, a bowl of food, and fresh flowers beside it on a little stand.

Quetzal let out a little squeak and flew right to it and settled in to chewing on some seeds.

"Wow," was all I could muster at the moment. "Just wow."

"Tell the boyfriend you'll be there by five Saturday afternoon. I know a place to have a lovely lunch by the ocean. We'll leave early Saturday and take the One-o-One. It will take longer, but it's far more beautiful. You should see more of California. I'll pick you up outside Aunt Augusta's front door at eight sharp."

He was right about seeing California. So far, I had only seen the airport when I arrived; the school—a small campus made up mostly of an admin building and kitchens; bits of town within walking distance; and this cottage. And now The Manor, of course.

And then, all of a sudden, he said he had to leave and was gone. Quetzal happily munched away on her seeds and I texted Nick.

Ok arrvng Sat by 5. friend driving me down. Where 2 meet? Hugs

I thought I would have a hard time sleeping that night.

Chapter Nine
I Try Out Spell Casting

I was right: I had the weirdest dreams all night long. When I got up, Quetzal was preening her tail feathers.

"I don't want to sit here all day waiting for you," she told me. She sounded peeved. "Leave the window open so I can get in and out while you're gone. I like to visit with the other birds sometimes, even though they're all pretty dumb."

Was I supposed to be carrying on conversations with her?

"Um," I started, but she cut me off.

"No need to engage with me," she said and hopped over to take a drink of water. "As far as I'm concerned, this is no different than any job."

"Have you, um, worked as a companion for others?" I felt idiotic asking a bird about her work history. It was grotesque.

"Ha," she tipped up her beak and opened it wide. "The stories I could tell you. Actually, I started with Tessa. Can you believe that? That woman could not get a spell right if her life depended on it. I once saw her turn a squirrel into a washing machine. And she already had a washing machine. It was one of those very old wringer-type washers. You probably never even saw one."

"What was she trying to do?"

"Well, she was attempting to transport herself but with a vehicle. She wanted one of those scooters. She was younger then. I had to help her by getting someone to give her a lift to where she wanted to go. I don't even remember where it was. Lord, that woman. I was never so glad for a reassignment." She leaned over and picked up a sunflower seed and worked on cracking it open with her beak. She was very good at it and soon had the sunflower nut in her mouth.

"How many assignments have you had? I mean, they said Tessa was very old."

"She is very old. So am I. You're certainly rude, asking my age."

I opened one of the small windows that had a tree outside it, and she flew right over.

"If you need me, you can either call or whistle. I'll hear you anywhere, anytime. Lord help me."

I thought I heard her sigh, but I wasn't sure. How could a parrot sigh, anyway? She flew off and landed above my bathroom mirror, where she could barely fit. She just sat there watching me dress. I vaguely wondered what she was going to do all day. I mean, how does any parrot spend the day? When I slipped a green sweater over my head and pulled it down to my hips, I swear I heard her snicker.

"You're wearing that?" she asked and tilted her head to one side as if to say I was a total freak.

"What's wrong with it?" I was asking a parrot for fashion advice. Couldn't sink much lower than that.

"Welllll ..." she drew out the word. "If you can't tell, look at yourself in the mirror. Those are not cool jeans. That sweater belongs in a thrift store. And you're wearing—" here she stopped for emphasis—"I don't even know what to call those shoes."

I looked down at my shoes. She was right. I hate to say that about a talking parrot, but it was true. I had gone through a kind of makeover when I came out of my goth period, but people out in California had a really different look. More stylish, to say the least. I would have to smart it up. But I wasn't about to let Quetzal know she was making me rethink my fashion choices. Besides, wasn't she supposed to do what I wanted and not the other way around?

"You're supposed to help me with magic, not critique my style choices."

"Well, far be it from me to butt in when you're making yourself into a frump," she snorted and flew out the open window and landed on a live oak tree next to some other tree that had some little orange fruits ripening on it. She plucked one of them with her beak, held it with her foot, and pecked at it until I saw juice squirt out. She seemed happy eating, so I let it go.

But she had made me think about my paltry wardrobe. Back East, money had been really tight at first. Then, after Foxy had rented out the two apartments, things loosened up some. But her shopping obsession ran so deep, even running an "antique" on the street-level space of our building—which allowed her to travel all over the world to buy things to sell—didn't satisfy it. I swear, it seemed like the more stuff she bought, the more stuff she wanted to buy. I guess that's what an addiction is all about, right? So, no matter how much money she was making, there was never much left over for me. I saved every cent and badgered her to put away at least enough to pay for my first semester and living expenses for culinary school. I figured that, after the first half year, I could at least get a job cooking at some hash joint to make ends meet. It wasn't like I had to study and write papers. I would have extra time to get a job. Then I got the scholarship money, so that helped. And the cottage was incredibly cheap.

I'd be seeing Nick soon and I wanted to look good. Even though we'd grown apart since he went out to college, I figured this was our opportunity to get back to where we'd been. I was still too young and naïve to realize you can never go back to what you had; you can only move forward. But that day, in my mind, he was still the same Nick and I was still the same Amanda and nothing had changed us. Well, unless you considered my new status. But, so far, that hadn't made any difference.

When we students first arrived at NCC, the school had handed out a schedule of classes. It wasn't like college, where you had American Studies first period and then a physics lecture or something. For students at NCC, the schedule was a list of different cooking classes. Tuesdays were pastries all day, which was why we had been making Bundt cakes the day Emilio arrived. Wednesdays were basics of managing a kitchen and tools of the trade. Later would be challenges with Mr. Batchelder and Chef Emilio. Thursday morning class, meats. Afternoon class was specialty recipes. Friday was fish and stocks. We'd also been promised to learn classic French specialties. And, of course, California cuisine. NCC was not a traditional culinary school; it was a bit all over the map, especially in the first year. They said they wanted to prepare us for as wide a career in food as possible, so we had to learn a bit of everything and then, in our last semester—which happened at the end of our second year—we had to choose a specialty and really dig into it.

I'd been thinking about pastry as my specialty until that disaster of a Bundt. If I couldn't even do that, maybe I should stick to something less temperamental. Like fish. But

I guessed I could mess up anything, so I put it out of my mind for the present. I had plenty of time. And now I had a new priority—or, anyway, a new *something*—and it was big, maybe a whole lot bigger than a culinary career. Problem was, I really loved cooking. So maybe I could find a way to combine these two callings (which was an odd way of thinking about what I was becoming—could you call witchcraft a calling?). I mean, what was it? Not something you could plunk down on the last line of a resume: "Loves playing guitar, skiing, and hexing people into oblivion." Not what any employer would be looking for in a new hire. It occurred to me that maybe I wouldn't have to worry about supporting myself anymore. Couldn't I just zap myself up some money whenever I needed it? And what about clothes and stuff? I decided I would spend the drive to Pasadena asking Emilio to explain the fine print on this new contract. That is, if I had really signed up with them. I still wasn't sure. But it seemed like Emilio and Aunt Augusta assumed I had, so maybe. Until then, I had time to think about what I wanted to do with my new powers.

And that was something to think about on its own. Okay, so I was still tied to cooking classes. I mean, if I wanted to get a good job after pouring all this time and money into school, I'd better do well while I was there.

Class that day was in a different kitchen, but all the same students were there. Eight of us. There were sixteen in the first-year class, but they split us up into groups of eight for the cooking classes. Too many cooks would make for a crowded kitchen. We each had our own workstation, sink, tools, pots and pans, and oven. It was kind of cool to be able to practice like that. I was hoping Emilio would be our teaching chef that day, but I didn't see him when I got there. Just the other students so I decided to take survey them.

There was Bette. Short dark hair, a big butt, and loud voice. She always looked nervous, like she was afraid someone was going to criticize her. During orientation she told us she'd been named for both Bette Davis and Bette Midler, so we could call her either Bette (without sounding the e at the end) or Bette (with the e on the end). *That* was confusing. I tried to imagine what middle school must have been like for her, but the word "butt" kept creeping in, and the picture was way too ugly to contemplate for more than a second.

Next, that guy Armand, from France. He had a strong accent and talked with a big 'tude that irritated me. I could see him getting really competitive and mean, so I'd have to watch him.

There was a woman, closer to my age, named Clare who seemed sweet and too soft to be a chef. She was so thin I thought a light breeze might knock her over. With ash blond hair and really pale skin, I thought of her as Wispy Clare. I wondered how she could be so thin and turn into much of a cook.

Most of the others were still a blur, but the thing was, even if you wanted to get friendly with the other students, they graded us on each lesson and, at the end of each semester, there'd be a cook-off for extra credit. There was a point system and whoever got the most points could intern with a famous chef for six months and maybe get a job offer after graduation. Yeah, they were pitting us against each other, for sure—making class a survival-of-the-fittest sort of thing. Now I had a real edge. I sat there trying to decide when it would be a good idea to use it, but then our teacher walked in, holding a huge side of bloody beef. I thought I was going to barf right there in my shiny stainless mixing bowl.

That French snot, Armand, leaned over and whispered, "It's not an anatomy class for med students, you know. You can't throw up like they do at the sight of some meat on a bone." Except he pronounced "they" as "zay" and his accent (okay, along with his attitude) squelched my gag reflex. Right then, I decided he would be my first test case.

Turned out, the side of beef was for a lesson in how to butcher meat properly so your recipes will come out right and beef dishes won't look like slabs of barbecue from a Houston hoedown. Who knew there were so many different ways to skin a cat—er calf—er steer? So now that we'd been educated in the fine art of disguising the fact that these cuts of beef were once connected to a whole animal, it was time to take one of those steer parts and make something fabulous. With sauce. Okay, I was up for it.

We were each given two beef tenderloin steaks and told we would be cooking an entrée complete with red wine sauce, sautéed mushrooms, and pommes Parisiennes. By the time Mr. Batchelder was through describing the dish, I was so hungry I could have chewed up a paper towel and happily swallowed it. It was a mystery to me how I'd ever be able to work around fabulous food and not balloon up to about a thousand pounds. Portion control, my eye!

We got down to business: preparing the tenderloins, seasoning them, and then searing them in a heavy frying pan. I followed all the instructions, as did my neighbor, Mr. French chef, Armand. Matter of fact, he kept looking over at what I was doing—every once in a while shaking his head and smiling to himself. I began to think I might be doing things wrong, especially when it came to those pommes Parisiennes, which he seemed to know how to make before Mr. Batchelder showed the rest of us. You had to peel the potatoes and then, using a melon baller, you scooped out little potato balls and set them in cold water until you were ready to pan fry them in clarified butter.

I got through these steps and also made sautéed mushrooms as the second side dish. But the red wine sauce stumped me. I must have had the heat too high because my shallots turned blackish and then the butter sputtered when I tried swirling it into the pan the way Mr. Batchelder showed us. I must admit I snuck a few glances over at Armand to check out how he was doing with his sauce, and there it was: dark reddish brown sauce bourguignon sauce and glistening to perfection.

But instead of offering me any encouragement, he looked over at my pitiful lumped up shallots and dried wine and whispered, "The race is to the swift and competent, little girl. You Americans have not zee talent for cooking."

Without thinking much about it, and just as Mr. Batchelder was approaching our table, I blinked once as hard as I could and muttered under my breath, "May the sauce in your pan dry up and wither and may mine take on the sunset glow of a river."

Wow, I did it. I really did! And the look on snotty Armand's face was worth it. He had taken his eyes off his pan when he saw Batchelder approaching. I imagine he was anticipating a rave review and congratulating himself like he'd just won an Oscar. He stepped aside to let Batchelder see his masterpiece entrée and sides and there it was: the sauce stuck to the pan like it had been laid down at a glue works. The tenderloins had overcooked, and the little balls of potatoes had shriveled to raisins. It was all I could do to hold back from laughing.

"What happened here, Armand?" Mr. Batchelder asked as he leaned over the pans of ruined food. "I'm quite surprised. Certainly, you've made pommes Parisiennes and beef tenderloin with a red wine sauce before. These are incredibly basic. Well, try harder this afternoon when we make soufflés."

He moved on to me next and gazed in admiration at my perfectly browned tenderloins covered in a delectable red wine glaze with adorable little potato balls browned to just the right hue.

"Oooh," he beamed. "I must taste just one." He plucked one of the potatoes and popped it into his mouth, then scooped up a forkful of the sautéed mushrooms and slid it along the wine sauce. He downed that in one smooth motion and yummed his way to the next table. Before he looked at theirs, he turned back to me and said, "I see real promise here. Good work."

Did I feel guilty or in any way like I'd cheated? Hell no. I would have left it the way I really cooked it, because everything but the sauce had been fine. I would have if Armand, the snot, hadn't been so obnoxious. Anyway, I felt sure that, with a little practice, I could make that sauce. It wasn't hard. And it was my first day. Okay, I did rationalize a little but, given the shot I had, I was glad to have taken it.

I happened to catch Armand glaring at me and it was the oddest thing. I thought his eyes actually looked red and glowed a little. I dismissed it and cleaned up my stuff—after eating the meal I'd made, of course. And let me tell you, it was really good. This cooking thing was going to work out just fine. I had a little fantasy of Nick and me married, me cooking fabulous meals, and Nick adoring me. Mmmm, it was a delicious image, but it got cut off abruptly by Armand.

"You did something. I know it. Turned up the heat when I wasn't looking? From now on, I'm watching you like a hawk." He was cat-spittin' mad, as my Georgia-born mom would have said.

"I don't know what you're talking about," I shrugged, acting as nonchalant as I could, given that I *had* done something. Not that he hadn't deserved it. "And I don't know why you've decided to be competitive with me. It's not going to get you anywhere. You're already a professional with a job waiting for you."

"It would suit me fine if you never made it into the profession. People like you should go into clerical work."

Now he was sneering openly as Mr. Batchelder started to tell us about the afternoon class: soufflés, but with a California twist. And we'd better make them stand straight and proud and light, light, light as a cloud, he was saying. Armand shot me a triumphant look, which I interpreted to mean he had this down and would show me who the real chef was in this room. He could knock off a soufflé in his sleep, I thought. At that point, I decided to ask thin-as-a-blade-of-grass Clare to switch stations with me so I wouldn't have to contend with Armand, the kitchen gladiator, any more than was absolutely necessary.

We broke for lunch and I made it my business to fall in next to Wispy Clare, who walked as if she was leaning into a headwind, tilted forward like one of those weather guys reporting from a hurricane on some beach all churning with foam.

"Hi," I said, and she jumped a little because, so far, none of us had chosen up buddies since, basically, we were in competition with each other—and who wanted to have to beat out a friend? I'd thought there would be more camaraderie out there. At home I'd had all kinds of notions about what culinary school would be like. It wasn't anything like what you heard about first semester in college when the high school class ahead of you came back for homecoming and spilled all the tales of binge drinking and sex. We would have wine tastings on Fridays but that was hardly the same thing. They were really wine-and-food pairings to get us in the mindset of what we were there to do. Hardly a bacchanal.

"Oh, hi," she nodded and kept walking into the imaginary wind.

"You're from Seattle, right?" I'd memorized the station chart and looked everyone up in the class roster.

"Yes." She was downright verbal, this one.

"Is that where you went to high school?"

"Actually, I grew up in Vancouver. My dad's Canadian. They moved down to the lower forty-eight when I was twelve. My mom was homesick, which is kind of weird because Vancouver and Seattle are a lot alike. I think Vancouver's prettier, though. Have you ever been?"

Yikes, she had untied her tongue in a real hurry, so I fell into the groove.

"No. I'm from back East and this is my first time on the West Coast anywhere."

"How do you like it so far?" she asked. Her pace slowed and she seemed to stand up straighter.

"The weather's amazing. Flowers all the time, no horrible mosquitoes. Not humid like the East Coast. And I like the fog. So far, it's great. But also different in other ways. I don't know yet. I don't have a car. Maybe that's keeping me from really experiencing California."

"I'm heading over to The Daily Grind—you know, that coffee place on Tremore Avenue. Wanna come?"

"Absolutely." I was thinking how great it would be if I could get her to switch places with me, and then I felt kind of bad about it. What was I turning into? Some kind of sneaky witch? The thought almost made me smile, because I didn't really feel that different. But then again, I was different. Ruining Armand's wine sauce had proved that. I wondered what Wispy Clare would say if I told her. She looked over at me and smiled, and then I felt really bad. It seemed she was only looking to make a friend, and there I was trying to maneuver her into something.

"Hey," I said, "what do you do when you're not cooking?"

She thought for a minute and then said, "I like to go to clubs. The noisier and wilder the better. I love to dance."

Wow, I thought. You really couldn't tell what was going on inside a person from the outside. Or, at least, in some cases you couldn't. Not in this case, for sure. Wispy, thin Clare had a rebellious side.

"I used to be goth," I told her, since we were now sharing confidences of a sort.

"I'm not surprised. You probably didn't have any friends in high school. Cooking was something you could do on your own, right?"

"Sort of. I also had a mother who thought Chinese takeout was a balanced meal. Why did you think I didn't have any friends?"

"I don't know. Wanting to pal up with me for one thing. And you just seemed like kind of a loner. I am, too; don't get me wrong. There's nothing the matter with not being a crowd-gatherer. But sometimes ..."

She broke off there and we just kept walking. I thought about D.C. in the spring and fall. Especially in spring when the cherry trees bloom and it seems like the whole world comes to see them. It's a pretty city and, for all the politics that goes on, it's kind of a pleasant place. But it can be dismally hot in summer, and winters are no fun. Walking to The Grind, we passed lovely wooden houses with flowers blooming all over the place, cute porches, fruit trees, and the sun was shining in a blue sky. We had on light jackets and this was just perfect. By the time we arrived at The Grind, I was thinking I could get used to this.

It was one of those laid-back-looking places with coffee prices that could have fed a whole family. The indoor and outdoor seating with benches and big tubs filled with flowers surrounding artsy metal tables and chairs appealed to California types who like to look relaxed while they're making gobs of money. That was one of the things I'd noticed right away. Everyone looked casual but, in a low-key way, kind of well heeled—like the climate or something softened the harsh outlines of West Coast life. A crowd was waiting in line, with lots of people sitting around reading or talking or checking their iPhones. I could see why so much of the country had migrated west to California. Who cared about earthquakes when you could be affluent, attractive, and busy with gadgets everywhere?

We found a small table and sat down with our lattes. This was a huge splurge for me, but I figured—what with my new spell casting talent—I could certainly afford to spend some of my meager savings. It seemed a bit presumptuous to right-off broach the subject of trading workstations, but sometimes what seems like a tough puzzle to sort out just falls into place on its own. Which is what happened: Wispy Clare actually brought up the subject. But not right away; first, we did the four-one-one on what had gotten us where we were. At least the parts that were G rated—G being general interest.

She had a pretty normal life, with parents and everything, except that her mom had been driving to the grocery store one day when some lunatic ran a red light and crushed her spine between the steering wheel of her Toyota and the back seat, which shoved up to the front seat, pinning her inside. She'd been in a wheelchair ever since. It had happened when Wispy Clare was twelve, so she had to take over a lot of the household chores and learned how to cook by helping in the kitchen.

I guess it was inevitable that we'd become friends, both of us having to take on the role of mother to our mothers. Of course, mine was because Foxy had an allergy to anything domestic, while Clare's mom had actually taught her how to cook. Anyway, Wispy Clare liked cooking so much she had decided on culinary school pretty much the way I did. So that's how the conversation led to school and the subject of our cooking stations and Clare asking me if we could switch because she thought it might help her to watch what Armand did this semester. And I was like, cool, yeah, go for it, which is when she really surprised me.

"Why don't you like him?" she asked as she polished off her latte and crunched the last bit of her biscotti.

What was I supposed to say? He's a competitive snot who's out to bury me? Anyway, I didn't really know why or how we'd gotten off on the wrong foot. And it seemed odd, now that I was away from class, that he'd developed such a heavy negative in my direction. After all, he couldn't possibly have had any inkling of what I'd done.

"I guess he expected to come over here and ace everything and make us all look like amateurs, and when his meal got ruined today, he had to blame somebody, and I was closest. He's too competitive to be likable, so maybe you want to rethink trading stations?"

"No, I'm not worried about being in the line of fire. I saw what happened today. I think he took his eyes off the burners for too long while he was waiting for Mr. Batchelder. He was showing off, I guess. Or something. Anyway, he won't think of me as a threat like he does you. No one thinks of me that way. I kind of fade into the background."

That sounded funny coming from her, because I'd always felt that about myself—or had, until Nick. For me, there was "before Nick" and "after Nick." So it wasn't just me who thought I was different. I was getting to like Wispy Clare. Everybody needs a friend, and it was about time I had one. Question was ... how much could I really let her into my life now that it had taken this weird turn?

"I noticed you," I told her. It was a neutral enough way to tell her I didn't think of her that way. She seemed to like it, because she smiled and sipped at her latte and just sort of looked around at the crowd.

"Do you want to be a chef? I mean, is that what you love doing?" Before I could answer, she went on. "It's kind of a hard life, in a way. You work at night mostly. Or really long days that spread out into the night. And you're always working on holidays and weekends when everyone else is off. I mean, for me, it doesn't matter because I never cared about that stuff and never hung out with a bunch of kids or anything."

She stopped there, but it got me to thinking.

"I don't think I ever really considered the nuts and bolts of being a chef. I kind of think I'd rather do pastry. You know, concentrate on that. But who knows? At this point, when we're just starting, it's hard to know what offers we'll get."

"If any," she said. "That's why I want to win that internship. I'd hate to have to go back home and tell my parents I failed at this. And then hear them say I should have gone to college." She put her mug down and sighed, then gathered her bag and scarf. "I guess we'd better get back for the afternoon session."

I stood up, too, but happened to glance out to the other side of the street, and there was Ramos, the gardener from Aunt Augusta's, walking Bauble on a glittery leash that looked like something from a 1930s movie with Ginger Rogers or someone dressed up in ostrich feathers and tap heels. And Ramos was watching me, too. It gave me a chill up my back and prickled my scalp.

"What's wrong?" Wispy Clare asked. She looked concerned and that kind of rattled me, too.

"Nothing," I said. "Just I know that guy across the street." I don't know why I even told her that much. I mean, it wasn't like I couldn't have said "nothing" and let it go. Maybe the fact that she seemed concerned about me made me feel like we were connected somehow, and I didn't want to lose that. Anyway, whatever it was, all I knew was it felt good to have a new friend.

"What a cute little dog. I've never seen one like that before. It's so tiny. Is it a toy Chihuahua?"

"I don't know."

I was trying to steer her away from Ramos and Bauble, but, OMG, they were crossing the street in our direction.

And Bauble had started to yip when he saw me—or maybe smelled or heard me—because it's hard to tell with a dog, you know. He yanked at the leash Ramos held until they had crossed to our side and came up right in front of us, where Bauble stood up on his tiny hind legs and tried to jump up into my arms.

"He likes you so much, Miss Amanda," Ramos said and nodded to Wispy Clare.

"How are you, Ramos?" I thought if I stayed calm and cordial they would move on.

"I think he wants you to pick him up," he told me.

"I'll hold him." Clare bent down and scooped him up, but Bauble had other ideas and immediately started pawing the air to get to me. He was like some baby who doesn't want to be taken away from its mother. And it was weird. I mean, when did this little bug of a dog get so attached to me? Anyway, there was nothing I could do but hold out my arms to let him jump in. Which is what he did. And then he settled down and poked his tiny cold nose into my palm and licked my hand. After a few seconds, he looked at the ground and it was obvious he wanted to be let down, so I gently put him on the sidewalk. He calmly walked over to Ramos, dragging his leash behind.

Ramos nodded to Clare again and said, "So nice to see you." He and Bauble wandered off down the street and it was at that moment that I realized there was something stuck to my palm.

"We better get back," Clare said. "Boy, that doggie is really attached to you. How do you know them anyway?"

"I rent a cottage on an estate and he's the gardener. I just met them yesterday. I can't figure out why he got so attached to me." I shrugged as we walked back to class, but I kept rubbing my fingers against whatever Bauble had left in my palm and I was dying to see what it was but afraid to do it in front of Wispy Clare, because she was already asking too many questions.

"Well, yesterday must have been quite a day for you. Meeting a cute little doggie and a gorgeous chef from Tuscany all in one day. What did you think of him?" She didn't wait for my answer. "'Gorgeous' doesn't begin to do that man justice."

Chapter Ten
I Use a Spell (but the wrong way)

It was a flat, green thing—very tiny—that looked maybe like a frond from a fern, except that it had this glittery quality like the iridescence of a hummingbird's wing. I didn't know what to make of it, but the thing was I couldn't get it to come off my hand, so there it stayed for the rest of the afternoon.

We made soufflés. But California style. Avocado soufflé. Artichoke soufflé. Cauliflower soufflé. Ricotta cheese soufflé. Rhubarb soufflé. We were all assigned something different. I got a main-course soufflé made with salmon. And we had to make a sauce to go with each one. Mine was a dill yoghurt sauce. Some of the soufflés came out too tall and kind of burned on top and not cooked enough in the middle. Some were too flat. The soufflé from Bette, that loud girl, came out all runny and the avocado was lumpy. Ick.

Wispy Clare and I had traded places, so she got to watch Armand. He had the ricotta cheese and it came out perfect. I didn't even try to hex him since I was busy concentrating on my own. Clare's was okay but mine was absolutely fabulous. I was worried because salmon can be tricky, and I'd never ever made a soufflé before or had to make a sauce. But I just followed what Mr. Batchelder told us to do and it worked out. That is, until Mr. Batchelder left the room and Armand made a point to come over and sniff at mine.

"Oh, so you made the salmon? It's no challenge (he said "shall-anghe") to make a fish soufflé. One day you may have to make something difficult and then let's see how far you get."

He wandered off around the room as if he was the teacher and we were all under his thumb. Wispy Clare grinned at me and stuck her tongue out at him. I was liking her more and more. But it irked me that this guy was so determined to upset me, like he was playing some elaborate head game. And then in walked Emilio followed by Batchelder, and they proceeded to taste-test each of the soufflés and sauces. Except that they skipped the ones that were an obvious abject failure, which luckily wasn't mine.

Seeing Emilio again was funny in a way, because now that I knew who and what he really was, I felt like I had an enormous edge on everyone else. But I also had this immense urge to let Wispy Clare in on it. I fought that urge, though, because I realized it would make my life that much more complicated. Still ... it would have been fun to have a gal pal to hang with and let in on all the secrets. I hoped I could stick to my guns, but it was going to be hard. I still had Nick, though, and he was the best more-than-a-friend a girl could have.

Unfortunately, Armand's soufflé and sauce got the best marks of the day—but mine did come in a close second. He was going to be insufferable, and I'd just have to stay as far away from him as possible. After class, on our way out, I found a few seconds to practice a little mini hex by pointing to a spot just in front of his right foot as he approached the doorway. Under my breath I whispered: *Let the shoes that land on that spot stay tied together like a knot.*

He tripped and fell forward, catching himself on the door jamb just before he collapsed. He let out a yowl and everyone laughed nervously, but I noticed no one rushed to help him. So maybe everyone thought he was kind of a jerk. I looked up to see Wispy Clare grinning at me. It was almost like she *knew* something. I waved to her but wanted to get out of there fast so I could text Nick about Saturday and maybe get my act together a little. It had been a long time since I'd even thought about how I looked or what I was wearing, if I needed a haircut or any of those girly things. And I had to figure out what that green thing in my palm could do.

Wispy Clare caught up with me outside.

"Did you see him trip? It was awesome."

I just laughed.

"I have to do some stuff, but give me your cell number and I'll text you later," she said.

We exchanged numbers and I took off for my little cottage. The green spot in my palm had started to itch, and I thought I would wash it off when I got home. I vaguely wondered if I had a magnifying glass to study it more carefully, then I remembered that Aunt Augusta had a huge one at her house. She'd said to come over anytime. Maybe now was the time. I could learn some more spells and maybe zap myself up some sweet traveling clothes for the weekend trip.

By the time I got back to my cottage, I was excited to get started. I couldn't unlock the door without a key yet—a spell that must have required some advanced skill—so I used the heavy old key I'd been given to let myself in. Or at least I started to use it; the lock was old and rusty and the key would never slide in easily. Then, when I got it in all the way, it was hard to turn and I hadn't gotten used to it yet, since I'd only been there a few days and everything was still new. I could never remember which way it turned to open the door, and it even seemed to open to the left on some days and to the right on others. So I was standing there with my backpack half off one shoulder trying to get the thing open when Quetzal swooped down and landed right on my other shoulder.

"Where have you been?" she squawked, while she adjusted her feet until she was holding on firmly. "All my sunflower seeds are gone and I'm tired of listening to those stupid swallows chirping about absolutely nothing of interest all day long."

"Sorry," I said. Being kind of intimidated by a bird seemed stupid as well, but I let it go. "I can't get this key to work. I think the lock needs some oiling or something."

"Why don't you simply hex it? Or is that too difficult for someone who wears those tired things out in public? Just push it with that green spot on your hand. That works for almost anything until you get the spells in your feeble mind." She tilted her head so her right eye was looking straight down at the tattered leather shoes I'd had for years and years and were way past when I should have deep-sixed them.

"Well, A) I don't know how to hex a lock, and B) these shoes are way broken in and very comfortable." I took hold of the door handle, making sure the green leaf touched it. Bang, the door popped opened.

"Well, you don't have to get all snippy about it," she flapped her wings.

Okay, having Quetzal around could prove extremely stressful. After I dropped my bag and filled up her seed bowl and she was crunching happily away, I glanced at my old comfy shoes and had to agree that they should be in the trash can behind my cottage. She must have seen me eyeing them because she stopped and mumbled something with her mouth full of seed and I saw her looking smug. At least that's how it looked to me, if it's even possible for a parrot to look smug.

"And your plan for the weekend is what?" she asked as she carefully extracted a large sunflower seed from its shell by working it around and around in the tip of her beak until the shell dropped down to a plate under her perch. I noticed she was quite neat about it. Besides living with an oversized, green bird in my little one-room cottage, I was about to have a discussion with her about my weekend plans. I had officially entered the realm of super weird.

"I learned how to make a soufflé today." I don't know why, but I didn't want to let her know I would be leaving the next evening. Thus the new subject, but she was too clever for that. She made a face and dropped a sunflower shell onto the plate.

"Cooked air," she sniffed. And don't ask me how it's possible for a parrot to sniff, because I would have to admit it was probably impossible. Add it to the list.

"Okay, so I'm going down to see a friend Saturday." I had now lost an argument with a bird. Things were sinking ever lower.

"Friend?" She cracked another shell loudly for emphasis.

I kicked off my old shoes and sat down in the one chair I had left that had been supplied by my landlady.

"Well, sort of a friend. Okay, more than a friend. But I don't really know where we stand right now. I haven't seen him for a while. And maybe things have changed." What, was she now my love counselor? I really had to get a grip.

"You could always put a spell on him." She chewed up her seed and then actually cackled as if she'd made a huge joke.

"I guess I could," I mused aloud. "And you could help me, right? Like you just did with the door."

She flapped her wings like mad, as if something had upset her and she was about to take off. Then she settled down and cocked her head to one side.

"Didn't they tell you?"

"Who? And tell me what?"

"The Tuscan and the aunt. Didn't they tell you about the danger?"

"What danger?"

"Of fooling around with love."

"What do you mean?"

"Isn't it obvious? Don't do it. That's all."

I tried to remember everything that had happened the previous day at The Manor. I remembered some of it very clearly, but then there had been all that wine—or whatever it was they kept pouring into my glass—and a lot of that visit was just foggy. There had been a vague warning but nothing specific.

"What is the danger? They didn't tell me anything. At least I don't think they did. So you can tell me."

"Sex is okay," she said.

"I know. So they told me. But what's wrong with love?"

"You say you're leaving tomorrow? When will you be back? And where oh where will you be spending the night Saturday, may I ask?"

Before she had time to explain herself, or I had time to consider what she was asking, there was a soft knock at the door.

Chapter Eleven
I Learn Love Has Dangers

Tessa stood there and I noticed immediately that her hair was tilting to the right side today. She held a scraggly broom.

"Miss Augusta told me to come over and clean up for you." When she peeked around behind me to see what exactly she'd be cleaning up, she spotted Quetzal on her perch. "Ack, that nasty bird. Won't be touching any bird cages now. You'll have to tend that yourself."

Her gaze shifted to me and the look on her face said there was no arguing with her about the bird cage. I wasn't about to say anything, so I stood aside but wondered how effective she'd be at cleaning, having observed her serving mishaps the previous day. I imagined exploding vacuum bags and dust bunnies the size of potatoes left underfoot. She went right to work, beginning at the far corner of the kitchenette area, where she went down on all fours and started poking at something along the baseboard.

"Um, I have to do some stuff," I said, hoping she'd get the hint.

"Go ahead. Am I stopping you?"

Quetzal made a rude noise and then raised her voice in a squawky rasp. "Old woman, you should be retired by now. When are you going to the home for old witches anyway? I hear they have a room ready for you with a view of the toadstool garden." She laughed at her joke and flapped her wings back and forth a few times for emphasis.

I was thinking maybe Tessa could tell me about the danger, so I walked the few steps over, to where she was bent over, and cleared my throat.

"If you got something else to say, spit it out. I'm ignoring that bird, though." She didn't look up or turn around.

"I was wondering about something. Something they said yesterday. But I can't think if I got any details."

"Well?" She stood up slowly and took hold of the broom handle but didn't make any move to sweep. "Don't know why I should clean in here. With that bird making a mess with her seeds, it won't be long before it's all undone again, anyway. But," she sighed and pushed her hair over a little, "I do what I can. What do you want to know?"

"About love," I said. Keep it simple, that's my motto. I gave her a lot of room to embellish, hoping she'd fill in all the blanks, which is mostly all I had so far.

"Love," she repeated to herself. "Love makes the world go round. My love is like a red, red rose. Love makes all things easy. All you need is love. Love keeps the cold out better than a cloak."

I thought she was going to spurt samplers forever, but she ran out of steam and stood there, holding the broom handle and looking like a stunned sparrow who'd just smacked into a glass wall. I felt kind of sorry for her, but I didn't really know why except that she seemed so far out of it that her confusion obviously wasn't her fault. Like maybe she'd been hit on the head by a passing meteor or maybe someone had cast some kind of haywire spell on her and she'd never been able to shake it.

I was about to say something, but she jumped in first. "It wasn't always this way, you know."

"What wasn't?" Okay, here was my chance to dig for some dirt.

"I was once young like you. And pretty."

I didn't know what to say to that.

"Yes. Yes, I was. Young and pretty and gifted. Terribly gifted. Why, I could change a lion into a butterfly. I could cast a spell on a troll and turn him into a toadstool. Just like that." She snapped her fingers and a plate came flying across the room and almost clipped me across the head. I ducked just in time, and the plate soared past me and crashed into the front door. Quetzal squawked once and tilted her head.

"She once was a gifted spell caster, but now she's a menace with a broom." She let out a high-pitched screech and fluffed her feathers.

I didn't even want to think what might happen if Tessa's spells screwed up even worse. But the very thing you don't want to think about is the thing you can't help thinking about, so I couldn't help picturing the roof falling in and a powerful vortex sucking us all up and dropping us somewhere way off on a Pacific island surrounded by coconut trees and lots of Quetzals. Well, at least one of us would land in our native environment. And poor me, I didn't even know what my native environment was anymore. I mean, where do spell casters belong, anyway? Certainly not with Foxy, and maybe not here at culinary school. Maybe there was a special place where spell casters lived together, like in some magic-making commune where they could just snap their fingers and anything they want would come to them.

As if she somehow knew what I was thinking, Tessa spoke up, glaring across the room at Quetzal. "I may not be the best spell caster in the universe anymore," she sneered at Quetzal, "but I still know a thing or two. And ..." here she turned to face me, "I could teach you a few things. That is, if you can control that molting feather bag."

Quetzal squawked again, but this time she took off and flew out the window, presumably to annoy some of the birds outside because I heard a chorus of alarmed chirps from somewhere in the trees.

"Okay, she's gone. I really want to know all about this." After a few seconds it occurred to me that there was something else I wanted to know about. "And what spells have to do with love. But maybe you could just explain everything to me. It might be safer." I almost ducked again in case she twitched and released another plate my way.

"All right, then. Sit you down at that table and let's get right to it."

I did what she told me to do and, pretty soon, there was the oddest assortment of items in front of me on the little table in that part of the cottage designated as a combination kitchen, dining room, food prep space, and general entertaining area. Not that I had any plans to invite guests in for dinner ... but still. That there was room for Quetzal's perch in my little cottage made no sense; however, nothing much in this newly discovered life of mine was making much sense.

"All this," Tessa waved a hand over the table, "is just a start. Spells don't necessarily follow a recipe like a cake; they vary with each practitioner." She gave me a piercing glare, as if she were trying to see inside me.

"How do you know what kind of spells are right for you, then?" I asked. She waved a hand at me and closed her eyes, so I shut up to see what she would do next.

And so began my induction into that extraordinary, if unconventional, confederation of spell casters, as they preferred to be called, since "witch" and "warlock" carried so many negative connotations that had plagued my forbears for centuries—or so Tessa told me. Still, in reality, we were all witches, for witchery is what we practiced.

Spell casters, I learned, inhabit a space that is neither earthly nor heavenly, neither underground nor above ground. They travel among ordinary people in the everyday world and, if encountered, no one would ever suspect anything beyond what they seem. There were even cases, Tessa informed me, cases like my own, where a spell caster, for reasons as obscure and complex as what happened in the past and what may happen in the future, are not aware of their own powers. The spell casting community terms them "the unleashed," and spell casters usually let sleeping dogs lie, so to speak, leaving such people to discover their powers—or not—on their own.

"But why was I singled out?" I wanted to know.

Tessa shrugged and tilted her head, and a spoon suspended itself in midair and then did a little loop-the-loop before settling down as gently as a feather on the table in front of me. At this point I couldn't see the precise value of being a spell caster if all it meant was hurling stuff around the room or moving cutlery from one place to another. Of course, I could become a ten-second media sensation and end up in a carnival somewhere like a performing seal. So much for my culinary career.

Turned out, it wasn't at all what I thought. There were magic potions, but they were an insignificant part of what made us special. Same with toad eyes or bat wings. I didn't have to twitch or spin around or raise my arms like an angry zombie. In fact, based on Tessa's instructions, it was really simple. At least, as much as she could remember. Mostly it was up to me to get in touch with what she kept calling my "gift." All the stuff she'd laid out on my little table turned out to be ingredients for a meal she zapped up for herself. She said she wasn't showing off. It was just the way she'd learned to cook, and she didn't know how to do it any other way. Based on what she made, I was glad I'd decided to enroll in culinary school. "Blech" is all I can say to that meal.

Anyway, back to my gift, which turned out to be something deep inside me as shapeless as fog, that I could neither touch nor feel as long as I was consciously trying to get in touch with it. Sounds weird, huh? Well, it was. Tessa told me I had to lose myself in order to get in touch with my gift. She said it was, in a way, like getting rid of my conscious mind so the gift could take over. This sounded a little iffy to me, especially since, on most occasions, when she got in touch with her own "gift," it seemed to get away from her and act entirely on its own. But I didn't want to hurt her feelings, so I didn't say anything. I tried to concentrate hard, to find that place inside me where this gift was living a life of its own.

So there I was, sitting in the middle of my tiny cabin, with what I'm sure was a weird look on my face, telling myself to think "gift," "gift," "gift." All I got was a big zero.

"You have to let your mind go. Don't think. Don't try. Just become one with the gift," Tessa whispered, her head cocked to one side like a robin listening for a worm in the earth.

So I was supposed to become a what? A Buddhist monk like some lama in the Himalayas? This was all feeling more unlikely, and I was about to hang it up, when this strange feeling came over. Well, that's not exactly accurate. The feeling didn't come over me. It surrounded me, but from inside, if you can imagine that. I mean, there was me in my cottage next to Tessa. And there was another me inside of me that wasn't really occupying space the way I was. I mean, the "I" that was me. Oh, man. It was freaky. And totally wonderful, at the same time. Maybe that's what they mean by an "out-of-body experience." Except this "out of body" was within my own body.

I sat there for what seemed like forever and then I noticed Tessa looking sideways at me, her eyebrows raised as if she expected something to happen, like without talking she was saying, "Well?" and then the oddest thing happened.

Quetzal flew back in through the open window and landed on my shoulder. It was as if she and I had some mystic connection. She opened her beak, but no sound came out. Then I heard myself say, very softly, "Quetzal, I want Nick to call me."

Then everything went blank.

Chapter Twelve
I Appreciate the Value of Spells

When my cell phone rang, I snapped out of it and I wasn't even a bit surprised. It was like it was all the most natural thing. I reached for my phone and, when I looked up with it in my hand, Tessa and her broom were gone and Quetzal was on her perch—her head tucked under one wing, as if she was unaware that anything had happened, and I was lying in bed, the rumpled covers over me. I didn't have time to think much about it because I saw Nick's number come up on the phone. He almost never called me—said he didn't like talking by phone—and I thought this gift—whatever it turned out to be—could really improve my life. It hadn't yet struck me that there might be a downside. But that's what it's like when you start a ride on the whirlwind: You just don't look down. I forgot about the little leaf stuck in my palm and soon I didn't even feel it anymore. And then I realized that the really oddest thing had happened. I'd advanced in time.

"Hi."

Nick sounded far away, but that didn't worry me. He had a soft voice anyway, unless he was upset; and if you weren't with him in person he tended to be kind of reluctant to talk. Even texting wasn't his thing. He just thought of it as a waste of time. Once, he told me he needed to see me, to feel my presence, to talk. And if we couldn't be together, he'd just rather wait. That was one of the things I loved about him. When he was in the right mood, he would really talk. Not like some guys who have no clue and just want to brag or talk about sports and stuff.

"Hi, yourself." I had no trouble with the phone. It was great just to hear his voice. "I miss you like crazy," I told him, which was probably a mistake that would make him clam up even worse than usual. But then he did something that really surprised me.

"Manda Bear," he whispered into the phone.

Okay, I'll admit it: I just melted right there. I had to lean back against the pillow and pull up the covers to be sure I wouldn't melt into a pool of briny tears. Foxy was the only person who ever called me that, and Nick knew it. It was Foxy's way of showing she could mother me like she did when I was little. After she'd married Anders, she gave me a big stuffed bear and I used to take it to bed with me every night. That's when she started calling me "Manda Bear." I didn't like to think about those times. I think I shut off somewhere inside me when we moved to Virginia to be close to his team. He never did anything bad to me, at least until that day when the shit hit the fan and the tabs splashed his naked butt with a big black band across it on their front pages. Yeah, until then, he just wasn't there most of the time. And when he was there all he did was eat and watch sports and lounge around or go off to practice or travel with the team. In the off season, he trained. I mean, the man was nothing but a walking exercise machine. And when he retired after his left knee got bashed up, he became a TV announcer and was still never there. That is, until everything fell apart and Foxy finally got it through her head that all those years he'd been out of town, he was really running around on her. And that wasn't the half of it.

Poor Foxy. It's not that she was exactly deluded. I mean, she must have sensed at some level that something was wrong, that what they had wasn't a real marriage. I think it's that Foxy was one of the last remaining southern belles. Being gorgeous and from the South was like a double whammy. Foxy never looked beyond her beauty queen years except to think of marrying some big-name jock so she could lavish herself with all the things she'd been told she deserved.

And when I came along, from the beginning we must have been oil and water. Of course I don't remember, because I was a baby. But she took off her spring semester when she found out she was pregnant, and I was born in August. She left me with my grandmomma and the first time I actually remember seeing her was at my fourth birthday party, when she came to get me and take me back with her. I mean, I must have seen her before that, but it's all pretty dim, and memory can play funny tricks.

She breezed in wearing some frothy yellow dress with a wide-brimmed straw hat that framed her face like a picture I'd seen in one of Grandmomma's magazines, and I thought she was prettier than any of the dolls in my closet or pictures of fashionable ladies in those magazines. When she tipped my chin up to look at my face, she smelled like a summer garden, and her smile seemed to surround me like sunshine. And then I sensed something behind that smile. I didn't realize until years later, after she took me away to live with her and the jock from hell, that what I'd sensed was disappointment and that she was disappointed in me. I wasn't gorgeous like her, or sparkly and lively like her, or attractive to men like her. I was awkward and plain and not good at conversation, and I couldn't have flirted my way through a stag party. She spent years trying to get me to dress better, style my hair, and wear makeup, but all I had was a sharp tongue and I used it on poor Foxy every chance I got. What would she say now, I wondered, if I ever let her in on my new secret?

"I miss you, too, Manda," Nick was talking again. "But you'll be here this weekend, right? And I'll show you everything and we can talk."

"I got a ride down so he'll drop me off wherever you say." I should have explained it better. I realized that right after I blurted it out.

There was a long silence. Long even for Nick. I held back from breaking it, but it was a struggle.

"Better meet me at the physics building. That's where I spend most of my time. I'll text you the address."

"Nick? Are you upset? It's just one of my teachers. He offered me a ride and there's no reason not to take it." I had so much I was dying to tell him. It was all I could do not to explode with it.

"Amanda," he said, "you don't owe me any explanation. You do whatever you think is best."

"What's that supposed to mean?" This was not going well. I had a knot in my stomach by then and no idea what to do about it. "He's just one of my teachers, is all. Are you jealous?"

"I have no right to be jealous," he said softly.

"That doesn't answer my question. Are you?"

"Let's talk about it when you get here. I ..." But he didn't say anything more and I heard someone else's voice—definitely female—in the background. Maybe I was the one who should be jealous.

We said goodbye, and the knot in my stomach felt like a flame-thrower had taken up residence down there. After all, Nick and I hadn't seen each other in months. We hardly ever talked. And he'd been away at college for over a year. He was alone and probably lonely. I didn't know what to expect when I would get down to Pasadena. All I knew about that place was an old Beach Boys song. It might as well have been the Moon—except for buildings packed with brainiacs instead of green cheese.

We were barreling along in school. I tried out six new recipes in class that week and learned how to make sauces for five main courses. I figured out all on my own how to use flour as a hexing tool—a pinch of flour between thumb and index finger, a sideways look at your target, a very quiet intake of breath with the tip of your tongue against the roof of your mouth to make a hiss like a little snake, then flick the flour and make up a little rhyme about what you want to happen. I made Armand's butter pastry gummy (rhymes with "yummy"); I made a wine glass crack (rhymes with "hack"), and I helped Wispy Clare's piquant sauce come out perfect (tough to rhyme, but I came up with "select"). She got the top mark in sauce class that day.

By Thursday, Emilio hadn't shown up again, and I wasn't sure he would be picking me up on Saturday for the drive down to Pasadena. But at the end of class, Mr. Batchelder said Chef Emilio would be conducting class Friday, so we should expect to be tested vigorously. "Woo hoo!" was all I could think. Wispy Clare and I went out for coffee to celebrate her high mark.

"I can't believe what happened." She sipped at her iced latte with this little hesitant smile on her face. Even after a triumph, she was still reticent about her progress.

"You deserved it," It was a little lie, but it felt good.

"Armand was pretty distraught," she almost whispered it as if someone might hear her.

"He's a jerk."

Armand had looked over at my pastry dough when I was right in the middle of it, and I saw him snicker at me. That was when I decided to ruin his pastry. Maybe I shouldn't have been playing around with my gift, but it sure was fun to see his face fall when his dough got all clumpy on his rolling pin. I could barely keep from laughing.

"Yes, but there's something about him. I can't quite figure it out. Like he's got some secret."

"You mean besides the secret that he's an arrogant prick?"

"Oh, Amanda, you're so sure of yourself. I wish I could be that way."

"You're wrong about me," I told her. "Until near the end of my junior year in high school, I was a real shadow. I mean, I never talked to anybody, and I was sure everyone was always laughing at me."

"What did you do to change? I mean, I would so like to, you know, remake myself and be more, you know, confident."

"I'm not really sure why it happened, but one day I threw out all my black goth stuff and got my hair styled and bought some new clothes. Actually, it did start before that." I was thinking about Nick and how he'd offered to give me a ride home from school one day. That was when it started. Yeah, it was Nick. "I met this guy. He was really nice to me and things just started to shift. I wouldn't say I'm all that confident. I still question myself a lot. But being out here has made it better. Just getting away from Foxy."

"Who's Foxy?"

"My mom."

"You call her 'Foxy'?"

"Literally everyone calls her 'Foxy.' You would, too, if you ever met her."

"My mother would disown me if I called her anything but 'Mom.'"

"Yeah, well, Foxy's not the apple-pie mom type."

"Why's that?"

"Here." I pulled my wallet out of my backpack and flipped it open to a small picture I'd taken of Foxy right after last Christmas. She was dressed in high black boots and a short skirt with a bright green scarf wrapped around her neck over a cable-knit sweater and she was laughing at something. Of course, she looked like a gorgeous movie star or something, glamorous and beautiful at the same time.

"Wow," was the one word Wispy Clare could find to utter.

"Yeah," I said. "That's Foxy."

We left it there since we both had to get home. She gave me a hug when we stood up. It was a little awkward, like she wasn't sure how I'd take it, but I hugged her back and everything was okay. Being beautiful was a kind of gift, I figured, but my gift could give that a run for its money. If only I could find a good use for it. I was already questioning whether going around hexing pastries and stuff was really why I'd been singled out. Maybe I was destined for some big save-the-world moment. Oh, sure thing, I thought: Amanda Anders, born to save the world. I'll get on that right after I walk back to my little guard cottage at Aunt Augusta's mansion for the supernaturally gifted.

On my way I managed to silence a yappy dog and caused a squirrel halfway up a tree to drop the peanuts he'd stuffed in his mouth. That one made me giggle, watching the nuts rain down on a BMW parked under the tree. I could just see the driver come back to find peanuts all over his precious Beemer and say "WTF?" Oh well, it was fun being a clandestine troublemaker. That is, until I reached the gates of Aunt Augusta's estate and saw her standing there, hand on her silver-tipped cane, wearing—of all things—white lace gloves like some Victorian grand dame. But it was the look on her face that stopped me half a block from the entrance.

She squinted at me and raised her hand in a gesture that instructed me to come forward. Which is what I did, reluctantly. Where else was I going to go? It would look stupid to turn around and run. She knew I'd seen her. Besides, something about her demeanor sucked the free will right out of me. A hex on the hexer, you might say.

Chapter Thirteen
I Learn My Gift Has Obligations

"You haven't been made aware of your gift just so you could play silly pranks, you know."

We were walking along the path outside the walls of her estate. I must say, it was extremely pleasant, with the fragrance of jasmine every now and then. Aunt Augusta thumped her cane with every other step, and I had the feeling she might use it on me if I misbehaved. The gardener and Bauble were nowhere in sight, and we had the whole place to ourselves. I didn't know if her remark required an answer, so I stayed silent.

"This is not a game," she added.

"Yes, ma'am," I said very softly, so as not to rile her any more. I had never called anyone "ma'am" before, and it sounded odd. I wondered if she thought so, too.

"We didn't expose your gift to you to be frivolously—" She didn't finish what she wanted to say. I had the feeling she was a bit anxious about something.

"We haven't got much time, and the time we do have should be spent perfecting your craft. I understand you're going away for the weekend. That my nephew plans to drive you south along the coast. An excellent time for you to learn what you need to know. I want you to be very cautious about your behavior from now on. We don't want any suspicions about you. We've managed to keep it quiet all these years in preparation, so you must be careful, studious, and, above all, effective. My nephew has great talent, but nothing like your father's and most likely yours. He is primarily an instructor in spells rather than a practitioner. Do you understand?"

"Not really," I ventured. I did have a lot of questions. I mean, who wouldn't? It hadn't yet occurred to me that I might be in danger. Matter of fact, I really hadn't experienced any danger in my life. Inconvenience, yes. Because of the mess Pete Anders had made of our life. And of course Foxy's shopping habits and her inability to hang onto one red cent for more than an hour (or until she saw the next pair of Louboutin pumps for a bazillion dollars). So it was only just beginning to dawn on me that maybe I shouldn't just take this gift and run with it until I knew exactly what I was getting into.

"I mean, I don't understand what you all expect of me. What am I supposed to do, anyway? You keep telling me there's not much time, but for what?"

"I was hoping my nephew would be here to help with this part, but I suppose I'll have to explain it by myself. Tomorrow you can get the details from him while you're traveling, although, if it were up to me, I wouldn't have allowed you to leave right now. It only complicates things. But perhaps it will work out better than I expect."

As she was speaking, Bauble ran up out of nowhere and circled us like some little fly that couldn't make up its mind where to land.

"Hush, Bauble," Aunt Augusta shook her finger at him, and he fell in step with us.

We walked through the huge iron gates, and they shut behind us. I didn't question how they opened and shut anymore, since opening and closing things seemed not to be an issue in their world. Aunt Augusta led me to the side of the house, where we sat on a bench under a huge old live oak. It was beautiful late in the afternoon, with the sun at a low angle and all the shadows lengthened. The grass was a delicious dark lime green, and the flowers nodded cheerfully in a slight breeze. It was kind of intoxicating, and I just accepted that I was now a part of this special world and looked forward to learning more spells. But in the back of my mind was that nagging worry: What did they really expect of me?

"The equinox happens in less than two weeks from the time you moved into the cottage." Aunt Augusta's voice was flat. Bauble let out a tiny yip.

"Really? I don't keep track," I offered.

"Will you be still?" she sounded irritated. "This is important."

I didn't say anything else.

"On the equinox, twice a year: That's when we are in the most precarious position. And it's when your father will begin facing his final test. I know you've wanted to know about him at times in your life. Your mother couldn't give you much information because she didn't know it herself, so she made up a story. You were a little girl, and she wanted to protect you. It is true that your father was more than smitten with her. He was enchanted. But she was not able to reciprocate in the same way, and he couldn't take her into his confidence. Your mother is not a person of depth. That happens sometimes. It is no fault of hers. Just an accident of birth, one must suppose. But because your father did not receive love back from her with the depth of his own, he was weakened. His powers began to lapse. And to preserve what was left of them, he disappeared to join forces with another who promised him—and many others—salvation. But, probably because he was so disappointed by his love, or perhaps because he had been so weakened by it, he chose badly, and the salvation he hoped to find was nothing more than a kind of hell on this Earth."

She stopped talking. Bauble had begun to growl very softly.

"Wow," I sort of said it under my breath, but I knew she heard me, so I just went for it. "That's a heavy load you just lowered on me. I mean, phew, you know?"

She still didn't say anything and just kept stroking Bauble on the head with the tip of her cane. After a minute or so he jumped up into her lap and snuggled in, making a little kind of purring noise like I'd heard from him before. Well, since she wasn't talking, I thought why not take this chance to get some more info, so I sucked it up and just came out with a whole bunch of questions.

"Okay, so first of all, what does the equinox have to do with anything? And what is that anyway? And second of all, are you saying Foxy didn't love my father at all or what? I mean, I know she's full of herself and not really into being all mushy and cozy and stuff, but she does have feelings, and she always told me she was crazy about my father and, when he died—because that's what she always told me happened— she was devastated and that's why she married the football star. He was handy and willing and she'd had a child. She was a beauty queen, after all, and she was really gorgeous and everything, so I guess old Pete Anders thought he was hooking up with a winner."

Aunt Augusta smiled at me and nodded. "That's how it must have been. Except that, for one of us, to marry is quite a step. And we cannot do it without being absolutely sure that the one we've chosen can fully grasp our lifestyle. Your mother could never have done that. Just think of it: With her shopping habits and her need for new things all the time. She never would have been able to control herself, and it inevitably would have led to your father losing his power." She sighed, as if it was a lot for her to consider or remember or something. "And if she had known about his gift, she would have married him for it and that would have led to absolute disaster. No, in the end, your father was right to leave. Sadly, he left in the wrong direction. I believe he was too lovesick to make much sense of what he was doing at the time. He simply threw himself into that new situation hoping for relief from his broken heart. We were all distraught over it. He'd had such brilliance and then, to see it squandered ... well, it was too painful to see, but then you were born and we could watch you grow from afar. I must say you had your rough spots."

Rough spots, my eye. She couldn't have been watching me very closely. More like mini minefields.

"Couldn't you just zap him up and out of there, wherever he was, and away from this trouble? I mean if you—I mean we—have all these gifts and powers, how come we still have trouble we can't just poof away?"

I must have sounded like a total goof. Anyway, I felt like one, asking such a question, but Aunt Augusta didn't laugh. Instead, she looked very serious and put Bauble back on the ground at her feet.

"We have power to do certain things," she began, but I interrupted her.

"I know. Move things, change things, and create things. That should be enough to solve any problem."

"There are restrictions on the use of those," Aunt Augusta said.

Oh, oh, the fine print. Now we were getting somewhere. "Like what?" I asked her.

"There's no way to answer that, I'm afraid. Each of us has to find that out on our own."

"You mean, I might be in a situation where I need to zap someone or something and all of a sudden discover I forgot how?"

"Not exactly. I can't predict when you or any one of us will hit the wall, so to speak. But it will happen. And when it does, you'll know it right away. But there will be no warning. That's just the way it is. And beware the equinox—our most vulnerable time. Our powers begin waning leading up to that day, and they immediately revert to full power again when the dawn comes.

I was too embarrassed to ask when the equinox was exactly. I guess I should have learned that in school. Like the phases of the Moon and whether it was waxing or waning depending on whether the half-moon was on the right side or the left side. But I never could remember which it was, so I wasn't about to let Aunt Augusta know that, so I made a mental note to find out later. As it turned out, Quetzal knew the answer. She told me the equinox happens on the two days of the year when day and night are the same length. She didn't even sneer when she explained it. But she did kind of harumph at me behind my back. I could hear her tail feathers fan out the way they do when she's making fun of something.

It was funny, when I stopped to think about it: Before I could get any more details about what exactly happened to my father and where he was—that is, if in fact everything they had told me so far wasn't just a big fat pack of stories just to get me hooked to whatever it was they really wanted from me—Aunt Augusta suddenly got really tired and said she had to go inside and rest. I mean, honestly? With all that power, she couldn't just poof up a little extra energy? It was useless to argue over it, so she went home and I went back to my little cottage where Quetzal was waiting for some cashews.

She just loved those, so I had bought a big bag of them on my way home before Aunt Augusta had nabbed me.

While Quetzal was crunching her cashews, I tried out a few recipes mixed with spells. I was getting better and feeling pretty confident after I managed to zap up a strawberry shortcake and hide a knife inside it like I was some kind of jailbird with an escape plan, and I roasted a stuffed capon in only five minutes and then changed it into a live bird that ran squawking around the cottage until Quetzal made such a fuss that I zapped it into an antique lamp. After that I went on a real tear—zapping everything in the cottage into something else, moving stuff around, even commanding Quetzal to bring me a gorgeous silver necklace from Mexico and a large uncut emerald from Colombia. I really wanted to keep that one, but I didn't know how I'd explain it, so I made it evaporate. I thought about zapping up a car—only a small one—but I realized I didn't even have a license, so what good would that do me? I assumed if I zapped up a license, that wouldn't also put it in official records, so I was beginning to wonder just where the limitations were on this sort of thing. I mean, it was pretty heady, I have to admit, and I was really flying after an hour or so.

Chapter Fourteen
I Have a Friend

Class that day was about pastry making, which thrilled me so much I can't even express it. I had never thought about how pastry spanned cultures and countries, but we learned that every culture on Earth loves sweets of some kind.

Mr. Batchelder had us watch a short film of men in Nepal who suspend themselves by ropes they make out of vines and hurl themselves out over the edge of cliff above a steep ravine to swing back to where bees make enormous nests in the cliff sides. First, they hurl themselves with flaming torches so they can smoke the nests free of bees, then another guy swings in with a machete and hacks a huge chunk of hive off, and the men on the cliff haul them back up with their prized honey. One false move and down they'd fall with no hope of survival. I don't know if I'd go that far for a sweet dessert, but it made me think even more seriously that pastry might be a good career choice with an endless guarantee of employment.

We got to choose our pastry genre, if you can call it that. Strawberries seemed very popular. Wispy Clare asked for strawberry shortcake. Someone else decided on a strawberry tart. "Big butt" chose a strawberry cheesecake. And the twit Armand opted for a French classic, a napoleon, which I have to say was bold because the flaky pastry is a challenge if you don't buy it already made. But I wanted to really go for it, so I opted for a croquembouche. If you don't know what that is, try one sometime. I saw one in a pastry shop near Foxy's den of destruction and had to go in to ask what it was. If I'd had the money, I would have bought it and downed the whole thing by myself. So this was my chance. It looks so elegant you should be able to wear it as jewelry. The trick is how to wrap it in spun sugar. It's pretty complicated to make. I followed a recipe—well, you'd really have to. You make pastry puff balls and cream filling and assemble them in a tower on a form and then spin sugar all around it until it looks like a spider dipped its legs in liquid sugar and then danced around as it cooled, encasing the whole pastry in a web of thin glittery hard candy ice tendrils. It should end up looking kind of like a pastry Christmas tree without tinsel. When I announced my choice, I definitely heard Armand snicker, which only made me more determined to make the winning pastry.

We worked for three hours, taking the whole class time. The easier desserts were done before mine and Armand's. But mine took the absolute longest to finish. Using a tiny pastry tube, I filled all the little puff pastries with the pastry cream, then I had to place them on the cone and bind them to it and to each other with caramel that I made using a candy thermometer. Once that was all assembled—and it took a long time—there was the final step, spinning the sugar, at which point Armand was just finishing his napoleon pastry so he came over to inspect what I had done. He made what I can only call a French sneer and huffed his way back to his own workstation. I ignored him and, using two forks, I dipped them into the caramel and started spinning. If I could have crossed my fingers, I would have, because spinning the caramel could end in disaster, and I didn't want to use any spell to make it a success; I do have my pride. Once I got going, though, I spun that caramel like I was a seasoned candy maker, and it came out really beautiful. I was so proud of myself I could have puffed myself into a human pastry.

When Mr. Batchelder called time, we all stood at our stations awaiting the decision from the judges—Mr. Batchelder and, for this class, Ms. McCracken joined in—on whose would get the top mark.

"Well," Mr. Batchelder beamed at me, "Not only did you choose a real challenge, but you also mastered the croquembouche. Simply spectacular, I must say."

They placed a blue ribbon at station number eight and Armand came in second. I thought he was going to burst out crying, and I knew from then on he would never let up on me.

After we broke for lunch and came back, we all tried each other's desserts. Everyone agreed—except Armand—that mine was the best. I will say his Napoleon was also very good. Light and fluffy and not overly sweet. I thought one day I'd like to make one.

Chef Emilio took over the afternoon class and lectured about food science. We all took notes, and he demonstrated a few new recipes based on health science and food. We all tried the baked salmon with fennel and grapes. I liked the mashed cauliflower, which Emilio told us is one of the foods replacing wheat and potato recipes for a healthier lifestyle.

By the time we left class, I was stuffed full, and it was later than usual for ending school. But it had been a good day, and I was happy. I headed back to my cottage, intent on trying more spells and getting a good night's sleep before the drive to Pasadena, but then my phone buzzed with a text from Wispy Clare. She wanted me to meet her at this bar near her apartment where a lot of up-and-comers from the office buildings liked to hang out after work, which ended late for these tech geniuses. So I changed my plan and agreed to meet up with her at ten.

I got to the bar ahead of Wispy Clare, and guys started hitting on me right away. It was the oddest thing. My social life was really picking up. This was so totally new to me that I didn't know what exactly to do about it. So I let them order me drinks and preen and fuss and compete for my attention.

Maybe my magic is still working on its own and it's having some kind of weird effect on men, I was thinking, when Wispy Clare slid in beside me at the bar and whispered, "Wow, what perfume are you wearing, and can I borrow some?"

I laughed and asked if she wanted to go to a table, so off we went with a few of them trailing us like the tail of a kite. This was a whole new world for me. The social world, dating, bars, attention from guys. It's hard to describe just how mind-blowing it was, so all I can say is, I lapped it up like a hungry kitten at a bowl of cream. The other thing that surprised me was Wispy Clare's nonchalance, like she'd been doing this all her life. Maybe I'd misjudged her completely. This wasn't the Wispy Clare from school or from lunch the other day. Was it possible she had a secret life, too?

At that moment I had an almost irresistible urge to tell her everything. I mean, unroll the whole enchilada. But then there was so much swirling around us that it was hard to keep my mind on one thought and, by the time we got to a table, it was too late. Three guys sat down beside us, and Wispy Clare slammed into fifth flirt gear with the guys hanging onto every giggle and head tilt. When one of them turned to me, it was all I could do to remember I was supposed to be heading to Pasadena to see my boyfriend in just fourteen hours. I snapped back to attention when the three of them took a leak break to the men's room.

"Clare," I turned to her, "I've got to go back. I have something early tomorrow and then ..."

She didn't let me finish. "I know," she wagged a finger at my face. She was more than a little drunk. "You're going to run off and leave me with these guys and I can't decide which one I like best."

"Clare," I started again. "You've had an awful lot to drink. Why don't you let me get you home?"

I'd never been to where she lived, but I figured it had to be close by since I'd had the impression she walked to school and everywhere else. Besides, from what she'd told me, she didn't have any more money than I did, so how would she have a car?

"Sure thing," she muttered. "But first, l just have to freshen up a little."

When she got up, she wobbled and then stumbled and, just as the three guys came back to the table, she crumpled onto the floor. They just stood there, staring and then one of them started to laugh and the others joined in.

"Hey," I looked up as I tried to lift her to her feet. "Help me get her to a cab."

But they backed off, and I was left there with Wispy Clare passed out at my feet and not one of those twits would help. Then someone came up behind me and I saw strong hands reach down and take her by the arms and pull her up until she was leaning against him, mumbling something under her breath.

"Young ladies should never drink more than two glasses of wine," he said.

It was Emilio.

"What are you doing here?" It was all I could think to say.

"Come," he nodded at her purse. "Collect her things and let's get her home."

Turned out, Wispy Clare lived in a studio apartment so tiny that Emilio and I couldn't both fit in there half carrying her. It was barely five blocks from school—a ground-floor room with its own entrance off the back of a small house with a little garden. The owner must have added it for rental income, but it couldn't have brought in much, I figured. We found her address in a bill in her purse. Emilio carried her to a daybed against one wall while I stood in the doorway.

As he backed out the door, he pointed at her and uttered: "Let her lie now, sound asleep, when morning comes no memory to keep."

He shut the door and took me by the arm.

"And now," he began.

"You're not going to lecture me, are you? After all, as you said, you're not my father and you have no right to run my life."

When he ushered me down the sidewalk without saying a word, I began to get a definite feeling of pressure, as if the air around me was about to implode.

Chapter Fifteen
I Take a Car Ride

The next thing I knew, Emilio and I were in his car driving along this beautiful road by the ocean. I had no memory of anything in between. I have to admit it seemed more than a little weird. I mean, who knows what he had done with me—or rather *to* me—while I was in some kind of fog. If you want to know, I never even got drunk or used drugs in high school or anything like that. I never wanted to be that vulnerable.

But now the oddest thing was also happening, especially after the way I simply lost it like I'd been hit by a two-by-four when I first saw Emilio. He was still drop-dead gorge, and maybe it happened after he kissed me in my cottage that one time, but I just wasn't feeling the same *Oh my god, I can't control myself* vibe. It was like I had this really handsome, smooth uncle who was charming and everything but ... just an uncle. It was definitely weird. Another thing I would have to sort out for myself. Maybe it was because I was about to see Nick again, after all this time. Yes, that must have been it, I guessed.

Anyway, when I woke up in his car, Emilio acted like nothing was different. I kind of yawned and then I was wide awake.

"Good morning," he said with such a cheerful voice that I immediately felt guilty for even thinking any salacious stuff.

"What happened?

"Well, let's see, we took your friend back to her mouse hole of an apartment and then we went to your cottage and packed for the trip and you fell asleep."

"And you left?"

"Well, Quetzal wanted me to stay and amuse her, so we played some games. She's used to being a companion to someone who's around all the time. She gets bored easily. She wanted to come with us to Pasadena, but I said no to that. I told her I'd arrange for Tessa to visit, and she could go over to The Manor and visit with Bauble. That satisfied her, so I left the window open and she can also visit with her bird friends outside."

I thought about Tessa alone in my apartment. What would I find when I returned? Smashed plates and Quetzal's tail feathers and maybe a big pot of some stew? Well, it would be interesting.

"I don't get it; if I fell asleep in the cottage, how did I just wake up in your car? And where are we anyway?"

"That's the Pacific Ocean." He pointed to my right.

"Oh really? And here I thought it was Chesapeake Bay. Pu-leaze, give me a little credit."

He laughed and nodded.

"Ok, so you know we're in California. And we're heading to Pasadena to see your boyfriend. Nick, right?"

"Yes, Nick. But how far have we gone? Because I'm hungry."

"I suspect you are. After all, you had no breakfast. We'll stop early before a regular lunch time. I brought brunch food."

"This is a pretty dope car. What is it?"

"A Ferrari Purosangue. It literally means "pure blood" in Italian. But as to the car, it means "thoroughbred." It was a gift from an admirer. Someone I helped out when she was in trouble. She was most grateful."

"I guess she was. Is it very fast? It's so luxurious. I bet a lot of guys stop to admire it."

"Supposedly it can reach speeds of one hundred and ninety miles an hour and go from a—how do you say it in English—stock stand ..."

"Standstill?"

"Ah yes, that's it. From a standstill to one hundred and fifty miles an hour in less than fifteen seconds."

"Wow."

"But there's not much use for that in this country. In Italia is where she really performs."

I wondered about what it was like in Italy. Or anywhere, really. You'd think I'd be more sophisticated, but Foxy never took me anywhere on all her buying trips around the world. Just left me alone with her assistant who'd rented the basement apartment and had parties with who knew who (but always men) when Foxy was away. He was still there when I'd left for California.

"We shall stop soon for lunch."

We'd passed rocky cliffs and grassy hills with pine trees and places with names like Pigeon Point Lighthouse and Shark Fin Cove and Point Lobos. There were lots of state beaches and parks. I would have liked to explore some of them. Maybe all of them. One day Nick and I could do that together, I mused to myself. I was daydreaming about that when Emilio downshifted abruptly and pulled off the road at a sign that said "Garrapata State Park Bluff Trail." There was also a sign for a waterfall, and I looked out to see a trail that led to the ocean on a high bluff. I'd never seen anything so wild and beautiful, and all I could do was stare.

When Emilio opened his door, the sound of the sea came to me and there was a slight briny scent in the air. Waves rolled in and landed against rock cliffs that must have been there since time began. I felt as if I had landed where I was supposed to be. Not in a city. Not on the East Coast. Not swallowed by people rushing around all the time. Here was a new world for me, a place of possibility, a true new beginning. I imagined—without realizing I was even thinking about the future—myself finding a place to live and work in this gift of a country by the ocean. For the first time I didn't feel like a child anymore, not some faceless goth girl trying to hide herself from the world. Right there, still sitting in that impossibly elegant car, I could see a future for myself.

"Come; we'll go on the walkway to a spot where we can sit over the ocean and eat our brunch."

A canvas bag hung over his left arm and, in his right hand, he carried two flat folding chairs that looked like something you'd take to watch your kid play soccer.

"Can I carry something, too?"

He handed me a folding table that was also very light and a bottle of something in a chilling bag.

"Hey, why are we carrying all this stuff? Can't you just poof us up a lunch?" I was sort of kidding but sort of serious, too. I mean, what's the good of learning all these spells and finger-pointing if you don't use it to make life easier?

"We'll talk about that after we have la scampagnata."

"La who?"

"That's Italian for "picnic," although the word "picnic" has become commonly used in Italy, too, along with many Americanisms. I recently saw a list of words Americans add to the word 'shit' to make so many meanings you need a dictionary to understand them all."

"Like what?" By now we had left the car far behind and were walking along a packed dirt trail toward the ocean. The trail wound around following the cliff until, in front of us, I could see a narrow bridge over a fairly steep ravine. When we reached the bridge, I saw water flowing under it from a waterfall farther back from the trail. I thought it was lovely that a waterfall emptied right into the ocean, and that made me think about all the places I'd never seen and what a big world it really was.

"Oh, let me see if I can remember some of them." He paused as we walked and then he raised a finger in the air and said, "Oh, yes. I remember these. "Shit storm." "Shit for brains." "Shit stirrer." "Bull shit." "Horse shit." "Shit show." "Shit load." "Hot shit." "Shit happens." So that's a bit of them. And the amazing thing is they all mean different things. You can imagine how difficult it is to learn American English."

I cracked up laughing. This elegant, gorgeous, Ferrari-driving stone-cold fox reciting "shit" expressions. It was too much. I stopped on the bridge to catch my breath I was laughing so hard.

"Did I say something wrong?" He looked lost for a moment.

"No," I gasped for air. "That list just sounds so funny coming from you. I mean, holy shit." I broke up again and we waited until I got back to normal before we continued on the trail until we came to a point overlooking the ocean.

"We'll set up our lunch here." Emilio opened the folding chairs and the little table.

"I've never seen anything so wonderful. And listen to the waves hitting the rocks down there. Woosh woosh. It's like the start of a symphony or something."

Of course, the food he'd brought was amazing. A whole lot of little bite-sized canapés—some with smoked salmon, others with cheeses. There were Italian olives and prosciutto with thin slices of melon, and some dip with manicured crusts of bread that had the faint taste of rosemary. And wine. He'd brought a cabernet that was so smooth I could have polished off the whole bottle. It was good to start learning about wines, because pairing was going to be one of our classes second semester. Anyway, I couldn't get enough of the view, the food, the drive, just everything. And now that I'd stopped thinking about Emilio as anything other than a really good-looking uncle, I was relaxed and able to be myself without stumble-bumbling around like a moron. It turned out that was lucky, because Emilio was about to lay a responsibility so heavy at my feet that, if I'd been in any other frame of mind, I would have run to that beautiful road and hitched a ride back to San Francisco—maybe all the way back to Virginia.

Just as we finished everything Emilio had brought for our brunch, my phone buzzed. It was Nick.

Wen do u arrive

I turned to Emilio. "Nick wants to know when we'll be there."

"It's about five hours from here, so before dinner time I expect."

I looked at my phone. It was only eleven.

I texted Nick back *Mayb 4 txt u wen ½ hour away?*

Nick gave a thumbs up to that and then a heart. He was so sweet.

"Can you open that Ferrari up and make like the wind?" I smiled at Emilio.

"I'll see what I can do."

He looked serious all of a sudden, like something was bothering him. Anyway, his mood had definitely shifted.

"Are you okay?"

"Ah, you are so sensitive. I am okay, yes, but you are right to ask. Now that we have enjoyed our brunch and I know you are eager to start the rest of our drive to see your Nick, I must tell you some important things. I admit I have been putting this off, but Aunt Augusta was right that day at The Manor. Time is a factor for us, for you, for all of us."

I tried to remember what Aunt Augusta had said. So much happened. It was kind of a fog. I did remember Tessa. And Bauble. And some weird stuff I drank. But time? What had she said about time? Something about the equinox. Quetzal had to tell me what it was. When day and night are equal. Of course about my birthmark. A few times I'd thought about calling Foxy to tell her about it. Then I'd catch myself because, knowing Foxy, first she wouldn't believe me, and then she'd want me to use it to get her more stuff. Expensive stuff. No, telling Foxy was an idea that came and went pretty quickly. But when she did call me—and she hadn't yet because she's about as motherly as a clam—she might figure something was up, so I decided to be chatty and just tell her about school. Maybe I could mention the tiny cottage I'd found to rent because, after all, even though it was a paltry amount, she was sending me money to live on, so I owed her that much. But that might lead to telling her where it was and about The Manor, so maybe I should just say I found a safe place to live.

My mind was racing a bit, and I forgot about Emilio wanting to tell me something.

"Oh, sorry," I said. "I was thinking about something. Trying to remember what Aunt Augusta said that day. It seems like a long time ago, now, but it was only a few days. Funny how so much has happened." I finally shut up. It was embarrassing sometimes the way I could run at the mouth like some word river.

"Let's pack up. We can talk while we drive. I'm sure your Nick is anxious to see you."

Chapter Sixteen
I Like The Ferrari

I have to say it was exciting to be riding in his Ferrari. I imagined it must feel like when a horse is thundering down a racetrack heading for the finish line. I'd watched a couple of those races with Foxy. Of course, she liked racing. And betting. I wanted to think I missed her but really I didn't. Whenever she was around, it was the Foxy show. Like nothing else in the world mattered. It could be tiring. I never felt there was much space for me. But now, I had a whole new life. And power I never even imagined.

"Amanda, that day at Aunt Augusta's, she implored me to tell you more about your powers."

"Oh, right. Now I remember. At least some of it. And she also told me not to waste them on frivolous pursuits. Whatever that means. And now I remember she said something about why I came out here."

The road whizzed by. I looked at the ocean. Wave upon wave curling up and then breaking in a wash of white. It was mesmerizing.

"Aunt Augusta summoned you to come to California. As she summoned me. That is her special power. To summon when there is a need."

"I don't understand. Didn't the school ask you to come here to teach culinology this semester? I mean, Ms. McCracken was so gushy about you being here and teaching us."

"Yes. That's true. But Aunt Augusta made that happen, too."

"How did she do that?"

"She used Bauble."

I sat there while the car sped on, thinking about this information. It really was too much to comprehend.

"Are you saying she summoned us, using Bauble, that prancy little airhead of a fluff ball? How in hell did she do that?"

"Aunt Augusta has been practicing spells for over four hundred years. But she saves her power for the most important cases. She's right: It's not to be used for frivolous reasons. Like what you did to Armand. I can see why you did it. He was being an idiot. Why, I can't say. Perhaps he's just that way with everyone. There are people like that. He's annoying but harmless.

"But Aunt Augusta said we don't have much time, and that's what I must talk to you about now. Do you remember I said we would talk about why I didn't—as you say—poof us some lunch?"

I nodded. "Yes."

"We spell casters follow an astronomical cycle. Twice each year, our powers are at their lowest and highest. When day and night are equal, our powers are recharged. Do you understand? There's a natural weakening of spell casting power leading up to the fall and spring equinoxes, and when that is past, the power restores itself.

"You mean, like, when your TV remote rechargeable battery goes dead and then you recharge it and, boom, your remote works again?"

"Well, that's a simple way to put it. In reality, it's a much more complex process; but, yes, there's an ebb and flow like the tide. But in addition, the more you use your spells, the more they deplete. If it's just little spells, like what you did to Armand, the drain is not much. But if you're called upon to perform some really powerful spells, it happens much faster, although only temporarily. I know it sounds confusing."

"Wait a minute. Are you saying there are different levels of spells? I can't believe we're talking about this. A week ago, I was just a girl entering culinary school and now all this spell stuff comes at me and I'm expected just to fall in line and do what I'm told. Like this is my destiny or some weirdo thing."

"It is certainly a lot for you to absorb all at once like this. And I am sorry about that. But there was no other way. You see, we had to get you to California quickly. Since you like cooking, the school seemed to be the most viable choice.

"We did not bring you here for some minor reason; otherwise, we could have waited until a more opportune time to tell you about your powers. But really, what would have been a better time? No matter how we did it, you would go through the same shock and confusion. That's common. Each of us has had to learn about what we are. And each one of us had to experience a transition in thinking, in behaving. It impacts every second you are on Earth and all your involvements, human, animal, plant, everything."

"Well, what if I didn't want this gift? What if I wanted to get rid of it?"

Emilio looked straight ahead at the road and it seemed we were going a hundred miles an hour, yet the ride was smooth.

"I understand what you're asking. The answer is it is not possible to—as you say—get rid of it. Not once you know you have it. It's lain dormant within you all these years like a treasure stored in an old trunk put away in an attic. But now the trunk has been opened, the power has been discovered, unleashed. It will be with you, part of you, forever."

"Will I be able to get married? Have children? Have anything like a normal life?"

"That depends on who you marry. It has to be someone incorruptible. Someone who can accept who you are for yourself and not for the power you hold. That is why your father disappeared. He could never marry your mother. He was elevated among our caste, one who was born to greatness."

"What do you mean 'born to greatness'?"

It seemed like the more Emilio told me, the more there was to tell. I began to feel like I was tumbling down a rabbit hole that would never hit bottom.

"There is a complicated explanation, but let me try to simplify it for our purposes. Our caste—you may think of it as a group or clan or whatever word you wish to assign it—dates back many hundreds of years to those islands now known as The Hebrides. Some say these islands have mystical properties and that these properties came from the Norsemen who invaded and intermarried with the indigenous women. No one is sure when or how a small number of the inhabitants were imbued with special gifts. Gifts to cast spells. Gifts like yours, in fact. Over the many centuries these islands were inhabited, there were wars and power struggles which, in certain years, resulted in waves of emigration to America and Canada.

"During one of those prolonged struggles for supremacy, a spell caster called Zorn migrated from Europe and what was then called the State of the Teutonic Order. He was highly gifted but became greedy and corrupted by his unbridled need for power. There came a time when your father, Jack, was tasked with overpowering him to restore order to the islands. He used his more advanced magic to overcome Zorn, who was subsequently banished from the islands after his power had weakened to the point where he could no longer cast spells but only influence others. He is said to have wandered for a long time, looking for converts to manipulate, until he arrived in America, where he found fertile ground to create a base and expand his unscrupulous enterprises."

"So, he's not in our caste?"

"That's right. But he has set out to destroy our caste—and especially your father."

"Why?"

"Because, like all corrupt beings, he wants power and control. Not for any good purpose or to improve the lives or wellbeing of any living thing, but singularly to have power to wield as he wishes. And he seeks revenge."

"Sounds to me like a real jerk."

"I wonder, Amanda, what would you do if you came upon someone like this?"

"I have no idea. I just hope I never have the pleasure."

Chapter Seventeen
I Meet Up with Nick

I should have asked more questions during that drive,
but it was a lot to absorb—with what Emilio had already told
me and, to be honest, I think I didn't want to know more
about castes and spells and all that stuff. I was excited that I
would soon see Nick again, so that occupied my thinking for
the rest of the drive. Emilio stopped giving me info, so that
worked out okay. I mean, really, what did I care about
waning powers and being gifted with spells? I'd started to
think it was better not to let anyone know about all that
anyway. It was a secret I could keep, for once in my pathetic
life. Which, by the way, was turning out to be not so
horrible since I'd moved west. I liked it. The weather was
nice all the time. The school was fine for what it was. I
wasn't looking for some ivy-covered campus with a bunch of
sorority girls trying to outdo each other for dates, and I was
learning a skill I could use. So all was fine and dandy. Now,
if Nick and I could keep seeing each other, that would make
this the perfect decision, no matter how it got made. The
first one of my adult life. A good way to start.

We drove on in silence and, pretty soon, we turned
east, away from the Pacific at Ventura and followed signs to
the Pasadena Freeway.

"How much longer until we get there?"

Emilio didn't answer right away. He seemed to be
thinking about something, but I couldn't tell what. Finally,

he turned his head a little toward me, still keeping his attention on the road.

We have less than thirty minutes to reach Pasadena. Then a little more to arrive at the school."

I pulled out my phone and texted this info to Nick. He immediately answered: *great meet me at Caltech hall. U cant miss it. Tall white bldg long pond in front. Go from e cali blvd at lite past physics bldg takes u rite there*

I pulled up the map on my phone and zoomed into a map of Cal Tech. Yes, I could see where he was talking about. It was the middle light.

"Go to East California Boulevard. It runs along the south edge of the campus," I told Emilio.

"I know the area," he said. "I've been here before. While you are visiting with Nick, I will also visit an old friend. I will drop you off at the correct light so that you can find your way."

The miles dropped behind us until we turned off the freeway. I was so excited I could barely sit still. I wanted to fly right out of the car.

"Amanda, while we have a few more minutes, I have to warn you."

"About what?"

"While you're visiting here, be careful what you do or say."

"You mean about my powers? About the spells?"

"Yes, but more: While you're here, I believe you will be tempted to use them. You must resist this temptation. Soon, you will need all your power. And, as we approach the equinox, it will diminish anyway. So you must protect it and yourself. You will be tempted to tell Nick about your newly discovered gifts, but this is not wise unless a situation arises where you are both in grave danger."

"You're giving me the willies."

"It is for your own safety that I tell you these things. Nothing that happens is an accident. Remember that and you will stay strong."

"One question: When you say my powers will diminish, well, how much? I mean, would I still be able to poof stuff?"

Emilio laughed. It was the first time he'd eased up since we left.

"You could still 'poof stuff,' as you say. But nothing big. Nothing important. And you would not be able to save yourself if you came up against someone stronger, more powerful in spell casting. When we're back at school—at your school—you will continue to learn how to combine cooking with spells. There is much power in that. And much danger if misused."

As usual, his answer didn't completely make sense to me. But we were on the street where I was to leave, so I let it go because, anyway, nothing mattered to me at that moment except seeing Nick again.

And then, just before Emilio was to drop me off, my phone buzzed again and, when I looked at it, the text was from Foxy. *Oh God*, was all I could think.

He was sitting on a stone bench, texting on his phone, so I saw him before he saw me. I took mine out of my bag and texted him. *i m here*

When he looked and saw me walking toward him, he jumped up and it was pretty much what you'd expect. We were both delirious, which was good because you don't want to be the only one who's acting like a fool. Especially if there's a chance he doesn't feel the same way he did the last time you saw him. So, phew.

We walked around the campus, taking our time in the afternoon sun. It was kind of overwhelming in a beautiful way. We passed people wandering around and he told me that a lot of local people came to the campus to walk their dogs or push their baby strollers or just to take some time away from the city. It was like a park, only with a lot of buildings. Finally, he led me to this sort of lake with rocks and a gentle waterfall and roses and trees with branches hanging down that reflected in the water. It was shady and cooler than the rest of the walk, so we sat on a flat rock overlooking the water and were quiet for a few moments.

"Do you miss your dad?" I asked him, although I hadn't planned on talking about that. It just sort of popped out.

"Yeah. Sometimes. But, you know, it's been a while now, and I've been occupied and busy since I got here. I'll tell you one thing. I don't miss the East Coast at all. I really like it out here. The weather's always nice. Summers are really hot, but I don't mind that. Anyway, maybe I won't stay for the summer. Maybe I'll travel somewhere. Now that I'm out West, I'd like to see more of it. What about you? How's San Francisco?"

He took my hand and held it with our fingers intertwined. I ached to tell him about everything. It was all I could do to contain myself. Secrets really bite.

"I like the culinary school. I feel like I'm learning something useful."

Yeah, I was learning something useful, but it was excruciating not being able to tell him about the rest of it. Bundt cakes and reduction sauces were hardly worth mentioning when you considered spells and magic.

"Where are you living? Did you get an apartment or are you sharing rent with someone from school? I'm still in student housing like last year. They expect us to stay on campus and be collaborative in everything. We study and work in teams."

"Do you like that? I mean, being around others all the time?"

"I don't really think about whether I like it or not. I thought, after my first year, the math would be less intense, but it isn't. And now, physics is just as hard—but exciting, you know? I mean, everyone here is really smart and incisive. It's so far from high school you can't imagine. What about you?"

"The school housing office found me a tiny cottage near school. It's on an old estate with beautiful gardens. I was really lucky. It just sort of fell in my lap. And the rent is practically nothing."

Now I felt like I was almost lying to him. I never imagined being together would tie me up in knots like some criminal with a guilty conscience after a big heist.

"How about Foxy?"

"Oh crap. She texted me just before I got here. I did let her know I arrived okay but maybe she needs to hear from me again. I'm almost afraid to call her. Who knows what's on her mind?"

"It can't be too bad." He patted my hand and I just wanted to hug him. He must have sensed that, because he put his arm around me and kind of nuzzled my neck.

"You know," he said in a low voice, "Foxy may be less than the perfect mom, but at least you have her."

I didn't know what to say, so we just sat like that for a few minutes. It was super hard not to tell Nick everything, and I had to remind myself to back off of anything that would lead to Emilio or Aunt Augusta or, God forbid, Quetzal. I wondered how she was doing. I was pretty sure between Ramos and Tessa they'd keep her food dish full and change her water. It suddenly occurred to me: What if Nick wanted to come up to visit me? I had a slight feeling of panic and then thought I'd better ask Emilio how to handle all this secret stuff in my new life.

"Is anything wrong?"

Nick was staring at me intently and I'd not even noticed it.

"No. Of course not. I'm really happy to see you. I've wondered how you were doing because you suddenly went silent."

"Yeah, I know." He sighed and lowered his gaze to look at the water burbling in front of us. "Look, I've had a lot of things on my mind. I mean, besides physics and math. But that, too. This place is really intense, you know. They expect a lot from us. I guess because everyone here scored so high and it's tough to get in. It's a pretty small school. I mean, undergrads is less than a thousand. So I've really had to keep up. Not that it's too hard for me. But it's relentless."

"This is a beautiful place to be," I said. "I didn't imagine the campus would be so lush or so inviting. I guess I thought it would be more sterile because everyone out here is so concentrated on abstract stuff and thinking in math terms and everything." I felt like that was safe ground to discuss, since pretty much everything else in my life felt iffy.

"I know what you mean. It's easy to assume that people who're inside their heads constantly concerned with breaking atoms and how the universe was formed wouldn't need to see flowers and hear birds calling, but that's not the case at all. I still run three times a week and I like seeing flowers everywhere year-round. It's especially important just because I spend so much time in a classroom or a lab working on complex ideas and formulas. The more I learn in physics, the more I'm stunned by the beauty of the universe and everything in it."

I could have asked him about his classes and stuff, but we both knew I wouldn't understand any of it, so I kept silent.

"You know the reason I came out here to Cal Tech, right?"

"You thought maybe you could find your mother."

"Yeah, well, after the first year out here, I got so involved with school I kind of forgot about it. But it's always in the back of my mind. Kind of nagging at me. Like some mathematical equation I can't solve that feels like I'm near an answer. So—and don't go all ape about this—back at the beginning of August I hired a private detective agency to try to find her."

"You what? That's so bold. I never would have thought of that. How long have they been looking? What have they found out? Anything at all?"

Nick looked up at the sky as if he was searching for answers way beyond the planet.

"I'm not sure, now, if I want them to find her. I mean, she left us and I have no idea why. Maybe it's better if she stays just a memory, even if it's not a good one. She could be some horror show. Or just crazy town. I don't know. What do you think?"

Oh man, he was asking me—the one who was keeping this huge secret life, the one who couldn't really tell him much of anything. The thing was, I wanted to tell him to dig as far as he could because knowing the truth is better than not knowing what happened. Even if the truth is ugly, even if it's not what you hoped to find, even if it doesn't solve what happened in the past, it's better to face it down so you can come to terms with it. Anyway, that's what I wanted to tell him. When I hesitated, he looked straight at me like a knife going through me and coming out the other side.

"I think it's better to know than to wonder," I told him. "Because if they can find her—and it's been a long time now—at least you'll know what happened. Don't you think that's better than not knowing?"

"I guess."

"If you knew you didn't want to find her, you never would have hired these people to look, would you?"

"That's true. I could have just let it go a long time ago. But it nags at me sometimes, especially when I'm out running. It repeats in my head like a song I can't get out of my mind."

"And you probably think she didn't love you."

He looked so sad when I said that, like a little boy. I leaned over and kissed him on the cheek and he put his arms around me and just hugged me tight. At that moment it felt the way it did when we were in high school. So much had happened to both of us, but we were still the same.

Nick wanted to show me all around the school, so we walked the paths as he pointed out physics buildings and mathematics buildings and all the others. This one donated by that person and another donated by this gazillionaire and the ones where Nobel Prize winners did their work. It was all kind of overwhelmingly brainy, and I began to wonder why Nick was still interested in me with my dumb-as-a-bag-of-rocks math brain and my shop-til-she-drops mom. And I wondered what he would think of me if I ever told him about the spell stuff. Really, to be honest, I didn't know whether I wanted this incredible gift or if I just wanted to renounce it—if I could even do that. But then there was my father. My REAL father, the one I'd never known but who had been like a ghost in my life, hovering in the background, a vaporous being I wanted desperately to know but only thought of as Pasadena Man. Now here I was.

I made a mental note to ask Emilio for more details.

Then I saw this tall, blond-haired girl walking toward us on the same path. She seemed to be heading right for us, as if she knew Nick. She was smiling and running her fingers through her curls as she got close enough to speak to us.

"Why Nicky, here you are. I've been looking for you."

Nicky? Nicky? Who was this? She was pretty, I was sorry to see. And wearing what I considered a fashionable outfit.

"Oh, Mimi. Hi."

Nick sounded not the least surprised to see this ooey-gooey girl who called him "Nicky." I was surprised, though, and thought about when I'd called him and heard a female voice in the background.

"Is this your little friend from home?"

"This is Amanda. She came down from San Francisco to visit."

All of a sudden, Nick sounded lame. And I was in no way delighted to be referred to as his "little friend from home," like some high schooler who'd been let out on a weekend pass. My index finger started to twitch and my mind ran through a long list of possible diseases I might inflict on her. Mimi. Not a name I would have associated with anyone I knew.

"Amanda, this is Mimi. She's my physics lab partner. We're working on an experiment together."

An experiment? My mind was racing by then. I just bet you're experimenting. She looks like a real scientific type.

"Nicky, you make it sound so clinical. Physics can be highly stimulating in all sorts of ways. Maybe you can explain it to your friend. I'm sure she'd be interested in how atomic power is released when a **neutron collides with a uranium atom and splits it**. Wouldn't you, er, Amanda, isn't it?"

Okay, that was it. No matter what Emilio or Aunt Augusta had said about weakening my power leading up to the equinox, it was only eight days until September twenty-third, when I'd be at full capacity again, and I was not about to let this atomic gamma girl go without a taste of some of my own power to split stuff. The question was only what to split.

At that moment, my phone buzzed. Well, I knew it couldn't be Nick, so I looked at it and saw it was Emilio.

Be careful, Amanda. Don't squander your gift on nonentities.

I had no idea how he knew what was happening. Or that he even had my cell number. Or that he even had a cell phone. But then, Emilio had his own power, so I supposed he'd been keeping track of me somehow. I mean, if they could get me to come all the way out to culinary school without my realizing it, then they could certainly track my own—shall we say—experiments.

"Who is it?" Nick asked, glancing over at the phone in my hand.

"Oh, it's my teacher. The one who drove me down here. He wants to know when I want to drive back."

"How sweet," Mimi piped up. "Your teacher takes a special interest in you. I wish I had a teacher who'd drive me five hours to see my high school buddy."

Okay, this was too much to resist. My finger was actually twitching uncontrollably.

"Well, when you're really special, teachers recognize it and they want to nurture it in any way they can."

"I suppose in cooking class, that's so," Mimi snake-smiled at me. "Nicky, is she going to bake you a cake while she's here?"

"Hey, Mimi, let it go, okay? Amanda, are you getting hungry? There's a good Greek place not too far from here."

But Mimi was not about to let it go. "Well, Amanda, see how much Nicky cares about food? Any old Greek diner is fine with him. But I suppose you've learned how to cook up a five-course meal by now. That must be awfully stimulating for the mind, don't you think, Nicky?"

"I hope they have kolokithokeftedes. I suppose you like that Greek dish, too?" I smiled at Mimi, sure she would have no idea what that was and glad my culinary interests back home had included cooking some Greek dishes.

Just then I spotted a man with two small dogs on leashes heading our way. As he approached, Nick took my arm as he moved to the side of the path to let the man pass. I'd been holding back for so long it felt like I was about to burst. I raised my hand a little and pointed at the dogs and whispered, under my breath, "May she making speeches get tangled by leashes."

The dogs started yapping. They pulled at their leashes so that the man had trouble keeping them apart until they ran one on either side of Mimi's feet and then met on the other side in front of her and then crossed again twice, pulling her down. When she fell, they yapped like crazy. The man tried to untangle them from Mimi but couldn't, and they dragged her onto the grass, yapping and leaping.

Nick went over to help the man and, together, they got the dogs and their leashes straightened out while Mimi sat on the grass looking stunned. Tears came down her face as she glared at the man.

"You shouldn't be allowed to walk your dogs here if you can't control them," she yelled at him, her face red with rage and embarrassment.

"I'm so sorry," the man said. "I don't know what got into them. They've never done anything like that before. Usually, they're so well behaved. Are you okay?"

Nick took Mimi's arm to help her stand.

"She's okay," he told the man. "Just a little rattled."

By now the dogs were calm and harmless, standing silently by the man, a confused look still on his face. I watched the whole scene with secret glee.

"Maybe you'd better go back to the dorm and take a break," Nick told her.

He walked over to me and said, "Let's get something to eat at the Greek place. Okay with you?"

"I'm not a food snob." I didn't look back.

Chapter Eighteen
I Get Astounding News (and so does Nick)

In the middle of our Greek meal, which I have to say was incredibly good, my phone buzzed again, so I took it out and saw it was Emilio. I made a mental note to ask how he knew my number. I couldn't imagine what he could want now.

Nick looked at me as if to say, "Again?"

"Sorry. I have no idea what he wants. Should I just let it go to voicemail?"

"No. Of course not. Maybe he wants to coordinate when you're driving back. Text him back. I don't mind."

This just reinforced all the feelings I'd always had for Nick. He was steady and unshakeable. Not a quality you often find in guys. But this also made me think about what he and I hadn't discussed: where I was going to stay. And for how long. I did have to be back on Monday for classes. Did Nick expect me to stay in his room? And that led to the other obvious question, which had not come up since he'd left for college. Anyway, I held my phone and read Emilio's text.

We leave early tomorrow. You must meet my friend. Go to 23 Oak Grove Terr. Use code 5297 at gate

I was about to tell Nick, but then his phone rang. He used a funny ring tone that sounded like smashing glass. He dug into his pocket and pulled it out. It took longer to read his message than mine had taken and, as I watched him read it, he got a really weird expression on his face, like he was upset but also worried.

"What is it?" I couldn't imagine, but then I thought about Mimi, that maybe she was tracking us.

I was about to make a snarky comment when Nick raised his head—he looked like someone had hit him with a board. I thought he was going to cry, so I reached across the table and just touched his hand with my fingertips. Tears welled up in his eyes, just to the point of spilling over.

"Nick," I whispered. "Tell me what's wrong."

"They found her. The investigators found her." He cleared his throat and wiped at his eyes with the back of his hand. "I can't believe it."

He handed me his phone so I could read the text for myself.

Mr. Weyland, it started, which was funny to think of Nick as Mr. anything.

We're texting to report that we've located your mother. It would be good to meet so we can show you the details. The sooner we meet the better, we believe. Please respond asap.

I looked up at Nick. It was pretty stunning—after four years of wondering what had happened to her—but it still didn't explain why she'd left or where she was.

"What are you going to do?"

"I don't know. It's really a shock. I never believed they would find her."

"What was she doing before she disappeared?"

"Oh, you know, just housewife and mother stuff. And work. She was always really smart."

He grew quiet. I could see he was thinking. Maybe thinking back to four years ago, before I ever met him.

"I vaguely remember—you know, when you're in high school, you're not really aware of what's going on with your parents, I mean beyond where it concerns you. But I think she was going to some meetings somewhere. I don't really know why. At the time I thought it was at a church. But it's all kind of dim."

"I would want to know what they found right away, especially after so many years of wondering. How do you feel?"

He looked bewildered now. "I'm not sure. But yes, I want to know. If I wait, it'll gnaw at me, I'm sure."

"Well, Emilio texted me just before yours and he wants me to meet him at his friend's house and that he has to leave early tomorrow morning. How about we both go over there and you could have the investigator meet you there, too?"

At that moment, my phone buzzed again.

Amanda, when will you arrive?

"It's Emilio again. He wants to know when I'll arrive. Should I text him back and tell him you're coming too and meeting someone else there also?"

"Would that be okay with him? And what about his friend? I mean, I don't want to just bust in on them."

"I'll text and ask. He's not shy. He'll tell me if it's not okay."

bringing Nick he needs to meet up with someone so he'll give them the address OK?

"Oh, he sends a thumb up, so we're all set."

"Thanks, Manda. I'm glad you were here when I got this news. No one I know at school would understand."

"Not even Mimi?" Okay, so I had to toss that snark in after all.

"Mimi's only my lab partner. We were preassigned by the physics professor. She's smart but she's a pain."

I didn't expect it, but a wave of relief swept through me and I totally relaxed. We finished our food and thanked the owner for a fabulous meal, which made me want to learn more Greek cuisine. Before we left, I texted the address of Emilio's friend to Nick, and he texted it to the investigator and wrote to meet us there in an hour.

"That's not too far from here," he said. Let's walk back to campus parking so I can pick up my car and we'll drive over."

"Do you still have your dad's old beat-up Beemer?"

"Yeah. It runs fine. And I don't have to worry about getting carjacked because no one would want it but me."

He laughed. I was glad his mood had lightened.

"Is the investigator local? I mean, can he be there in an hour?"

"It's a she and, yes, she's local." His phone rang again. "She's texting she can make it. But may take more than an hour."

As we walked back to pick up Nick's car, we didn't talk at all. My mind went through about a million machinations about his mom and then about my father. Nick walked faster than I did, so I had to kind of hop every once in a while to keep up. I guess being a runner made him walk faster, too. I could have zapped him to slow down or myself to speed up, but it was becoming clearer to me that it would be better not to waste my power on such small matters. It had been awfully satisfying to wrap those dogs around Mimi, though. I smiled thinking about it and wondered what Nick would say if I told him how it really happened. This was all so new to me that part of me couldn't stand holding it inside. And another part of me was terrified by the idea of anyone—other than someone else with these powers—finding out.

"I keep wondering where they located her. And how," Nick said from out of nowhere.

"Well, isn't that what they're experts at? I mean, otherwise, why hire them?"

"Yes, but, if they could find her in a month, why couldn't she have looked for me during all those years? I'm not even sure now if I want to find her."

"Not like some nice, neat physics experiment, is it?"

"No. Not at all. If I follow this logically, I come to a sort of crossroads. I could leave it as it is and live with it like I have for the past four years. Or I can confront her. So then what?"

"You can't know what happens then. Because it's not in your control. Ignoring the situation is in your control. But it doesn't satisfy you and doesn't make you happy."

All this was coming out of me without admitting that my own situation was eerily similar. I had no idea where my father was or what it would be like to meet him. I was even more removed from him than Nick was from his mother. After all, he'd lived with her for years before she'd walked away. I had never met my father. I wasn't faced with finding my father, though. At least not right then. If Emilio was right, that would happen and, when it did, I would have to face exactly what Nick was facing now—or maybe worse. It was all so lame anyway that maybe I'd just renounce my powers and live a normal life. Who wanted to live with such a secret? If I could even do that. I wondered how that worked. Another thing I'd have to ask Emilio.

"You're probably right," Nick was saying as we reached the garage. "I've gone this far to find her. I might as well go the whole nine yards. I mean, what could possibly happen? She'll either want to see me or she won't. If she doesn't, I'm no worse off than I've been all these years when I assumed she didn't want to see me or else she wouldn't have left. I've been sad and angry long enough. I'm glad you're here and we'll find out together. I feel more confident about it with you around."

We got in the car. It looked just like when he used to drive me to school. It even smelled the same. Old leather and pine needles from when he worked for a landscaper after school and on weekends. I'd bet some of those needles were still in the trunk, along with bits of burlap infused with pine sap. As I was soaking up the scent, Nick put his arm around me and leaned in, his face close to mine, and, when I turned to look at him, he kissed me. It was a long, slow kiss, the kind that can lead anywhere.

It only took fifteen minutes to reach 23 Oak Grove Terrace, but we must have sat at the security gate for another five minutes just gaping before we even punched in the code. I mean, who lives in a place like that?

Two filigreed gates at least ten feet high slowly swung apart to let us pass like we were entering the palace grounds. Once the gates clanged shut behind us, we inched forward on a long, curved driveway made of perfectly fitted bricks ground so smooth they seemed to be all one long piece. This driveway was wide enough to accommodate three cars next to each other as it curved gently toward a house that seemed to go on forever. Once we were in front of the house, we saw that the driveway was even wider, and we could see that the house had wings on either side. It was so massive I couldn't even grasp how many rooms it could have or what those rooms could possibly contain. The grounds were so manicured I figured it took a crew of a dozen working from dawn until dusk, but I didn't see any around. It was sure nothing Ramos could handle, even with spells.

Nick slammed on the brakes and sat staring at where Emilio's Ferrari sat in the sun.

"Whoa," he almost yelled.

I'd never seen him get really excited before. He'd always been sort of a thinker. Not a reactor. Not someone who shows emotion easily.

"That's a Purosangue. A real one. Holy cow."

He pulled over next to it and turned off his car, then jumped out and approached that car as if he'd just found the key to the universe. Okay, I admit it was a nice car. I liked riding in it. But the way guys go nuts over cars is way beyond understanding.

"Amanda!"

I got out of Nick's car just as Emilio called from the front door of the palatial estate. And, by the way, the door was painted red, of all colors. For some reason I found that amusing because the shutters were charcoal gray and there were two awning-like things overhanging large one-story tall French windows on either side of the front door, and they were also charcoal gray. That was the main house. Off of the right side there was an extension, just as big as the main house, and it had no shutters at all. The house itself was a very pale gray.

Emilio, dressed in slacks and a navy blazer, waved as he briskly walked over to us. I looked at Nick in ratty jeans and a Cal Tech T. He was wearing running shoes, of course. At least I had thought about what to wear before leaving my cottage. Quetzal helped me coordinate a teal jumpsuit with a white T-shirt. She also zapped me a new pair of sandals with little seashells on the straps. I looked pretty cute, but she said I shouldn't go around with a big head. Anyway, I didn't feel totally lame going into this ginormous fancy house.

"And is this Nick?" he said when he was close enough for an introduction.

"Yes. Nick, this is Chef Emilio, my teacher from school."

Nick was still in the throes of his love scene with the Ferrari, but he managed a weak smile and handshake.

"Ah, you're admiring my car."

"Is this yours? She's a beauty. I've never seen one. Must be amazing to drive. What year is it? How fast have you driven in it? Is it a smooth ride?"

"Would you like to see for yourself?"

"If you have time to take me out in it."

"No no—I mean, for you to drive me. Would you like that? We could drive up to the hills. Once you get to the ridge there are some roads that never get used, where you could really test it out."

"Are you kidding?"

"Not at all! Let us go now. I'll just take Amanda into the house and introduce her to my friend. All right?"

"All right? God, yes."

All of a sudden, Nick was someone I didn't even know. A drooling doofus. Because of a car. Who could understand men?

153

"Your friend?" I turned to Emilio. "Are you just going to leave me here alone?"

"You'll be fine. We won't be gone long. And I'm sure you'll be well cared for. My friend is a most charming and interesting person, and she's eager to meet you both. Come, we'll all go to the house."

If Nick can tear himself away from the Ferrari, I thought, as we walked toward that inexplicably red door.

✳

I had no clue what to expect Emilio's friend to be like but, based on the house, if she carried a scepter and wore a crown, I wouldn't have been totally shocked.

When she opened the door, I was surprised, but not in any way I'd expected.

"Ahhh," she said in a voice so soft I had to lean in a little to be sure I could hear her, and I did pick up an accent somewhat like Emilio's, so I assumed she was also from Italy. "You have arrived at last. Emilio, bring them into the library where we have some sweets and tea set out."

She waved us ahead and, as she walked in front of us, three orange cats with extremely long hair, their tails erect and waving a little, appeared from somewhere. They bounded ahead and stopped every few steps to keep pace with us. "Walked" is not precisely a good description of how the woman moved. It was like watching some slow-motion dancer. Her steps were precise, but she almost seemed to float. I guess the way I would describe her if I had to choose only two words would be "elegant" and, I think, "serene." She just seemed goddess-like. A total match for Emilio, I thought, and then it dawned on me. Oh right, she's not just his "friend."

I felt like an idiot by the time we made it down a long hall past a lot of doorways until we finally reached the library. And what a library! It was not your everyday working library; this one had floor-to-ceiling—very high ceilings—shelves of leather-bound books of all sizes. It was not so much a library as it was a museum. One summer, Foxy had sent me to an art appreciation course at one of the DC museums. So I'd learned some stuff about European and American art and couldn't help but notice a smallish (for him anyway) Rodin sculpture in one corner. And that wasn't all. The room was studded with sculptures and artifacts that looked ancient and decidedly foreign.

"Oh, no," Emilio said as Nick and I examined the room. I wondered what Nick thought of all this, aside from the car awaiting him outside. "I've forgotten to introduce you. Contessa Della Robbia, I'm happy to introduce you to Nick and Amanda. My new friends."

"So pleased." The Contessa motioned for us to sit on a plush couch in front of an enormous bronze-and-glass coffee table all laid out with food and an elaborately decorated gleaming silver tea set. I thought of the one I'd seen at The Manor and wondered if these two ladies ever got together for a coffee klatch.

The cats settled themselves on a small velvet chaise off to one side.

"And may I introduce you to Fluffy, Muffy, and Sam. My companions. They keep me from feeling alone in this big house."

She looked at Nick. "Do you know that your name in Italian—Niccolò—means 'people's champion'? Are you a champion, Nick?" She beamed at him in such a disarming way that Nick smiled back, and I thought I saw a blush spread across his face.

"I hope to be."

"Yes, a fine answer."

The Contessa handed him a cup of tea. The scent of it came to me. A mix of some sweet herb and rose hips. She turned to me with a cup that had the distinct aroma of mint and sage.

"And you, Amanda, what do you hope to be?"

She passed around a plate of small almond-scented Amoretti cookies.

I looked at Emilio, who was smiling broadly at the whole scene.

"I'm not sure. I came to California to learn how to become a great cook. I'm not sure how far I've gotten. I just started and, you know ..." I trailed off. Now was not the time or place to go into everything I'd learned lately.

"To be a great chef requires a certain magic, don't you think, Emilio?" She handed him a cup and I wasn't sure, but it seemed to me she winked at him.

"Ma'am," Nick began, "I, um I hope you don't mind but someone is going to meet me here. I'm not sure exactly when she may show up. It's just that she has some information for me that can't wait, but I can go outside the gate to talk to her. I mean, she doesn't have to come inside or anything."

"Yes, yes, Emilio mentioned something. Do not concern yourself, Niccolò. Your business can be conducted in the office at the other end of this hall. I'm sure it's important or you wouldn't have made the arrangement. And while you have your meeting, Amanda and I can visit my art collection."

Emilio then said, "But first, Nick and I will take a drive into the hills. Yes?"

"That would be fantastic," Nick said. He put down his teacup and stood. "Thank you for the tea. I enjoyed meeting you."

"Enjoy your drive, Niccolò. And you, Emilio, don't go too far."

As they left, the Contessa turned to me. "Come, my dear. Let me show you my treasures. Each has a special place in my heart."

"Are these part of your collection?" I motioned around the large room where sculptures were placed strategically here and there on stands.

"You have a good eye, dear. Yes. That Rodin is a maquette the sculptor did for a large piece. He changed it slightly from the study. This is more intimate, I think, and I like it better."

She led me around the library from piece to piece with Fluffy, Muffy, and Sam padding along next to her—every once in a while rubbing against her leg. I heard the Ferrari drive away, and then its purring engine faded. At one point, from out of nowhere, a tiny mouse appeared in front of my feet before heading to a slightly open French door. And then, I swear, it turned to look at me and let out the oddest little high-pitched peep. The cats just stared at it.

The Contessa stopped. "Oh, Norman, behave yourself," she told it and shook her finger at it. "He is always suspicious of new people. Pay him no mind at all."

The mouse scurried away. I wanted to ask if it was one of those messenger animals. I mean if dogs and birds could be, then why not a mouse?

"Is Norman a pet or something?"

She laughed at that. "Norman is a messenger. Like your Quetzal. Or Aunt Augusta's Bauble. Or these three." She pointed at the triplet cats.

So she knew. And that meant she was one of them, er us. Can't say I was surprised.

"Wow," was all I could utter. "Where did all this art come from? I mean, did you collect all of it?" What I really wanted to ask was about knowing what I really was and where she came from. But I guess I was afraid in a way because, every time I found out something else, it meant some kind of danger. So I was still wondering what good all these powers were if all they did was put me in trouble.

"Most of it came to me through the Della Robbia family. A long time ago, one of us was a gifted, innovative sculptor in Italy. His sons carried on the tradition for over one hundred years. What you see here are masterpieces. It has been my mission to preserve and protect the pieces that are not in museums. But, let us walk among these works and feel the sense of history they impart. You know, Amanda, when you are blessed with a gift, like an artist is, you must use it wisely, not squander it."

Everyone kept telling me about this great gift. Well, so far I didn't get what I was supposed to do with it. If I was destined to meet my father and all that, why couldn't we just get on with it? Not that I was itchy for a fight or anything like that. I mean, it was great seeing these huge houses and driving around in a Ferrari and all the other stuff I'd never expected or even dreamed of seeing or actually being invited into. But I felt like an intruder, somehow. It just wasn't me. But neither was Foxy and her world. All I knew was that being in a kitchen and cooking up stuff that people liked to eat made me feel good.

"Amanda, you're wondering about me. About us. That's only natural. I didn't discover what I really was until I married—and then only because my husband turned out to be from another caste. I was young then, and naïve. It was on our wedding night that he told me about himself and how he came to choose me for his bride. In fact, I was chosen for him. In those times, arranged marriages were not uncommon, especially among the elite families who wanted to keep their wealth and position intact. Until then I had no idea about spells or witching. He showed me the mark on my thigh that I'd always thought was a freckle. A silly little blemish that meant nothing. But once you know, it comes to mean everything."

I tried to understand what she was telling me, but there were still unanswered questions. Like where all this art came from. And how she ended up so obviously wealthy. I mean, be real: The only thing I knew about money was that Foxy never had any because, the minute a dollar hit her palm, she spent it.

"So all this art came from him?"

"After my husband died, I inherited his wealth. These treasures were passed down directly to me."

"How did your husband die? I mean, I thought ... well, how old are you? I don't mean to be disrespectful but, like Aunt Augusta and Tessa told me they're centuries old."

She nodded. "That's true. So was my husband. But even we have a life span. His lasted until it was over. And then I met Emilio. We became good friends."

"Is that how he got the Ferrari? From you?"

"Clever girl. Yes. It was a gift from me."

At that moment, we heard the Ferrari drive up past the gates. There was no mistaking that sound. I never thought

I'd have a car as a rival. Maybe I could zap its spark plugs or something.

"Come, Amanda. I'm sure the wanderers have adventures to share."

Chapter Nineteen
I Learn the Truth

It's weird how stuff that happens changes you. Like when Nick got back from driving that piece of art that just happened to have a motor and a bunch of things called pistons that were, and still are, a mystery to me. He was so wound up I thought he might bust a synapse or something.

Emilio just stood there smiling while Nick went on and on about what an amazing experience it was to drive that car. And then he said something that shifted the mood into low gear.

"Up in the hills there's a road that runs along the ridge. It's flat so we could really fly. It was the most astounding experience of my life. And you know, while we were up there, we slowed down when we passed this sort of enclave that looks like some kind of religious retreat. It was very weird and ..."

At that point all three cats leaped off the chaise and started to hiss. Their hair stood up like they'd been electrified and they hunched their backs and then spat at the air. The Contessa didn't seem at all surprised, but I was freaked out like you can't believe.

And then we all heard a buzzer.

"Kitties, hush," said the Contessa. "I believe your associate has arrived." She nodded to Nick as she walked to an intercom on the wall and pushed a button. Then she opened the front door and we watched the tall entrance gates slowly swing open to let a car through.

Nick looked at me, although I wasn't sure what was going to happen or what he wanted me to do. The Contessa walked out to meet the woman as she got out of her car at the front door.

She was nice looking, with wavy brown hair and glasses. She wore a crisp blue suit and matching shoes with short, fat heels. She looked about forty to me, which I thought of as rather old but, compared to the Contessa and Emilio and the others, I guess she wasn't really old at all. I mean, in witch years.

She carried a canvas briefcase and seemed quite businesslike and determined walking up the front steps to the door.

"How do you do?" she said and extended her hand to the Contessa. "Maxine McCarter, with McCarter, James, and Maggio. I'm here to see Nick Weyland."

"Yes, come in please." The Contessa stood aside. "Niccolò is just inside."

Nick stepped forward and shook hands with this Maxine McCarter, "I'm Nick. Thanks for coming all this way." He introduced all of us and then turned to me. "Amanda, would you come with us? To the office down the hall? Is that all right?" He turned to the Contessa.

"Yes, of course, Niccolò. The last door at the end of the hall that way." She pointed in the opposite direction from the library where we'd had tea. "Take all the time you need. Is there anything I can get for you? Drinks, perhaps?"

"Thank you, no," said Maxine. "I'm not sure how long this will take, so I hope it's not inconveniencing anyone. Usually, the client comes to our office for these meetings, but this is an unusual situation."

She clutched her briefcase with both hands, fingers twined around the handles as if she suspected someone might grab it away from her. I wondered if she carried a gun, and, if she did, where she would hide it. Since her suit had a jacket, I imagined she might have it hidden somewhere under her armpit. I wondered if she'd ever shot anyone, and then I thought what if her search for Nick's mom turned up the truth about me and Emilio and the Contessa. And the cats. And the mouse. Where had it gotten to, anyway? The cats had calmed down, but they stayed right by the Contessa's feet. What had gotten them so riled up? All these thoughts raced through my mind like I was on some mind-spinning drug.

"First, let me explain our method," Maxine said.

Nick led us down the long hall to the office, which was more like a den than anything that looked like a working room. There was a desk and chair but there was also a big couch and two chairs facing it, with a heavy, glass-covered coffee table and recessed ceiling lighting. Also, the room looked out through extra-tall sliding glass doors to a long pool and outdoor spa that all looked very inviting. There was a barbecue pit and a firepit with lounge chairs and tables—I guess to put your drinks on while you pampered yourself. I couldn't even imagine a lifestyle like this. Did the Contessa spend time out here with Fluffy, Muffy, and Sam? Or was she hostess to lavish pool parties for witches from all over the world?

From her seat on one of the chairs, Maxine opened her briefcase and laid a thick folder on the coffee table while

Nick and I watched from the couch. She opened it and turned it around so we could see the papers inside. Then she pulled out a sheaf of papers and began to read from notes.

"We followed the usual procedure in locating a missing person. I did most of the work myself but had some help in the initial stages from Gil Maggio, my associate. He checked all databases of hospitals and death records in the U.S. and Canada. He even did a search for Mexico and the Caribbean Islands as far away as the ABC Islands off Venezuela. At the same time, I did a maritime search of all shipwrecks, abandoned boats, missing boats with persons aboard, missing persons from boats. All those searches came up empty. We searched airplane manifests and that also produced no record of your mother, either under her married or her maiden name. That's when I took over solo and I concentrated on any outstanding vehicle tickets and did find a vehicle registration in her name, but it had expired. Ditto with a driver's license. Then I searched credit cards—and there, I did get some recent hits, so looked for how they were paid and found a bank account, but not in her name. I also contacted the list of names and groups you had given me."

She looked up at Nick. "I know you want me to get to the end result, but it's important that you're up to date on everything."

I was about to burst. I wanted to pick up the folder and look for myself. Poor Nick. I glanced over at him. His jaw was set hard as if he was waiting for some really bad news and he didn't want it to flatten him. I took a deep breath to try to calm myself.

"When we searched from the list of connections, we did come up with a few leads," she went on. "This category of leads is where foot work begins. I spoke to people who knew your mother and they all reported her falling off the radar at the exact same time. All except for one. A woman she grew up with, an old friend, agreed to speak with me as long as I didn't reveal her name or anything about her. After I agreed—in writing—she told me about a conversation she and your mother had right before she disappeared."

At this point Nick looked nervous. He fidgeted on the couch and, all of a sudden, stood up, walked around the coffee table and began pacing around the room. Before I could say anything, Fluffy, Muffy, and Sam ran through the partially open door, although I thought we had closed it, and pushed themselves against Nick's feet so he had to stop. When he couldn't move, he looked at me as if dumbfounded by their behavior. I didn't know what to say, so I called to them and they came over and jumped on the couch where he'd been sitting.

"Sorry," he said to Maxine. "It's upsetting, is all."

"I understand," she answered. "I know you'd like me to get to the bottom line, and I'd like that, too. But I think it's just as important for you to understand the scope of our search and how we got where we are. There are still hurdles. So knowing the whole background will be useful as we go forward."

"But did you find her?"

All three of the cats lifted their heads when I asked that. Since they were all orange, I couldn't tell which one was which, but one of them meowed loudly so I stroked its head and it settled down again.

"I'm getting to that," Maxine answered.

Well, okay, don't give me attitude, lady. That's what I wanted to say, but I kept it to myself. And I couldn't just poof her to get to the end. Then again, maybe she was right, and all this background would be important. I was always too impatient. I vowed right then to concentrate on being more forgiving and to hold still in the moment.

Nick saved me from getting too petulant when he asked, "What did this woman say?"

"She told me that your mother had called her the day before she vanished and said she had found a spiritual path that she felt compelled to follow. The woman asked her what she was talking about, but there was no other explanation, and their conversation ended abruptly.

"Well, that gave me another area to search, which I did. At the time your mother disappeared, there was an organization holding what were termed "enlightenment seminars" during the day in Holiday Inns in the Washington, D.C. area. I contacted all the Holiday Inns in Virginia and Maryland and DC. There are quite a few of them, but I narrowed it down to one that reported there had been seminars like that four years ago. They were held for three months and then they just stopped."

Nick was getting agitated again. "My father always said she ran away and joined a cult. I never believed it. I mean, she wasn't religious. And she was very smart. She used to work in a research lab. She was a chemistry whiz. She wasn't someone who could be talked into anything."

"If you'll please look at the folder in front of you, I'll go over the details of what we know at present," Maxine went on. "I want to tell you, also, that in my work as an investigator, I often have to provide news to clients that's hard for them to accept. Often, we come up empty-handed. In some cases, the person they're looking for is deceased. However, in the case of your mother, we've found her, she's alive and, from everything we can find, is in good health. So those are all positive pieces of news."

"What's the negative?" Nick asked. He picked up the folder and read through the papers inside it, leafing through them quickly.

"Where she is," Maxine answered. "It's not like she's a child; she can be wherever she wants to be."

Nick frowned as he looked at the last paper in the folder.

"What is it?" I asked him. I was beginning to feel a bit defeated by all this cloak-and-dagger searching with no answers. What was the point if Nick's mom wanted to stay where she was and not have any communication with anyone?

"It says here she's with something called The Zorn Institute. It's in—oh my God—Pasadena. It's here. She's right here."

When he said the word "Zorn," the cats started to hiss again; then, they jumped off the couch and ran out the door to the hall. I didn't know if it was registering with anyone but me that Fluffy, Muffy, and Sam had the inside track on Zorn. And it was beginning to dawn on me that there would be trouble ahead. I vaguely remembered what Emilio had said about The Hebrides and a power struggle among the spell casters. Could this be the same Zorn?

Chapter Twenty
I Make a Cosmic Find

"That folder is yours," Maxine told Nick before she picked up her briefcase. "If you need anything more from me, you know how to reach out."

She glanced around the room, then said, "I wonder what's going on with those cats? Oh well, who can understand cats? I've always been a dog person. I have two border collies."

We walked her to the front door. Emilio and the Contessa were there already. She thanked the Contessa for letting her meet Nick at the house, and then she was gone. We stood at the door for a few moments before the Contessa turned to me.

"You'll stay the night here, Amanda. Emilio tells me you have to leave very early tomorrow to get back for a special Sunday evening class. I was surprised to hear he took time off from his duties in Florence to come here to teach. But then, there were special circumstances, no?"

She smiled at me, and I worried that Nick might want to know more about these special circumstances, but he had opened the folder and was deep into it, reading every page carefully. His attention to details and thoroughness had always appealed to me. I guess if you're a scientific type, you have to like minute bits of information. Me, I always skimmed stuff in school. That's probably what attracted me to cooking. You can measure exactly or leave things a little up to chance. Sometimes that works out in a surprise new recipe. But now I was supposed to be learning about the intersection of science and cooking, so maybe I'd have to be more detail oriented like Nick.

As these thoughts ran through my mind, all of a sudden Nick almost shouted out, "Hey. Look at this."

He held up one of the pieces of paper from the folder.

"It says here, on Saturdays, people from the Zorn Institute have a booth at the farmers' market."

"And?" I asked.

"Maybe my mother goes to that. At least some people will be there. I could ask about her, maybe find a way to talk to her. But I've got to get back to my dorm now. I have a big research paper due on Monday."

I walked with him outside, closing the front door to the house behind us. When we reached his car, he stopped and leaned against the door.

"Do you think I should go?"

"To the market next Saturday?"

"Yeah. I mean, do you think it's crazy?"

I wasn't sure what I thought about most of this stuff. "What do you hope would happen?"

"That she'd be glad to see me. That she'd apologize for leaving like she did. That she'd ask about my dad."

"So you'd want to have a relationship with her again? After what she did?"

"I don't know for sure. I guess it would depend on how she'd act if I did see her. Just knowing where she is makes me feel almost hopeful."

"Are you angry at her?"

He sighed and twisted around as if he wanted to avoid that question.

"Yeah, I was angry for a long time. But now I don't think I am."

"You seem different, though. Not the same as when we first met."

He shrugged and turned away so I couldn't see his face.

"People grow up. I was a kid then. A high school kid worried about my next track meet. I closed myself off to feelings until I met you. Then I started to realize how angry and sad I was. When my dad got cancer and it went so fast, I had no time or space to think about much of anything."

"Oh, Nick. It must have all been awful for you. Makes me feel guilty for complaining about Foxy so much."

He turned back to face me, and I could see tears glistening on his lashes, about to spill over.

"You were the best thing in my life then. You still are. When I got to school out here, it was like finding a new world. Like discovering the Earth is not flat. All these incredibly smart people—the students and the teachers— made me feel like I finally had a community of common souls. But it all still had no weight. Do you know what I mean? We all need to feel connected to something solid. Something more than neutrons and protons."

I thought about my childhood fantasy about a large, loving family. I knew exactly what he meant.

"At this point, I think I just want—what do people call it? Closure. Seeing my mother would at least give me that, I would hope. It's a small hope, but I'm still hanging onto it."

"Then I think it's not a bad idea to go to the market and try to contact her. I don't see how it can hurt," I told him.

Nick hugged me. It felt really good.

"Hey, with all the great dishes you're learning, maybe you'll make one for me the next time we see each other."

He leaned in to kiss me goodbye. There was no uncle vibe about it.

That night, I had the weirdest dreams of my life. At one point, I woke up to find Fluffy, Muffy, and Sam curled up together at my feet. Then I went back to sleep, and the dreams continued. You know how sometimes you'll be having a dream and you wake up, but, when you go back to sleep, your dream picks up where it was? Well, that happened a bunch of times, and each time I tried to figure out what I was really dreaming about. And that was in my dream, also. There was some large man in the dreams. He seemed really menacing, like, if I didn't stop him, he was bound to do something terrible, but I didn't know what—and I wanted to find out. That's when I kept waking up.

Finally, the dream stopped and, the next thing I knew, the cats were jumping around on the bed. That woke me up. Dawn light and the cats were a signal that I'd better get going, although I felt kind of groggy. Then I remembered we were leaving early for the drive back to school, so I got out of bed and made it to the shower.

The room the Contessa had given me was pretty large, and the bed was a huge four-poster. I'd always wanted one of those. I felt like a princess climbing the little embroidered stool to get up into it. The bathroom was large, too, with a big white tub and a separate gigantic shower that had a marble seat and lots of shower jets. I wondered if I could hex myself one of those, but then it would never fit in my little rented cottage.

I was beginning to understand why I had to be careful using my new powers. If I used them to get outrageous stuff for myself that I wouldn't be able to explain to other people, I'd spend all my time cooking up lies that made no sense. I guess everything comes with a price of some kind.

Emilio was already eating breakfast when I got downstairs to the dining room—another enormous space. It sure wasn't a cozy house; every room was kind of cavernous. I had my little overnight bag, and I'd made up my bed as well as I could. It was hard to reach around the sides.

"There's food waiting for you over there," he said, pointing at a sideboard where a huge spread was laid out like a hotel buffet.

"Is all this just for us?"

"The Contessa says we can pack up whatever we want from this for the drive. We'll take the freeway back so we can make better time."

I was dying to ask Emilio more about the Contessa. Then, as if he'd read my mind, he said, "I don't need to have the power to read minds to know what you're thinking. You're such an open book; anyone could do it. The Contessa is an interesting case. She married a wealthy man. I'm not sure if she was ever in love with him, but they had a good life together. He was a widower with grown children from his first wife."

"Did she hex his first wife to get rid of her?"

"Now there, you surprise me. I wouldn't have thought it was the kind of thing you'd consider. The answer is no. She just happened to meet him at a resort in Tuscany. They got along and he was lonely. She didn't even know about his title until they were signing the marriage papers. He had only told her his family name was Robbia. She had no way of knowing the family history."

172

"So, if you're finished with your breakfast, are you ready to leave?"

"I'd like to say goodbye to the Contessa and thank her for letting me stay the night."

"She was called away on some business very early. She asked me to tell you how much she enjoyed meeting you and that you're welcome to come back any time and stay as long as you like."

"Amanda, do you remember what Nick said about what we saw when we were driving up in the hills?"

We'd been on the road about an hour, barely talking at all. It wasn't like when we'd driven down to Pasadena all along the ocean. This was a boring freeway with trucks and traffic. We passed a whole lot of farms on the east side and some mountains to our west. I fell asleep a few times. The hum of the Ferrari's engine was kind of hypnotizing. Emilio's voice brought me back to where we were, and I sat up a little straighter.

"Huh? I'm not sure what you're talking about. You mean how excited he was about driving your car?"

"No, not that. About the place he saw up in the hills when we were on the straightaway."

"What place? Did you stop somewhere?"

"Remember, he mentioned what looked like a religious retreat?"

I tried to remember what Nick had said, but it just wasn't coming back to me.

"Sorry, I'm drawing a blank. And, by the way, what class are they holding on Sunday evening at the school? I don't remember that being in the schedule I got."

"This is important, Amanda. It has to do with your father. Nick started to describe it. He said it looked weird, but ..."

"Oh, right. The cats jumped up and started hissing and their hair stood up and everything. That *was* really weird. I wondered why they reacted like that. But what does that have to do with my father?"

"Do you remember the other times the cats got spooked?"

I had to think about it. There had been so much going on in such a short time. It all kind of jumbled together. Finally, it came back to me.

"You mean when they heard the name 'Zorn?'" I looked over at Emilio. He looked kind of grim, like he'd heard some bad news.

"What is it?" I asked him.

"That's where your father is. In Pasadena at The Zorn Institute."

"Are you serious? You mean the same place where that investigator, Maxine, found Nick's mom? Really? That's some coincidence. Are you sure?"

"Yes. And we're going back today because you have a special cooking class. But it's in Aunt Augusta's kitchen. You need to learn some spells, and fast. We haven't got much time to dawdle."

As if I'd been dawdling all this time. Which, by the way, had been less than a whole week. I mean, come on, it was all a lot to absorb.

"So, you're saying that's the same Zorn? The one who got kicked out of the Hebrides a long time ago? That Zorn?"

"That's right."

"But how can you be sure my father's there?"

"The Contessa found him. She has a worldwide network. Funny that he'd be right here, but sometimes fate throws events together in an unpredictable way, almost as if there's a plan in the cosmos."

"What about Nick's mom? Is she part of that cosmic plan, too?"

"I think there will be revelations we can't predict and outcomes we never imagined."

Sometimes Emilio could be so cryptic that it made my head hurt; and now, along with everything else, I had to think about the cosmos.

Chapter Twenty-One
I Learn the Power of Cooking with Spells

So there we were, back at NCC, and me with no time to reflect on seeing Nick or finding out about his mother, or anything else, really. I hadn't tried a spell since the incident with the dogs' leashes. I didn't even know if I could still poof anything. I mean, maybe, if you didn't use the power, it dried up or just evaporated. Obviously, anything was possible.

Emilio dropped me off at the cottage and told me to be at The Manor in an hour for my private class. When I unlocked the door, Quetzal was napping on her perch, her head tucked under a wing. She looked up and squawked at me, ruffled her feathers, and opened her wings in a wide stretch.

"You're back," she rasped. "I didn't miss you."

"Well, nice to see you, too," I answered and dropped my overnight bag on the floor. "Have you behaved yourself?"

She reached into her food bowl and grabbed a sunflower seed. While she worked it open, she stared at me. "I suppose you found your boyfriend. And he was glad to see you. And ..."

"How do you know about him?" It was uncanny the way that bird got my goat. If it was anyone else, I would have tried some kind of hex. But who knew if it would work on a companion?

"Ha. I know all about you. For instance, I know that soon you're going to learn something useful. To both of us." She swallowed the seed and flew to the open window. "I'll see you later. I hope you don't screw it up."

She took off into a tree outside. I could hear some other birds chirping and singing. It was a mystery why any of them accepted her presence. Maybe I could request a more agreeable companion animal. Bauble seemed friendly and helpful, whereas Quetzal only complained. But she did seem to keep up with what was going on and seemed to know more than I did.

Nothing in my cottage had changed, and I was tired from the restless night and the long drive back. I texted Nick that I'd gotten home okay. I thought about calling Foxy, but the last time I'd talked to her she'd said she was going on an extended buying trip for the store, so I had no idea where she was or what she was doing. Besides, talking to Foxy never yielded any rewards, so I let it go. So I just texted her, too, and an hour went by quickly. Soon I was ringing the doorbell at The Manor.

Tessa opened the front door. Her hair was all skewed to one side and she held a wet floor mop in one hand and a bucket in the other. The fact that Aunt Augusta let her anywhere near a bucket of whatever liquid was in there made me wonder about the sanity of anything that happened in The Manor, but I walked in anyway, while Tessa spilled a little out of the bucket and swore under her breath.

"So you're back. I took care of that bird while you were gone. Ornery bugger, isn't she? What she's got her feathers in such a ruffle about all the time is beyond me. We all wait on her like she was a queen. Well, come on in. They're waiting for you in the kitchen."

She slopped her way in front of me—creating an obstacle course of puddles for me to navigate. I thought about telling her to be more careful, but then took into account that this was Tessa and I'd be wasting my breath. Then it occurred to me that maybe I could practice poofing on the way to the kitchen, so I pointed at the most recent pool of water and whispered: *Water sloshing from a pail, dry it up without fail.*

I was so tickled it worked that I wanted to shout! From then on, each puddle evaporated right after it hit the floor, and Tessa motored along, oblivious. When we reached the kitchen, she plunked the bucket and mop in a corner and said, "Here she is."

Aunt Augusta and Emilio stood to the side of the stove and nodded to me.

"Thank you, Tessa," Aunt Augusta said. "We won't need you any more tonight."

Tessa rolled her eyes and patted her hair, a few strands of which had escaped the loose bun and fallen in front of her nose. "I'll go to my room then," she said, and suddenly she was just gone. No walking out. Nothing. Just there and then not there.

I was about to ask how that could happen, but Aunt Augusta put a finger to her lips and shook her head, so I kept quiet.

"Tessa," she said softly, almost in a whisper, "come out now. There's no need to hide like this."

Tessa suddenly appeared again. She left the room, head down, frowning. When she was truly gone, I asked, "What happened? I couldn't see her. Where did she go?"

"It's very simple," Aunt Augusta said. "She uses a very old trick to become invisible. But I can still see her when she does it. She leaves an outline. Understand?"

"You mean like a police chalk line around a body? What kind of an outline? I couldn't see anything."

"The time will come when you'll be able to see it, too. But right now, we have much work to do here."

It seemed to me that being able to erase yourself from view must be the most valuable spell you could ever learn. But I could see arguing wouldn't get me anywhere. Besides, I could see pots boiling on the restaurant-sized stove and the aromas swirling around the room were impossible to ignore.

Emilio had a full chef's apron over his clothes and Aunt Augusta had put on a frilly white one with puffy sleeves. As I approached the stove, she reached out and handed over an apron for me, too.

"Wear this," she said. "As a precaution."

I had an idea that normal cooking splatters weren't the concern. Who knew what goo might find its way onto me?

"You can begin with any ordinary recipe," Emilio explained. "Come, stand by me," he added.

So I went over to the ten-burner stove and looked at the various pots and pans full of whatever was giving off delicious aromas.

"This all smells really good. What are we making?"

Aunt Augusta pointed to the pots and told me about each one.

"Here we have a classic bouillabaisse using haddock fillets as the main fish with peeled prawns. Now the entire ingredient list is long but, for our purposes, what you need to know is that saffron and leek will be what you'll use as conversion elements. Keep that in mind."

I nodded, although I had no idea what she was talking about or what I was supposed to do with this information. At least at school we had a sort of course syllabus and daily goals. And by the end of the year I'd hoped I could get a restaurant job.

"Leek and saffron will allow you to build a repertoire of spells. Of course, you'll have to learn the proper incantations," she sighed, as if I was too big a burden for everyone.

But then she said, "You already know much more than you think you know."

Emilio was cutting leeks into little pieces. On the stove, the bouillabaisse bubbled merrily. My mouth watered. I hoped we'd be the recipients of this meal.

"Now in this pot," Emilio pointed to a smaller one on a back burner, "we have begun an Italian wedding soup. A simple recipe that anyone can make. I've prepared the small meatballs already and the pasta to use is acini de pepe. But the ingredient for conversion is simple and readily available: spinach."

He tossed some, along with a bunch of other vegetables, into the pot. Steam rose in a single stream and I thought I heard a muffled sound like a cat meowing. Okay, this was getting weird.

"What is it supposed to do?" Maybe it was a dumb question but, really, how else could I get them to tell me what they wanted me to learn?

"Patience, Amanda," Aunt Augusta said. "Tonight, you will learn how to cast spells through foods. It's simple, really. First, you must learn which foods are conversion positive. That means, in the hands of a skilled practitioner, they can be used to evoke spells powerful enough to change outcomes or, in the wrong or inexperienced hands, to wreak havoc. So we must proceed with caution and care and make sure our aims are well defined and controlled."

I slipped the apron over my head and tied it around my waist, ready for whatever was next. They were right. There was a lot to learn. I ground dried herbs and spices, then mixed batches of them together as they instructed. I had to use an old-fashioned pestle to grind them into fine powders. Sometimes I breathed in the strong scents and felt woozy. Aunt Augusta made me move back until the powders settled. I watched Emilio chop fresh vegetables into tiny pieces. He put these into a dehydrator and then we ground those up, too. There were small jars lined up next to the stove. I was instructed what to put into which jars. Then we sealed them with screw-on lids.

We worked like that for two hours until all the herbs, spices, and dried vegetables were stored and labeled. I felt like a chemist in a lab. All that time different soups and stews and the bouillabaisse simmered on the stove. Then Emilio showed me how to bake cakes that we put into a large oven. Soon the kitchen smelled of chocolate and lemon and cinnamon on top of all the other scents.

"Now," he said as he took the cakes out of the big oven and set them on cooling racks, "for the spells."

I'll admit it. I was nervous. Spells. Just the word sent a shiver up to my scalp. Who was I, Amanda Anders, to think that being a witch was anything like normal or even acceptable? What would Foxy think? More important, what would Nick think? But there was no escape route now. Or maybe there never had been. I always wondered if life is predestined or if you can choose what you become. That's the biggest mystery to me. But I guess I'd been chosen to be something I never imagined. If I had imagined it, maybe I would have chosen it, though. Except for the part about not being able to tell other people—I mean non-witches—who and what I really was. It was like carrying around this big secret that totally impacts your life but not owning up to it. At least not publicly. In one way, it was like living a big lie all the time. In another way, it was like being a member in a really cool club. But those two things were in opposition to each other.

So far I had only mastered small hexes, like ruining Armand's boeuf Bourguignon. Fun, I'll admit, but hardly life-altering for either of us. I wondered how many levels of witchery existed but was afraid, if I asked about that, then I wouldn't get any kind of satisfactory answer. I mean, Emilio and Aunt Augusta—and maybe even the Contessa—were all probably way up there in the expert realm. But they'd been at this a really long time. Then there was Tessa, who'd also been a witch for eons, but look where she was: water-sloshing her way around The Manor. That didn't bode well for my future, but hopefully it would be way, way, way in my future. So I accepted where I was now and turned to Emilio.

"We'll start with a few experiments," he said. "Line up the jars of powders we mixed."

I lined them up in front of me. So far, so good.

"Now serve yourself a bowl of each one of the dishes on the stove."

Well, that was easy. I laid them out on the big counter. No wonder everything was oversized in this kitchen. It was like you had to prepare and then eat six meals at the same time. Once everything was lined up, things began to go quickly and, in some funny way, it was almost as if I wasn't there at all. Like it happened to me in a dream. And maybe that's what it was. I know for sure it wasn't like learning anything in school. Nothing was written down. There was no blackboard or whiteboard or a laptop I had to open. I don't remember any specific spells I had to memorize, or that Aunt Augusta or Emilio asked me to repeat any words or phrases. I don't even know how long we were there. I had shown up about an hour after we got back from Pasadena and, when I left The Manor, it was dark as ink outside and cloudy. A fog was rolling in from the Bay and I felt like a different person.

When I got back to my cottage, Quetzal was asleep again. I got undressed and put on my sleep pants and tee shirt and crawled into bed. I couldn't remember ever having been so tired that my bones ached. I closed my eyes and saw in the darkness of my soul that I knew something special and wonderful and dangerous. I shivered under my covers.

"So, you finally got the goods," Quetzal croaked at me. "I thought you'd never turn."

I sat up and switched on the light next to my bed.

"What do you mean?"

"What do you think I mean?"

"I have no idea." But I did have an idea; I just wanted to hear it from her.

"Go to sleep now. You'll know soon enough."

I watched her tuck her head under her wing, and it was obvious she would not tell me anything more.

Chapter Twenty-Two
I Am a Practitioner

At class the next morning, Chef Emilio (and I had to think of him as Chef Emilio in class; otherwise, I felt highly confused) was in charge of teaching the making of fruit tarts—French style. We could choose what kind we wanted to make. Half the class chose apple. Predictable. And why not? Two people opted for peach. Bette of the short hair and big butt wanted to know if the school would supply fraises des bois, but that was a no. Wispy Clare and I both decided on pear. We followed as Chef Emilio demonstrated making the pastry dough, then laying it in a round, flat baking dish with fluted vertical sides. Next, he cut up his fruit and laid it in a pattern on the dough. We watched and followed his lead.

"One tip," he announced, looking around the kitchen at our workstations. "You can make many different types of tarts—some using a pastry cream or a custard. Today, we will only use the fruit and a few other ingredients to sprinkle over the top."

While we each worked on our tarts, Bette frowned at her strawberries, trying to cut them evenly. Wispy Clare and I tried to control ourselves and not laugh at Bette. We shared the pears. I'd never made a tart, so I expected this lesson to be a bit of a stretch; but it turned out that I shouldn't have worried. A lot of stuff is like that in life, I was learning. Why give yourself more problems by construing scenes that probably won't materialize?

The snot Armand hadn't sneered at me once so far, but, as we placed our tarts in the ovens, he managed to get his next to mine and whispered, "I hope you have a prayer for not burning your tart. But I suppose, when you've been making French tarts as long as I have, you learn simple rules. N'est-ce pas?" His accent was so annoying I could have slapped him silent.

Wispy Clare heard and followed me back to my station, where she whispered, "I hope his looks like singed charcoal when it comes out."

If only Wispy Clare knew what had been implanted in me the previous night, maybe she wouldn't have said anything. Then again, maybe she would have delighted in what happened to Armand just thirty-five minutes later. The fall he took and the smashing sound as his tart pan spun across the floor was a beautiful sight. I thought Wispy Clare was going to applaud, but she contained herself admirably—only winking at me as Armand picked himself up and ran for a mop and pail to clean up the mess. The rest of the class admired their creations, and we got to go around the room and taste everyone's.

Chef Emilio congratulated us and we broke for lunch, although we were all pretty stuffed on tarts, so Wispy Clare and I bought some cold teas and sat on a bench under a live oak.

"I don't remember how I got home last Friday," she said. "Did you bring me or what?"

"It was a joint effort."

"Who had the joints?" She laughed and a little of her tea splashed on the ground. "I mean, how did I get home. It's a blank."

"I think someone slipped something into your beer. All of a sudden you were lying on the floor and a group of very drunk guys was huddled around you. I was afraid what they might do. And then Chef Emilio was there. From out of nowhere, it seemed. He stood you up and together we walked you home and put you to bed."

"I'm surprised we could all fit into my 'apartment,' which is an overstatement if there ever was one. More like a glorified closet."

I laughed. "Actually, I waited at the door. We couldn't all fit at once."

"This is embarrassing. That my teacher had to carry me home from a bar."

"He was very concerned about your safety. I'm sure it's not a big deal to him, so I'd just forget about it."

We finished our teas and sat there just enjoying the air.

"I wonder why that French twit Armand is so competitive with you. He seems hell-bent on singling you out for snarky remarks."

"I have no idea. But he started the very first day, so it's not like he knew me before or anything."

It really was a mystery. Maybe he was one of us but from a different caste? Or maybe he was just some snotty French skillet-slinger.

"Maybe it's his way of getting your attention. It's possible he thinks you're cute. It's weird how he's tripped over himself and made a mess twice now."

At that point I was about to burst. It was getting harder and harder to keep my secret. But if I told anyone—Wispy Clare or even Nick—I had no idea what would happen. To me or to them. So I stood up and told her we'd better get back to school. That was the safest.

In the afternoon class, Mr. Batchelder took over to teach knife skills. This seemed pretty basic, but I found out there were lots of different knives for preparing different foods. And that a good knife sharpener was an essential kitchen tool. At home, Foxy had two knives she had picked up in a thrift shop. But since pizzas came from Anthony's already sliced, it didn't matter much. Also, I learned I'd been holding knives the wrong way. And using the wrong ones for different foods. So it turned out to be a really useful class. As part of the tuition, we were each given our own set of knives to keep locked in a drawer under the counter of our workstations.

Speaking of tuition, I had convinced Foxy to support my trek west to study cooking by making a financial comparison of college and culinary school. I expected to be there one (maybe two) years, whereas college would be four years and prepare me for pretty much nothing practical. So she forked over what I needed for the first half-year's tuition, then I found the cottage. After meeting Aunt Augusta, I learned I wouldn't be paying rent, so that was some spending money I'd never expected. It was kind of like winning a small lottery. And then we learned from Ms. McCracken that there would be one full scholarship for the second semester awarded to whoever received the highest scores overall for their first semester. That might have explained some of the heat I was taking from Armand. So far we were tied, but the semester had just started. It was anyone's game.

After class, when I got back to my cottage, the door was slightly open and I could see Tessa inside sitting in front of my tiny workstation, which was just a piece of wood with a small chair facing it.

"Tessa, what are you doing here?"

"What's this?" She was pointing to my laptop.

"It's my laptop. But what are you doing here? Wasn't the door locked?"

"I may be old," she said, "and losing a lot of what I once had. But I can still unlock an old lock—and, besides, I once lived here."

"Really? When was that?"

"Never mind. And that bird gets more disrespectful by the day. I've a good mind to ..."

She trailed off as if she'd forgotten what she planned for Quetzal, who, at that moment, landed on the sill of the little window where she could fly in and out at will.

"She still here?" she squawked. "I was hoping she'd be gone by the time I got back. What does she want, anyway?"

"I was just trying to find out. So, if you'll close your beak for a few minutes, we can both find out at the same time. Well?" I turned to Tessa again.

"They want you over at The Manor. They sent me to fetch you. And don't think for a minute that I don't know what's going on over there with you and the recipes and all."

She stood up and smoothed her skirt, which looked like it had been made out of an old tablecloth. Then she winked at me. It was a funny thing to do, it seemed to me.

That is, until she pointed to my laptop and asked, "What does it do?"

"It doesn't do anything by itself. You can do a lot of stuff that wouldn't be of interest to you, I don't think."

She pointed at it and mumbled something. It flipped open and a screen came up with some weird characters on it. They looked like hieroglyphics.

"Hey, what are you doing?"

She didn't answer. Just flounced out the door and let it shut with a bang.

"Can't you keep her out of here?" Quetzal started working a large seed, holding it with her claw and using her beak around its edges.

"I wish I could. But I don't see how."

"Why don't you hex her?" She cracked the seed open and popped it into her mouth. "Yes. Hex her so she can't get in here anymore. Send her to another city on another continent."

"I don't think I can do that. Anyway, I wouldn't know how. All I can do is trip people and toss some things around a room. It's not much."

"Ha. Don't be an idiot. I know what's going on. At the big house. I hear things. You can't deny it. Pretty soon you'll be right up there with her." She pointed toward The Manor.

"You mean Aunt Augusta?"

"Of course."

"What do you mean by 'up there'?"

Quetzal flapped her wings out wide and looked sideways at me.

"They're preparing you for something. Seems to me it's something big. But don't take my word for it. Ask Tessa. She knows all about it. She's not as much of a ditz as she makes out to be. Except for sometimes."

"Where does Tessa go? I mean, when she's not snooping around in here."

At that moment my phone buzzed, so I took it out of my jeans pocket.

Miss u

It was Nick.

Me 2

evrything ok?

Sure u?

Y gotta go tho

He was so sweet. I had this very quick thought that maybe I should quit school and go down to Pasadena and just get some crummy job and forget about spells and hexes and poofing stuff.

"Oh oh," Quetzal squawked. "Speak of the devil."

"They want you up at The Manor," Tessa called through the closed door. And then it blew open as if a big wind had ripped through the yard. But there was no wind outside.

"And they say to come now."

I glanced over at Quetzal, and she bobbed her head up and down. "Told you." She turned her head sideways and looked like she'd just won the lottery. She jiggled her head back and forth, then picked up a seed and started working it.

"Tessa," I said, "will you please come in for a minute?"

"What do you want?" She stepped inside but left the door open.

"Why do they want me up at The Manor? What's going on?"

"I'm not supposed to butt in."

"Quetzal says you know."

"That bird is a menace. She should be ..."

"Should be what?" Quetzal squawked. "You can't touch me. I know things."

Tessa looked confused for a minute, then she went back out the door and turned to me.

"You'll find out. They have a lot of faith in you. I don't know why, but they do. Now come on or you'll get us both in trouble."

✻

This time, Tessa led me past the big kitchen to a sunroom at the back of The Manor. It was a lovely, tall space with potted palms and orchids hanging in baskets, their roots trailing and their bloom stalks heavy with exotic-looking flowers. There were giant ferns and a banana tree in one corner. Like everything else about The Manor, this room, mostly glass, was oversized. And it was humid—the air heavy with orchid scent. Aunt Augusta sat on a bench at one end with Bauble on her lap. Emilio was not present.

"Come, sit down by me," she motioned to the bench, which was a light beige wood with intricately carved arms and back. Bauble seemed to purr almost like a cat. "Tessa, thank you for bringing her."

"She wanted to know what you want with her, but I didn't say anything."

"Yes, very good, Tessa. You can rest now. You've had a busy day."

Before disappearing, Tessa glared at me. I expected her to knock something over, but she managed to exit without any catastrophes.

"I don't know why she's mad at me. I know she and Quetzal are always at each other, but I've never done anything to her."

"She's a bit jealous, I imagine. Her heyday is over and yours is just beginning. But, to be fair, Tessa was always a bit flighty. Even inept in some ways. But she has a good heart.

You see, Tessa is from a hard-luck caste that always seemed to end up at the bottom of some unfortunate calamity. Who can say why? I rescued her from one of those disasters and so she's remained faithful all this time. I suppose it's somewhat out of gratitude but also probably because she knows she's safer this way—that not too much can go wrong here with me. Perhaps she feels you're a bit of a threat to that sense of stability. She's wrong, of course, but who can change someone else's feelings?"

I sat down next to her, and she took my left hand in hers and turned it palm up. Somehow, I trusted her, but I wasn't at all sure why. She had a weird combination of grandmotherly warmth and royal demeanor that made me feel loved and honored at the same time. Somewhere I must have learned how to go my own way and tolerate other people's peculiarities without letting them make me crazy. But I'd always felt I was pretty much on my own. So being a part of this witch caste was new to me. I guess, if I'd had my choice of groups I'd wanted to accept me, I never would have imagined this one. But so far it was pretty cool.

"I know you've seen this mark in your hand and that you know what it means. At least you know that it makes you part of a special caste within a special group. But I want you to consider what else it means, Amanda."

I'd had a feeling this was coming. Finally, I would find out what this was all about.

"I was hoping you'd tell me. But I'm kind of afraid, too."

"That's because you have good sense and an intuitive way of feeling situations. It has to do with your father. That's another reason you're afraid. You sense that he's in danger. Soon you will meet him. There is nothing ordinary about your father or about the trouble he is in right now. The spells you learned here in my kitchen will help you, but your own power will have to guide you. Do you understand?"

"I don't remember any spells. That time is a blank."

"That's the way it's supposed to be. When you need them, they will come to you. Have faith in yourself. That's all you need."

"What do I have to do?"

"In a few days, you'll return to the Contessa's estate. There you will get guidance from her. Emilio will be there, also. One thing that has not been discussed is your friend Nick. The Contessa has told us that, perhaps, he should be told about you. About us. No decision has yet been made. He is a very serious young man—and in a field that would, by its nature, make him skeptical of anything you might tell him. He would require proof. It could go very wrong. There is, however, one factor that could have a heavy influence on him: his mother's situation. She is also in grave danger. So we will discuss it further. For now, it is enough that you are aware of what is ahead of you."

Chapter Twenty-Three
I Remember

The next thing I knew I was back in my cottage and the alarm was ringing to wake me up to get ready for class. Quetzal stared at me from her perch.

"You really are clueless," she squawked. She paced foot over foot from one end of her perch to the other and back.

I stretched. "What are you talking about?"

"You."

"But what do you mean?" By now I'd gotten used to having conversations with a bird and not questioning it. "What am I clueless about?"

"What they have planned for you."

With that, she turned and flew out the window—leaving me to wonder if it was worthwhile listening to what a crazy bird said.

"Today we will focus on pan sauces. But first you must learn how to bone a chicken."

Chef Emilio was back at the helm. And I must admit, class that day was truly exciting, although I had no idea what pan sauces had to do with dismembering a poor dead bird. I forgot all about my visit with Aunt Augusta, so I could concentrate on the pale-yellowish, floppy, raw chicken at my workstation. I'd hacked my way through a chicken before, but had never learned the proper way to bone one. This organic one with the neck and little triangle of a tail still attached was closer to a living thing than anything I'd ever cooked. We were lucky we didn't have to chase them around a barnyard and do away with them by ourselves. I'm sure that would have sent me to accounting school.

We took out our boning knives, placed washable cutting boards on a paper towel to keep slippage down, and washed our chickens before patting them dry. We had metal cookie sheets for the cut-up pieces. Chef Emilio insisted on a holistic approach, telling us that organization in the kitchen is essential to a professional chef. Growing up with Foxy, I was used to a disorganized—even chaotic—environment, so this was a good lesson for me.

We learned how to find the wing joints, staying close to the joint so as not to cut into the breast meat. Next, we watched as Chef Emilio demonstrated cutting thighs away from the body and then cutting the legs away from the thighs. We followed his lead and next cut the back away from the breast. Finally, we bore down on the breast with one hand and cut it right down the middle. I felt so pioneer woman I could have downed an elk and carved it up for a month's meal over an open firepit. Apologies to all vegetarians.

"Now, we're ready to cook the bird," Chef Emilio told us.

Pans at the ready over medium heat, we lightly salted our pieces and peppered them, then dropped them into the buttered pans. They sizzled and browned, and we cooked them until done. Which is how we got to pan sauces. We all opted for slightly different ones, but the basics were the same. Butter, olive oil, shallots, garlic, salt, pepper; some of us added a bit of white wine, and I added a touch of ground mustard. And guess what? Mine got the blue star ribbon from Mr. Batchelder. Armand was furious and Wispy Clare came in second. But this time there were absolutely no spells involved. I swear.

The best part was getting to taste each other's dishes for lunch. I was really getting to like culinary school. I even imagined one day working in a fancy restaurant kitchen, although that was surely a ways off. Still, it was fun to imagine it.

We had an hour off before afternoon class, so Wispy Clare and I took a walk down and up some hilly San Francsico streets. We looked in store windows and chatted about nothing in particular. It was a sunny September day, and the city was full of blooming flowers. Wispy Clare told me about her family and that she could only afford the school because her grandmother was supporting her.

"She's only doing that until I graduate, so I have to have a job the day after I finish," she said. "Wouldn't it be great if we both got jobs at the same place when we graduate?"

I thought about it for a second. "Yeah, that would be great. I'm not sure what I'm going to do, though. See, there's this guy from home. He's in Pasadena at Cal Tech. I mean, I thought about getting a job down there. He's only in his second year, so he has a way to go. But he's brilliant. I know he'll get work offers when he graduates. I just don't know about the future. One thing is sure: I like it out here."

"Oh. What's his name?"

"Nick. Nick Weyland. He means a lot to me."

"You're lucky. I mean, to have someone you care about. I always attract the biggest losers. I'm surprised Armand hasn't made a move on me. He probably will. It wouldn't surprise me in the least." She laughed and we decided to stop into a little clothing boutique we were passing. Not that either of us could afford much of anything, but we still had half an hour.

Class that afternoon was all about culinology. It wasn't held in the kitchen but in a lecture hall with the whole school, including second-year students. We took notes and watched a slide show and some interviews with food technicians working in food labs. It didn't really appeal to me, but then Mr. Batchelder gave a talk on salaries in the food industry and those guys were cleaning up. So I thought I'd better pay attention, because you never know when something's going to come in handy.

Chef Emilio gave a presentation on how the health field is crossing with the science of food to come up with healthier ways of eating and preparing foods. It was funny how I thought of him as Chef Emilio at school, like he was a different person from the one who drove me to Pasadena and stayed at the Contessa's, and any of the other stuff.

I listened to the lecture and took notes until the class ended. I had an urge to walk up to him and ask if he was going to drive back to Pasadena that weekend, but so many other students were crowded around him, it wasn't a good time. He was really popular—especially with the girls. Well, of course. So I left and walked outside, intending to go back to my cottage since school was over for the day. After I'd walked a few blocks, a strange feeling came over me. It was as if I was outside my body looking at myself.

And then Wispy Clare came up running behind me.

"Hey, why did you leave so fast? I thought maybe we could go out for dinner somewhere cheap. Like a food truck."

She laughed at that idea, then took my arm. "Amanda, are you okay? I called and called for you to wait up, but I guess you didn't hear me. Which is funny because everyone else on the street looked around, I was yelling so loud."

I heard what she was saying, but I couldn't answer her. I felt as if I was in a locked box with no way to experience the world around me. Yet I knew she was there talking to me. It was the oddest feeling I'd ever had.

She pulled me by my arm and led me to a bench off the sidewalk. She stared at my eyes.

"Are you having a stroke or something? Maybe I should call an ambulance."

She took her phone out of her purse, but I put my hand over hers and then it hit me all at once like a flashback from some trauma I'd heard people talk about. All these images started cascading in front of my eyes and my head felt like it was going to burst open. I seemed to be watching a movie about myself, but the images were unconnected until thoughts began coalescing into chants and rhymes. It was then I realized I was remembering something that had really happened.

I must have slumped forward, because Wispy Clare was saying, "I'm calling for a rescue squad. You're acting too weird. I think you're sick or something."

She began dialing but again I took her hand and pushed the phone away.

"Stop," I said. "I'm okay. It's just all these images are coming to me like a bad dream that I'm remembering all of a sudden."

"You mean like a flashback?"

"Yes. Yes, exactly like a flashback."

"From what? I mean did you have an accident or something?"

"No."

"Were you abused? Sometimes that happens to children who've been abused. I mean, did someone do something to you? Is it Nick?"

At that moment it all came back like a flash flood that I couldn't stop. I was at Aunt Augusta's, and Emilio was there. They were teaching me spells. All kinds of spells. With food and herbs and incantations. So many incantations. And I was repeating them all over and over. And adding herbs and other elements to the food. The food smelled delicious, enticing, impossible to refuse. I tasted it all and had the feeling I could do anything with anyone and to anyone. It was exhilarating and wonderful. And scary.

I turned to Wispy Clare. She looked like a bystander at a car accident, like she was shocked and had no idea how to help.

"I'm okay," I told her. "Thank you for being here. But really, I'm okay now. It just came over me all of a sudden and I felt like I was drowning for a few minutes. I think I have to go back to my cottage now. I can't go to dinner with you this evening. Maybe another time."

She looked skeptical. She may have been a bit flighty, but she was also smart. She knew something was going on that I wasn't telling her. Part of me wanted to share the whole story with her. And another part was sure she wouldn't believe it and would make me prove what I was revealing. If I did that, I had no idea what the consequences would be. For once, I held back. It was too big a risk. And it could have terrible repercussions for both of us. I didn't want to turn into some internet freak or put her in a position of having to fend off demands and offers just for being the friend of a witch.

"How about we go out tomorrow?" I asked her. "We'll find the best food truck in the city." I smiled, trying to act normal and defuse the situation. But my mind was racing, and all I wanted to do was get back to The Manor and confront Aunt Augusta.

※

I'd never gone to The Manor without being invited, but now I wanted to bang on Aunt Augusta's front door and demand an explanation. I didn't even get the chance; just as I got there and raised my fist to pound on the door—ignoring the obvious doorbell—Quetzal flapped by my head, squawking and batting her wings.

"Don't do it," she yelled at me and circled my head a second time.

"Go away. I'll do what I want."

"No, no, no," she kept on. Then she landed on my shoulder and pecked at my ear.

"Ow. Stop it, you crazy flying albatross."

"I am not an albatross. I'm beautiful. That is one ugly bird with a big fat curved beak. It's no wonder they have to spend most of their lives flying over the ocean. No one wants to have them in the backyard."

I raised my fist again to pound on the door, but the commotion must have signaled that I was there, because the door opened and Aunt Augusta stood there, regal and unruffled.

"Amanda." She said it softly, but there was a command in her tone and the way she looked at me. "Come in."

"I've come to get some things straight."

"Yes. We know. Send the bird back to the cottage and come with me to the kitchen."

I was determined not to let her defuse my distrust, and I was just as determined as ever to find out about the flashbacks and what they meant.

"Quetzal, go back home and wait for me." I turned slightly so I could see her eyes.

She cocked her head to the side and, if it's possible for a parrot to look skeptical, that's exactly how she looked.

"Remember, I warned you," she whispered, but I was sure Aunt Augusta heard her. Then she lifted off and flew back toward the cottage. As she flew away, I felt alone and wished she could have stayed.

I went into the house and heard the door lock behind me, although Aunt Augusta walked in front of me—leading the way to the kitchen. I had a brief thought about learning what spell would unlock doors, but Tessa appeared from somewhere and followed behind me so I was sandwiched between them. This weakened my resolve a bit, but then I straightened up, still determined to get to the bottom of everything.

The oversized kitchen stove was covered with pots of various sizes, all bubbling or hissing. Geysers of steam rose toward the high ceiling. In one corner I saw Bauble curled up in a velvet doggie bed, eyes closed. A mixture of scents greeted me. Garlic, for sure. But also sage, bergamot, rosemary, and others I couldn't distinguish, as they all blended together the closer I got to the stove where Emilio stood, wearing a chef's apron—a large spoon in one hand and a strainer in the other.

I began to feel deflated. With all three of them in the room, it seemed too gigantic a task to confront Aunt Augusta. Then Emilio looked up and my knees felt wobbly.

"Ah, there you are, Amanda. We expected you. But you have something on your mind. We'd very much like to hear what it is."

I opened my mouth to start telling them I wanted to know about my previous visits to The Manor but—and I couldn't explain this under oath on a witness stand in front of a judge and jury—instead of saying anything to them, I raised my hand, pressed my thumb and index finger together and made a continuous circle in the air. I watched as lids for all the pots on the stove lifted up and settled down onto their corresponding pots. All the burners turned off. A chair moved from one wall to where Tessa stood. I pointed to it and she sat down without saying a word.

And then, this was the most astounding part: I floated off the floor and over to where Emilio stood at the stove—hovering there while I pointed to one of the pots. Its lid lifted and a small spoon rose from the counter and dipped into the pot, taking a spoonful of the mixture and hovering in front of me. I lowered back down to the floor and took the spoon and ate whatever was on it. It was a delicious kind of a stew with a heady flavor that left its pleasant taste with me after I put the spoon down.

"Excellent," Emilio said. "Now we can truly complete your awakening."

I felt lightheaded. Also like I could do just about anything. Like there were no limits for me. Mixed with those feelings there was also a kind of fear. I couldn't have described it, because the feeling was as amorphous as a cloud that shifted, slowly evaporated, and then settled again like a night fog on a dark road, illuminated by headlights just as far as they reached to define patches, then clear spots, then dense gray.

Finally, after what seemed like hours, I felt I could speak; but, when I opened my mouth, what I'd wanted to say when I'd first arrived was completely gone. Instead, what came out was one question: "What do you mean 'my awakening?'"

"Come, Amanda, sit down over here."

Aunt Augusta led me to the end of the kitchen, where she motioned for me to sit down on a carved wooden settee in front of a tall, multi-paned window. I felt like I was about to receive a lecture, like I was a misbehaving child sent to the principal's office.

Emilio and Aunt Augusta sat in two chairs facing me. Aunt Augusta motioned to Tessa, who had been completely quiet since I'd entered the house, to stand by her side. Although I'd intended to go into The Manor making demands and stomping around like a child, now I felt ready to listen to what they were about to tell me. I will say, though, I hoped the feeling that I was about to be loaded with some task way beyond what I could—or even wanted—to do, would turn out to be one of those fears that you realize later was a waste of your energy.

Chapter Twenty-Four
I Awaken to My Destiny

"I remember my awakening," Tessa said to no one in particular, almost as if talking to herself.

"It was a cloudy day. I stood on a cliff in Scotland overlooking the North Sea, when a wind came up and nearly blew me over the edge. I was younger than you are now, and had no idea what was happening to me, until an old man walking with a large sheepdog came along and grabbed me before I fell into the sea. He said to me, 'Nah, tis not your time, lassie.' He and his dog led me back to his hut, and he instructed me to examine my palm. What I had always thought was a tiny birthmark turned out to be like yours. And if you look at your palm now, you'll find something else."

I had never seen Tessa so focused and clear-headed. I thought maybe I was dreaming all this but, no, it was real, and I was there with all of them. I realized, then, that my palms were clenched shut and that my shoulders felt so tight I could barely move them. Then I remembered back to the day Bauble had leapt into my arms and everything since that moment. I did what she told me and opened my palm. That's when the whole thing hit me as if I'd been Rip Van Winkled.

In my palm, a sparkling dot radiated tiny beams of multi-colored light that spun around, enveloping me in a warm glow. All I could do was gape at this display. No words came to me, nor any specific thoughts until, as the beams widened and the sparkling in my hand dissipated, I understood what they'd taught me about spells and hexes and incantations. It was as if the spells became part of me and I knew them all. I wanted to shout or dance around the room, but I also felt there was more. And then, Bauble jumped off his little velvet bed and into my lap. I looked into his round, black eyes and I saw the sparkle again. Then he jumped down and went to Aunt Augusta. That's when I found my voice.

"I understand," I said quietly. "I understand it all now. I remember the spells. And the recipes. I know what the herbs do and how to use them."

"From this day forward, you will never be the same," Aunt Augusta told me. "You will still be Amanda, but you will be more than you were, as if you were two people within one body and mind. Now that you've assimilated the spells, you will be able to create more of your own and, someday, perhaps, pass them along to another of our caste. You now have power, but beware, you also have vulnerability. Next, as one of our own, you must learn your first mission. But that's for tomorrow. For today, this is enough for you to contemplate."

The next morning, I wanted to try out what I'd learned, so I decided to find a secluded place to practice my new spell-casting powers. But where? Not back at the cottage, where Quetzal was sure to pester me. Not where anyone could possibly see me experimenting, or where someone could get in the way and maybe get hurt—or worse. What I really wanted was for Emilio to show up and help me get started. Well, maybe that was a good spell to try out: summoning.

Before I left The Manor, Tessa had handed me a package with some ground herbs from my first lesson. I stuffed it in my backpack and went off to class at NCC, where Mr. Batchelder started the class off with a lecture about different ways to cook food.

"Boiling, baking, roasting, broiling, deep frying, pan frying, braising, poaching, steaming, searing, sautéing, blanching, grilling," he recited the list while pointing to photos of different types of dishes cooked each way.

Then he went on to describe what types of food could be cooked in any number of ways. I noticed Wispy Clare taking notes in a small spiral-bound pad. Without realizing what had happened, all of a sudden Armand had moved next to my station. I had specifically tried to stay as far away from his workstation as possible, but there he was—like some turd on my shoe.

I tried to ignore him, but he spoke to me in a low voice that only I could hear, "I never would have bothered to come all the way from Paris to this school if I knew what a brood of amateurs would be here. Really, who has to be told what ways to cook food? In France, everyone knows all this without going to school."

I just couldn't figure out what he was after from me. If all these snide remarks were a come-on, he was just about the least smooth operator I could imagine. I just wanted him to leave me alone. So ... maybe it was time I practiced one of those spells. When I ignored him, he backed far enough away that it was possible to dip into my herbs and pinch a tiny bit between my thumb and forefinger.

When Mr. Batchelder dimmed the lights to show a few slides, I looked over at Armand and whispered: "Let he who pesters begin to fester." With a little flick of my fingers, I sent a bit of powdered herbs in his direction and turned my attention back to the presentation, which was actually interesting. Mr. Batchelder was turning out to be a really good teacher. I had even gotten used to his lisp and was finding him kind of endearing, like a little kid.

"Now," he was saying as he turned the lights back up, "we'll try out as many of these types of food prep as there are students in the class. I'll assign each of you a method of preparation and, for our afternoon class, you'll find your ingredients assembled at your workstations for you to prepare a meal."

He handed out preprinted cards with each of our assignments. I got poaching. I hoped I could make something with salmon. It all depended on what we found awaiting us when we got back after lunch. I snuck a look over at Armand but, so far, he looked the same. I soon forgot about him, because I still wanted to try summoning Emilio.

After leaving class by a back door so no one could follow me, I walked as fast as I could down to the Golden Gate Park to find a stand of redwoods, which I thought might give me good cover to try summoning. It being the middle of the week, the park was fairly empty when I got there, and the Redwood Grove was only trees as far as I could tell, so I walked around on the paths among the big trees just to be sure I was alone. I chose a tree that would give me good cover from all directions and stationed myself behind its gigantic trunk. Looking up to the canopy the branches formed, I got kind of a feeling of awe and wondered how many living things were as old or older than Tessa and Aunt Augusta and Emilio. Thinking of him then, I decided it was time to try my new skills. I took a deep breath and emptied my mind of all thoughts except the summoning spell I'd learned.

"Wherever you are and whatever you're doing, be by my side Emilio, or risk your undoing." I spread my arms wide and waited. The tree seemed to shake its leaves as if a wind had blown through them. I closed my eyes. When I opened them, Emilio was walking on the path toward me. I gasped. This was unbelievable. And miraculous. I'd never felt such a sense of power.

"You're quite pleased with yourself, aren't you?"

"I'm amazed, is what I am. It really worked."

"Of course it did. What did you expect?"

I shrugged. "I'm not sure; maybe a big nothing. But this is just fantastic."

"Do you remember the warnings that came with this ability?"

"I don't know. Let me think. I was so ready to try it out, I hadn't thought about anything else."

We stood there, under that giant tree while I tried to remember everything that had happened when they'd transferred the powers to me. And that, in itself, was a mystery. It was more like a cloud going through the space and some of the mist settled inside my head somehow. It was all kind of amorphous and vague, yet here I was with this new knowledge and the ability to use it. So, as I tried to remember, yes, what they had called "the cautions" came back to me.

"Oh right, now I have it," I said. "Let's see, there are rules. One, summoning is not to be used for personal gain. Two, spells must be tempered with mercy but can be employed if revenge is warranted. Three, powers decrease the closer it is to the fall or spring equinox and increase when the equinox is reached."

I grinned at Emilio, pleased with myself—but he looked so serious that my smile faded.

"What is it?"

"Do you remember the equinox comes this Saturday?"

"I hadn't thought about it."

"It's time you were aware of what will happen this coming weekend. And what is expected of you. Because you must realize, you've been chosen not only as a result of your heritage but also to gain the power to save someone important."

"My father?"

"Yes. And, tangentially, your friend Nick's mother. They are both in thrall to Zorn and he must be stopped—for many reasons, but also so they can be released. After school today, you will come once again to The Manor and learn everything you need to know. You must prepare for the equinox and your task."

He wouldn't tell me any more right then, so, by the time I got back to school, I was in an agitated state of mind, wondering what they expected of me. But most of all I'd begun thinking about my father, about what it would be like to finally meet him, about whether he would be happy to see me or would reject me or worse. All those years I had grown up without knowing anything about him had left a hole that I was on the cusp of being able to fill. But maybe the hole with nothing in it would turn out to be better than what I would find. Maybe knowing would be its own curse.

And that brought up the fact that I had missed my period. It was now officially three weeks late. I knew I couldn't possibly be pregnant but, ever since I was thirteen, I'd always been ultra-regular. I figured maybe it was the stress of moving west, starting culinary school, and then all the witchery stuff. So it hadn't concerned me. But now, what if it hit just when I was supposed to be some super-uber witch to deal with this Zorn character? Well, I would just have to be prepared when I got there. I was learning to accept a lot of what growing up meant. There was no way to get around it, so I just decided to go where it led me, which in this case was back to class.

Chapter Twenty-Five
I Learn the Power of Spells

All my resolve to handle things like an adult collapsed in class. I did not get salmon to poach; instead, I found three eggs, some fresh vegetables, an onion, a half loaf of some dark bread, butter, salt, pepper, and a chicken breast still on the bone.

Wispy Clare nearly ran to my workstation when I got back.

"Did you hear?"

"No, what?" I was preoccupied looking at the ingredients on my counter slab and trying to imagine what I could do with them.

"About Armand?"

I looked up then and noticed he wasn't in class.

"What about him?"

"He was taken to the hospital with some kind of weird sores on his face and hands. Maybe other places, but I couldn't see that. They were all oozing pus. He looked gross. Ms. McCracken was all a-twitter. I thought she was going to burst a blood vessel. It was like she thought maybe something was wrong with the food or the kitchens weren't clean enough. I have no idea, but the EMTs hauled him off. You missed the whole thing. Where were you anyway?"

"Oh, I took a long walk. I had to think through some stuff."

"The boyfriend?"

"Um, a lot of stuff. Hey, we'd better get started cooking."

"I know. I got pan frying. That's what I wanted. If I get the top grade on this, I move up to second. Of all things, behind you, now that Armand is out of the competition."

So my hex had worked on Armand. I smiled to myself as we both started working on our cooking assignments. I didn't relish the idea of competing with Wispy Clare, but I can't say that was what messed me up that afternoon. At the time I thought maybe it was the idea of poaching that threw me off balance.

I started by making a broth using the vegetables but had no idea how to incorporate eggs into a poached chicken breast. The only thing I could think of was egg drop soup, so I decided to save the eggs for later. Then there was the loaf of dark bread. I stared at it for a long time but not a thing came to me. I boned the chicken breast, cut it into thin strips and seasoned the broth. Once the vegetables had softened and the broth was simmering, I slowly added the chicken. It smelled good but looked downright dowdy. I considered removing the chicken so I could scramble the raw eggs and spin them into the simmering broth for an egg drop soup and then add the chicken back in. That left me with the bread. As I considered just slicing it and serving it on the side, I got a massive cramp and realized my period was about to start.

I grabbed my backpack and raced to the rest room just in time to deal with the gush that emptied itself into the toilet where I plunked myself down, almost falling in the process. I'd never had period problems before, but this was epic. The gushing was like a waterfall with no end. I sat there for maybe ten minutes until I could get a break long enough to fish out a tampon and a pad. I figured, if this was going to continue, I'd better double up. With no one else in the room, I hobbled over to the sink to get some water and paper towels to clean myself. All I could think was that men never had to deal with crap like this. I wondered how my poached meal was doing in my absence, and it occurred to me more than once that I could zap that mess into something reasonable. But, for some reason that wasn't clear to me, I held myself back from that path.

I got myself together and headed back to class, where I found everyone working on their own dishes and mine still simmering at station number eight. I spun the eggs into the broth as I had planned, dumped the chicken back in and stood back. It was acceptable, if not exciting. The bread just looked odd. I wished I had some cheese to go with it, but it would have to do.

Wispy Clare had made pan-seared salmon with lemon butter sauce with a side of a mini broccoli casserole and pan-fried sweet potatoes. It looked fabulous, colorful, and tasty. Big Butt Bette made pan-fried dumplings with a variety of fillings, both meat and vegetable, with a pickled plum dipping sauce. She won first place for that class. Wispy Clare came in a close second. Mine was second to last, followed only by some concoction I couldn't even identify by a student who had obviously chosen the wrong profession since he came in last or almost last in every class. I was sure this class marked the end of my quest for a scholarship for next semester, so I left class and headed back to my cottage to think through what I would do if I couldn't continue at NCC.

The minute I opened the door, Quetzal met me with a complaint.

"I need more cashews," she snorted, if it's possible for a parrot to do that. "And my water is old and smells foul."

"Please, Quetzal, I've had a bad day."

"Oh, boo hoo," she fluffed up her feathers. "Take care of me and I'll listen to your sorry self-pity party."

It was no use ignoring her. She'd just get even more obnoxious, so I refilled her water and gave her more of her precious cashews.

"So?" she said, while munching on nuts.

"Never mind. I don't want to go through it all anyway. And I feel awful."

That was the truth. The cramps had gotten worse, and I also had a headache, so I went to the bed and stretched out.

"That time of the month?" she cackled. "I'm glad I don't have that."

"Shut up."

"Oh, getting downright snippy, are we?"

She finished her cashews and flew out the window. I was glad to see her go. Then I heard a soft knock at the door.

"Come in. It's not locked." I just couldn't rouse myself to open it for whoever it was.

Because it was precariously perched at the very front of her head, sticking out over her face, Tessa's hair preceded the rest of her into the cottage where she stood observing me.

"Taken to your bed, I see," she said. "At least that blasted bird is out."

"What is it, Tessa? I'm really not feeling well."

"I know that. Why do you think I'm here? They told me to come over and educate you about just why you're—ahem—experiencing lady problems."

"Who told you?"

"Aunt Augusta and Emilio, of course. They know about your little pester fester spell. That's why you've been hit with cramps and all."

"What do you mean?"

"I mean ... they mean ... you can't go around hexing people without suffering some consequences yourself. When a witch acts with ill intent, the ill will snaps back like a rubber band, so be careful how you choose your targets, and be sure of your intentions. Of course, if your intentions are positive—if you're using your magic to help someone or to save someone or for other positive purposes where your intentions are in service of the greater good—then you won't suffer any ill effects and may even enhance your power."

"No one told me that."

"Well, I'm telling you now. And if you behave yourself, they told me I can remove the effects of your faulty intention."

She moved closer to my bed and spread her arms out. I shut my eyes. Knowing Tessa's past attempts at spells, I could only hope she wouldn't replace my uterus with a frying pan.

"Be gone this curse when I finish this verse." She sat down on the floor as if exhausted. Her hair moved to the left side of her head and she took a deep breath. "There. I did it."

"Yes. Thank you. Tessa. I feel better already."

"They want you up at The Manor now."

I should have figured she hadn't come by just to make me feel better.

Tessa led me to another room I'd not entered before. It looked kind of like a cavernous library but also like a laboratory of some sort. There were walls of books, but they were all enormous tomes that barely fit on the shelves. Along one whole side of the room were the kind of stands you might see to hold oversized dictionaries. I'd seen one of those before at a big public library. But these stands, lined up one after the other, had huge books—some closed, others opened showing strange writing, symbols, and images. I couldn't get a close enough look to try to decipher any of it. In the middle of the room, a long table had beakers and bowls and measuring devices, and I also saw lit Bunsen burner-type things, sort of the kind we used in chemistry class in high school, but these were taller and looked more impressive.

"Go on in and wait," Tessa told me. "They'll be here soon."

She vanished somehow and I was left alone in this odd space. I was about to try to get a better look at one of the huge, open books, but I heard Bauble's tinkling bell so I stayed put. He appeared, trotting happily up to me, and plunked himself at my feet, which is when Aunt Augusta showed up followed by Emilio.

"So, are we feeling better?" she asked me.

"Yes, much."

"And have we learned a valuable lesson?"

"Yes. I'll control myself from now on. It was just that Armand character was being so snotty and mean to me, I couldn't help wanting to get back at him."

"We have more important tasks for you. You mustn't squander your gifts on frivolity, especially when you're facing an existential challenge three days from now."

She led me to the long table, where flames suddenly spurted out of those weird burners. It felt like walking into a live caldera. Although I wanted to ask about a million questions, I kept them to myself, at least at that moment.

"Tomorrow, after class is over, we will make the drive down to Pasadena and stay at the Contessa's again," Emilio began. "That means today's lessons are the most important ones for you to learn. We would have preferred more time to help you through this transition; however, we are convinced this will work out."

It was funny how sometimes I noticed his Italian accent and other times I didn't. This was one of the times I did. But more than that, what he'd said made me feel edgy and unsure. I still didn't know what they expected of me—except for some vague idea that there was a guy named Zorn who was dangerous and that my father needed rescuing. But there were no details attached to that. At least not yet. So I waited, my stomach knotted and my brain racing to places better left in darkness. If I was being honest with myself, at that point all I wanted to do was run away someplace that felt safe, for things to be like they were before I'd learned I had these powers—when my life was only filled with the dissatisfaction of being Foxy's daughter and relying for my dinner on her scatter-brained schemes. But there I was with no way but forward. So I sucked it up and listened to what they wanted me to do.

They led me to the table in front of the flaming burners and, before I was really aware of what I was even doing, the flames in front of me died. With one wave of my right hand, they soared up and up; then, with a wave of my left hand, they died down again. They taught me incantations which, when I repeated them, made the flames burn a bright blue and then back to an orange glow.

"When you go up against Zorn, your weapon is fire. He is terrified of it and, with it, you can reduce him to a blubbering mass with no power at all. His power is in words, phrases, the tones he uses, and the fear he instills, in the way he finds weakness and exploits greed. He makes promises—empty ones—but that sound, in the way he presents them, as if he's a kind of godlike savior," Aunt Augusta was telling me, as I learned how to manipulate the fires in front of us.

"But the fire is already here," I told her. "What if there is no fire to begin with?"

"Then you must create your own fire."

With that she clapped and all the burners went dark. I wanted to know more about this Zorn creep, so I tried to ask questions. But before I could get the first one out, Aunt Augusta came over to me and took both my hands and turned them palm-up.

"Repeat these words, very softly," she said. "Through these palms, a life force that sparks a flame will appear when I say this name."

I did as she said but nothing happened.

"Now say the names of those you want to save."

"What names?" I asked her.

"When the time comes, you will know what names to add."

"And then what?"

"The fire will appear. Let it run its course until you and the named ones are safe."

"And then what happens?"

"It will die out on its own. But for the moment, add whatever name or names you choose."

I felt incredibly stupid even trying this, but she was insistent. So I stood back, turned my hands palm-up, and repeated the spell.

"Through these palms, a life force that sparks a flame will appear when I say this name." And then I added the name: "Tessa."

Flames erupted from all the burners and spread like a cloud together. The room heated up, and suddenly Tessa stood in the doorway, looking confused, her wayward hair all tangled as if she'd been asleep. The minute she stepped into the room, the fires died out and the room cooled. I stood there with my mouth open, dumbstruck at realizing what I could now do.

"But suppose there are no burners like these when I need to do this?"

Emilio spoke then, "There is always fire ready to come to life. You won't need the burners or anything else. The fire is in you. It will be there when you need it. We know Zorn is deathly afraid of fire. It will defeat him as long as his goon patrol is also neutralized."

Somehow that was a less-than-comforting thought. But I had no choice by then. And the other questions nagged at me, so this seemed like the time to get them out into the open.

"Where is Zorn?"

"He stays within the confines of his institute, only sending surrogates out to do his bidding."

"And what's so awful about him?"

Emilio sat down on one of the stools at the fire table. "It began when he was cast out of the Hebrides. He is an unscrupulous user and predator. He will use any means to control and then debase his followers. His protectors are paid well, so he holds that over them. And he carefully selects men who also have no principles, morals, or conscience. He abuses anyone in his control, including children. He uses young women as a harem to provide him with fresh victims he can groom for his needs. I cannot think of one redeeming quality to ascribe to him."

"So this is a cult, right? What about my father? How did he get roped into it?"

Aunt Augusta spoke up, "We're not sure about what happened. There are missing years when we tried to trace him but never could find him. And then we heard he had been located within the Zorn Institute. There was one story that he had entered to try to save someone else inside. But by then his powers were so deteriorated that, instead, he was captured by Zorn, who may have been systematically draining your father's power for his own use. We surmise he threatened to harm the person your father had wanted to save."

"Who was that person?"

"The Contessa just informed us that she's heard it was the mother of your friend, Nick." Emilio said. "We have not verified that yet. But it could be the case."

"And what do you expect me to do about all this?" I was feeling nervous again. Now that the power to create fire was a past accomplishment, I was not at all sure how I could possibly rescue my father, along with Nick's mother, and get us all out alive. It also occurred to me that Nick would have to know what was going on if I was even going to attempt this weird escapade. How—and if—that could happen was a mystery.

Chapter Twenty-Six
I Cannot Run from Destiny

My sleep that night was full of strange dreams and a
feeling of foreboding. I woke up feeling tired, as if I hadn't
slept at all. I had to drag myself to morning class, where
Chef Emilio was already set up and about to start the lesson.
Wispy Clare looked at me with her eyebrows raised as if
questioning why I was so late, but I just went to my station
and tried to concentrate on the ingredients in front of me.
We were all making the same thing, so there was no greater
or lesser difficulty and we were all in the same stew pot, so to
speak.

The assignment was ratatouille with potato boulangère
and sole en papillote. Baking anything in paper was new to
me, but Chef Emilio demonstrated all the steps. So far, we'd
learned the basics of French cuisine, but in the second
semester we'd be exploring Japanese and California recipes.

Emilio included a culinology science lesson as part of
this class—listing the health values of all the ingredients we
were to use. I tried to clear my head and concentrate on the
cooking tasks but, just before we began, in walked Armand.
I was too in my own head to notice that his station had been
prepared for his return. He went quickly over to stand next
to Wispy Clare, keeping his head down. As he inspected the
ingredients in front of him, he looked up for one moment
and glanced right at me. Once again, I saw the red glow in

his eyes. It lasted only a couple of seconds, but it was surely there.

We all went to work—cutting vegetables, oiling our pans, seasoning our sole, and wrapping it in parchment. Pretty soon the scents of ratatouille and garlic filled the kitchen. The fish was last to go into the ovens. When we were all done, we each arranged our meals on the supplied platters and garnished with parsley and sprigs of fresh rosemary. By the time we had finished the lesson, we were ready for lunch. But before we could sample what we'd made, Mr. Batchelder arrived for the tasting and grading. He brought three bottles of white wine and poured himself a glass. Then, with fresh forks in hand for each student's platter, he went from station to station, tasting each in turn—from fish to potatoes to ratatouille. After each tasting, he made notes in a little book and then took a sip of wine to clear his palate before going to the next. Eight stations. Eight tastings. Emilio watched from a corner.

When he was done, he spent about five minutes calculating the scores in his little book. Then he wandered around the kitchen until he came to station number eight and placed a small blue ribbon next to my platter.

"Excellent," he beamed at me. "Truly superb."

Then he went to Wispy Clare's station and placed a red ribbon next to her platter.

"Very good job," he told her.

Finally, he turned to address the class. "You are all to be commended. You're making very fine progress, and I encourage you to keep at it. Next week you'll be assigned to come up with meal plans based on what we've done so far. Look at the bulletin board in the hall for what categories fall on which days. We will have no class this afternoon, so I say,

'Eat up' and enjoy the fruits of your labor." He left chilled wine bottles for us.

Wispy Clare brought her platter over to my station and poured us each a glass of wine.

"Congratulations," she said with a grin. "But next week, I'm going to win at least two days. I'll beat you yet, Amanda."

I laughed and ate what I'd cooked. It was really good and made me feel a lot better than I had when I first got to class.

"You looked awful when you got here," Wispy Clare told me. "Why were you late and what have you been up to?"

"I just had a bad night. Trouble sleeping and bad dreams. I don't know why."

That was a lie. I knew why, but I couldn't tell her about what was going on beyond class. I was glad we had the afternoon off. I needed time to sort through everything Aunt Augusta and Emilio had told me.

"You know," Wispy Clare said as she swigged more wine and polished off her sole. "Chef Emilio gets better looking with every class he teaches. I wonder if he's married. What do you think?"

"I think it's not a good idea to fantasize about a teacher who's probably, like, twice our age."

"You're probably right," she nodded and sipped her wine. "And I shouldn't pry into a friend's life, but I get the distinct feeling something is going on with you besides cooking classes."

"That's silly."

She wagged a finger at me and winked. "I won't tell anyone about your secret life beyond class. As long as you don't spill the beans on me."

I laughed at her and put out my hand to shake on it but suddenly remembered the leaf still in my palm and just hoped shaking hands wouldn't send her into orbit somewhere beyond Neptune.

I finished eating and told her I had some errands to run. I got the feeling she was going to ask me to go to a bar later, but I didn't give her the chance. Any other time, I would have been into that. But not this weekend. Not with what I was facing. It was dawning on me that maybe they still hadn't told me everything. I decided to go up to The Manor and find out what else was going to happen.

It was long before sunrise and was still dark outside. Emilio opened the door at The Manor. I hadn't expected to see him there.

"Come in. I thought you would come back. You want to know more about our upcoming trip, don't you? Aunt Augusta warned me you would still be reluctant. We understand that, but you must know, the path has been laid out and there's no stopping it now. We can discuss it more on the drive to Pasadena."

I stepped into the hallway, and he could see on my face that I was not going to wait until we had already left to find out more. I shook my head.

"No more half explanations. If you want me to agree to go, I want to know exactly what's going to happen."

He led me to the cavernous laboratory. This time there was no fire and only the two of us. We sat on tall wooden stools at the long table, and he turned to me with a look I had not seen on his face before.

"You did very well in class this morning. And without any spells or magic of any kind. You have a natural talent for the craft. And I was relieved to see that you resisted any desire to inflict a spell on Armand."

He stopped talking, seeming to know I had a question about that.

I've never been good at keeping my thoughts or feelings to myself, probably because, growing up with Foxy, someone had to stay level-headed, and I was the designated adult—or at least the practical one.

"Speaking of Armand, when he looks straight at me and I catch his eye, I see them as red. But I know they aren't red."

"Ah, cara mia, so you do see that, too? It is part of your special gift, of which you have many."

"So what is it? Something with my eyes?"

"No. It is that part of you that can see inside the soul. You are sensitive to those who would do you harm. You see it in their eyes."

"But why would that Armand guy all the way from France want to harm me? It makes no sense."

"He knows you are talented in the kitchen, that you are his competition, and that he cannot beat you with the recipes but only by undermining your confidence. But he has no idea who you really are."

"No one else does, either. I can't tell anyone, and that's very hard. It's not a secret I want to keep."

"The day will come—and soon—when you will be able to reveal yourself to a special one."

"Nick?"

He nodded and folded his hands on the table.

"Now, tell me: What else do you want to know?"

"Suppose I refuse to go to Pasadena, that I don't care about rescuing my father? I mean, I don't know him. He never even tried to find me. He left my mother with nothing. Why is he even worth saving from this creepy Zorn?"

Emilio looked up at the ceiling, where we could see blue sky through the glass skylight above us. He took a long time before answering. I waited, expecting to hear how I had to use my gifts for good and all that. But so far I only half bought that argument. I still thought I could walk away from all this if I chose to and just continue school until I landed a job at some restaurant or bakery. I still thought this was some weird life detour and my true track was through food. What could be better than a life where I could use what I loved to support myself and bring nourishment and enjoyment to other people?

"I am sorry, cara mia, but you cannot run away from this—how shall I call it—responsibility. You see, because, from generation to generation, children carry the burden of their parents' decisions. You, like all children, carry within you what your father decided was best at the time. If he had stayed with your mother, it would have been to destroy you, a baby who had no resources to save herself. His gift, his energy, his very being would have been adrift, leaving him prey to any kind of exploitation or worse. He left to save you and your mother. I know that is hard for you to accept. But he knew you would carry within you the line of powers you now possess. And that it would one day blossom and grow.

"There is so much sadness and pain in this world; the powers and gifts you've been given must not be squandered on parlor tricks but to ease that pain whenever and wherever you can. Not that you are expected to be a saint, but that you use your gifts to some higher purpose—because that will enhance and strengthen them. Otherwise, you risk the gifts working against you.

"And the first steps in using your gifts for good are to free your father and Nick's mother from the grip of Zorn."

I listened and stayed silent. It was so much to absorb, and I tried not to fight against it because I was slowly realizing that would be futile.

"And what about Zorn? What am I supposed to do about him?"

"He remains inside the Institute, for the most part, to stay clear of any interruption or scrutiny of what he's doing. He's clever at evading the law and keeps his apostles close to him, guarded at all times and subservient. He supports his system by cleaning out the wealth of converts and also by trafficking in all sorts of illegal activities, both online and in the public arena. Because he uses cutouts and fake and stolen identities, so far it's been impossible for law enforcement to do anything about him. And without complaining witnesses, they have no first-hand corroboration of what he does and how he operates."

Before this, when they had told me what they wanted from me, it all sounded rather nebulous. But now I was getting the whole picture—or at least more of it. I may have been naïve, but I wasn't a complete dolt. This Zorn character sounded like a terrible thug with the ability to brainwash his so-called disciples. It was a bad combination.

"Nick was correct about the Pasadena farmers' market on Saturdays," Emilio went on. "Zorn sends two of his goons and four converts to stand at the stalls and sell the products they create. Trinkets, amulets, books on the benefits of joining the Institute, and wearable tokens that supposedly impart magical powers to wearers who've gone through Institute training. This is one of his recruitment venues. He holds these all over the country and we understand he is even expanding to Canada and Mexico.

"The Contessa has arranged for you and Nick to have a stall near theirs at this market. We understand that one of Zorn's favorite stall workers is, in fact, Nick's mother, so she will likely be there."

I interrupted him, asking, "But what do we do? Kidnap her, or what? We can't just march up to her and say, 'Run away with your long-lost son now.' I'm sure the goons would stop us and maybe even take some revenge on her when she's back in their custody. And what if they attack us?"

"The Contessa has a plan. There is no way to take them all on directly. But if you casually stop at their stall and show interest in the Institute, they'll surely try to get you to come back to the compound for a more detailed explanation and a personal tour. To get inside is the only way you can reach Zorn. We understand that he personally meets every interested potential convert. He would take one look at you and immediately want to convert you. He does it initially with drugs and sex before he begins the brainwashing system."

Okay, this was sounding more and more sketchy. And dangerous. And the very last person I was interested in having sex with was some cult scammer.

"How do you propose—that is, if I can get inside the compound—that I find my father and get him out? And, by the way, why is it so important to rescue him anyway? I mean, you're not exactly suffering, and none of the others seem to be, either. What's so important about him to you?" I shrugged.

Emilion turned away and stepped down from the stool where he'd been sitting. He walked a few paces away from me and then spun around. I'd never seen him confused or upset before but now he seemed to be struggling with some inner turmoil.

"He is my half-brother," he blurted out. "I made a promise to our own father before he died to find him and save him."

I was truly stunned by this. "That means you are my uncle—er half-uncle. And you've known that all along. Why didn't you tell me before? I really am family." I felt myself blushing, although I tried to hide it. Then I thought, What else don't I know? I was about to ask, when Aunt Augusta breezed into the room with Bauble hopping along behind her, his little bell merrily tinkling with each bouncy step. All of a sudden, I felt I was in some other worldly reality show where nothing is what it seems and everyone in it is really someone else, including me.

"I've spoken to the Contessa," she announced. "It's all prepared. When you get there tonight, she will give you the details. Until then, Amanda should pack and get ready for the drive south. And keep me informed as events transpire."

Chapter Twenty-Seven
I Face the Inevitable

I was up at dawn. The faint pink light from my open window cast a glow across the big four-poster bed where I had slept on our last trip. The orange cats had come into my room sometime during the night and were still curled next to the pillow where my head had left a hollowed-out form. That night, at midnight, the equinox would begin and, according to Emilio and Aunt Augusta, that's when my power would rise to its strongest.

I decided to give it a test. Since I hadn't hexed anything in a few days, I decided to try levitating some small object. Looking around the room, I noticed a brightly colored glass paperweight on a little side table. I concentrated on it and pointed my finger and simply thought about it floating up from the table.

Nothing happened, but the cats woke up and stretched the way cats do: paws extended, asses in the air—all three of them at the same time—and then jumped down from the bed. I watched them circle the foot of the bed and then wander slowly to the little table, where one of them leaped up and, very slowly, carefully, with definite intent, pushed at the paperweight until it came right to the edge of the table. With one last gentle nudge, over it went. But, instead of falling to the floor, it stayed suspended in midair.

I pointed at it again and crooked my finger.

"Come to me across this space, for I would like to see your face," I whispered.

It floated across the room to my upturned palm. I held it there for a few seconds, smiling to myself and, when I looked at it closely, I saw not the brightly colored designs inside but a man, dapper looking, wearing a tweed jacket and carrying a cane with a brass knob on the top. As I examined it, he seemed to me to be sad. Then he turned his face to look up and—yes—he winked. I knew right then, this was Jack Wiltshire, the same as the picture in the locket I had worn since the day Bauble had dropped it into my hand. The tiny iridescent leaf he had left with me had worn away, but this was mine forever. I touched it. So my power was there, if I needed it. This weekend, it would be strong and steady. However, this was a simple test. I wondered if I could do anything really difficult. I replaced the paperweight and picked up my phone to text Nick. On the drive down, we'd texted back and forth, and he'd agreed to meet me at the farmers' market.

C U soon, yes?

I waited, but my phone didn't ping. So I concentrated and thought, "Wake up, Nick, and do this trick."

Ping, he answered. *Yes. C U soon. Xcitd*

The Contessa had lots of local contacts. Besides the crew that maintained her landscaping, there was a greengrocer who delivered her fresh food and a butcher who found her the best beef and poultry and a fishmonger with contacts on boats.

She had a cook and a driver and a handyman, named Horace of all things, who looked like he was once a longshoreman, with huge biceps covered in tats.

After another grand breakfast laid out for us on the sideboard, the Contessa led us outside, where Horace pulled up to the house in a big red pickup with a German Shepherd calmly seated in the passenger seat. He told me to climb in the back and sit down on a stack of burlap bags next to crates of tomatoes and avocados. There were also collapsed tables and chairs stacked along one side of the truck bed, jugs of water, and a sun shade to cover our stand.

I must have looked skeptical, because Emilio nodded to me and went over to speak with Horace. I couldn't hear what they said.

"He'll watch out for you," the Contessa told me. "He's been with me for ages." She patted my arm and helped me into the back of the truck, then said, "Remember, there are spell casters with specific powers and a rare few who can harness all the spells, hexes, and powers. You, Amanda, are one of the few who have them all within you. When the time comes, do not be afraid to use everything you are, everything in your power."

"Aye," Horace yelled out the driver's window. "Off we go."

It surprised me that he had a British accent of some kind. The dog barked once, and Horace gunned the engine. I lurched back against the tables as he drove off through the gates, which closed slowly behind us. It was weird watching where we'd been instead of where we were going. I kept my head down in case we passed a police car, as this certainly was not an authorized way to ride in a truck. I should have been nervous but, instead, I felt excited, like I'd been preparing for this my whole life and finally I was going to get in the game. Plus, I was going to see Nick again. I had no idea how it would happen but, by the end of this day, he would know who I really was. Whether he could—or would—accept that was unknown, and that was the one thing about what I was heading into that made me feel queasy.

It looked like any farmers' market. Stalls and tables, most with some kind of canopy for the hot Southern California sun. People in overalls and jeans, sneakers, T-shirts, hats, and sunglasses. There were some families with kids milling around. And lots of produce of all kinds. Each stall had a hanging scale to weigh fruit, and bags nailed to some wood for people who didn't bring their own bags. One stand had live chickens in plastic crates. And one was selling canaries. I wondered how Quetzal would react to that. She'd probably let them all loose. From my experience with markets, this one was pretty large. I counted more than thirty stands before I could even see the end of them. Three stalls down from ours, two beefy guys with shaved heads and arms crossed stood on either side of their stall—just watching, from what I could tell.

Horace parked the truck behind our designated spot and helped me down from the back. I had to hold onto his arm. His bicep was too big to fit both my hands around. It was like grabbing a tree trunk.

He unloaded our tables and chairs and set up the stand with our own canopy for shade. It was my job to unload our produce and arrange it in some inviting way. As I unpacked the avocados and tomatoes, I found a lot of other saleable items that I hadn't seen at first. Baskets of hand-made soaps, scented candles with shells embedded in them, little ceramic birds holding place cards for a table setting. It was an eclectic mix, and I wondered how the Contessa had pieced it all together. But, more important, I wanted to find Nick, so I texted him the number of our stall.

Seated behind our table, waiting for buyers and browsers to show up once the market officially opened, I surreptitiously glanced over at the stall where the two bouncers stood guard. I suspected that was the Institute's table. I could see some leaflets stacked up. There was no one I could see actually stationed at their table to sell anything. But in the back I spotted a large, black SUV with windows tinted so dark it was impossible to see if anyone was inside.

"Hoi, Miss," Horace had quietly come to stand by my folding chair, the Shepherd at his side. "You want to be careful of that lot." He nodded in the direction of the Institute's stall. "A bad business all 'round that bunch." He stroked the dog's head with his giant sausage fingers.

"I know," I answered under my breath. "Where are the people who sell their stuff, though?"

The Shepherd growled a little.

"What's his name?" I asked, looking down at the dog.

"Duke of Gloucestershire, Miss. Ee's a good old boy who'll keep you safe."

It seemed the Contessa had set up more than a stall for me.

Nick arrived just as cars started parking, and people began wandering the stalls looking for products and produce. I spotted him looking for our stall and waved so he'd notice me.

"Hey, you," he grinned and hugged me tightly. "Missed you."

"Me too," I said. "This is Horace."

Nick reached out his hand, which looked like a baby's hand next to Horace's.

"And this is Duke of Gloucestershire." I pointed at the Shepherd.

"Duke, my man." Nick reached under Duke's muzzle and held it while he stroked the dog's head. I swear Duke smiled at him. It was obviously love at first sight. Duke's tail wagged like crazy.

"I'll do a little reconnoitering, Miss, if you don't mind," Horace nodded at me and off he went, followed by Duke, now leashed with a harness around his chest.

"So?" Nick raised his eyebrows. "Are they here?"

"Three stalls over that way," I nodded in that direction. "I've only seen those two bouncers so far, though."

"I brought this." He reached into his jeans pocket and pulled out a piece of folded paper. "It was in the packet of papers Maxine left for me. It's a picture of my mother. She took it with a long-range lens, so it's not as clear as it could be."

He unfolded the paper and we looked at it together. A woman of maybe fifty, with graying brown hair to her shoulders, dressed in what looked like some kind of prairie dress, buttoned in front, the skirt down to her ankles. Over the dress was a kind of loose smock with square front pockets. The dress was open at the neck, and it appeared she was wearing some kind of slender chain.

"Do you remember her at all?"

235

"Yes. She looks older here. It's been almost five years, but it's her."

He looked torn, like he wasn't sure what to think.

"I've been studying this picture for the past week. I just don't know how I feel about it. Or about her. How does a mother leave her son like that? I can understand if someone's unhappy in a marriage and wants a divorce. But just to disappear with no explanation ..."

"Was she unhappy in their marriage?" In all the times we'd spent together and talked, this had never come up. I was surprised Nick had brought it up now.

"I didn't think so at the time. But hell, I was fourteen. After she left, my dad did find a whole bunch of books on spirituality and finding peace and how to get in touch with your true self. Maybe she was searching for something and she felt she couldn't tell anyone about it. I don't know."

"What if she is here? Would you want to reconnect with her?"

"Yes, if only to get some answers. I've been carrying this around for too long. It's been nagging at me the whole time."

I didn't know what to say to that. But there was a much bigger unrevealed secret, and I had no idea how to let him in on it without wiping out all the confidence he had in me and ruining our relationship forever.

A woman stopped at our stall to buy five avocados. Then another bought some of the soaps. Nick and I were busy for a time. More and more people arrived, parking their cars in the big lot and walking around the stalls, browsing and buying all sorts of items. It got so busy I didn't notice that, by then, the Institute's stall had three people answering questions and handing out pamphlets. When I did look over, I saw Nick's mother. I was sure it was her. She looked just like the woman in the picture. I nudged Nick and looked sideways over at her. He followed my glance and, when he realized it was her, grabbed my hand and squeezed it hard.

"Oh God, it *is* her. I remember. What do I do now?"

The look on his face was something I'd never seen before. Confused, tentative, a little afraid; this was not the Nick who'd always been sure about what he wanted and didn't want.

"What if I just go over there and confront her? I mean, what can she do?"

"It's not what can she do, but what would those thugs do? She's probably there against her will by now."

"You mean it's a cult and she's a captive? What the hell? How can something like that happen? I'm going over."

He started to walk around from behind our table, but I took his arm to hold him back.

"Nick," I leaned in and spoke in a low voice to be sure I had his attention. "I have to tell you something. Well, really, quite a few things. Things I've been keeping to myself since I came out here and started school. Maybe this isn't the best time for this, but I don't know what would be a good time. Besides, seeing your mother here, like this, well, you have to understand some things about her situation, about where she's been and what danger there is. For her and for you—for us."

He stared at me as if I was insane.

"What are you talking about?" His eyebrows raised and he shook his head, as if to say I was making no sense. "What danger? Like she might not want to see me?"

We stood there as people wandered by, and some stopped to see what we had to sell. I felt like I was waiting for some sign that would tell me how to proceed. My mind whirled with the possibilities. If I began with, *Well, I'm a witch and I have amazing powers*, or, *The cult your mother's in is dangerous, and my father's been held captive by the same one, and I'm here to free him*, or, *I don't know how to tell you everything, so let me start with why it's dangerous*.

While I considered all these, some woman bought two candles, and I had to wrap them in tissue paper, make change, and put them in her bag. And then a man and his son bought six avocados. Nick gave them change and then turned to me as no one else stopped at our stall for the moment.

"Well? Is that the danger? Are you saying she might not want to see me? If that's it, I think I can handle it. She's been gone all this time and I haven't exactly melted away. If that's the way it is, I can accept it. I just want to know. For sure. And then I can move on."

"I don't know how she'd feel about seeing you. What I do know is I doubt she knew what the cult was at first. And maybe she still doesn't realize it. But it's a dangerous place run by someone named Zorn. That's what The Zorn Institute really is. It pretends to be an enlightenment center, but the people who go into it never come out. At least not alive. And he milks them for money and other stuff—ugly stuff, bad stuff."

"How do you know all this? That wasn't even in the report from Maxine."

Now he looked belligerent. I hadn't counted on that. Nick had always been so reasonable. So thoughtful. I'd counted on his reason, his math brain.

"Nick, you're a scientist. I know you base everything on provable facts. I understand that. But there are things in this world that defy proof and defy facts." I took a deep breath, knowing that would not be the end of it for him, knowing that he would ask more questions, demand more answers, and want proof of anything I told him. I raised a hand to stop him before he began questioning what I had told him.

"Nick, do you trust me?"

It was the simplest question and yet his answer would tell us if we had any future.

He looked at me for a long, excruciating time without saying anything.

"Yes," he said finally. "I don't know if I trust you because I love you or if I love you because I trust you. But either way, they're inextricably joined."

Okay, how to make a girl melt. Nick could totally write that book any day. At that moment, without warning, I felt all the power that Aunt Augusta and Emilio had said would come to me with the equinox. I knew then what I had to do to proceed.

"Then will you believe me when I tell you I want to free your mother from the grip of this cult and the one who controls everything about it? And that I need your help to do it?"

I thought he would take time to think about that, ask me more questions, want facts, but instead he just said, "All right. I'll help you. What do you need me to do?"

I figured the only way into the Zorn Institute would be to pose as a convert, so I would have to stop in front of their stall and pretend to be interested in spiritual growth. After all, it was called "The Zorn Institute for Enlightenment and Self Fulfillment." Some scam. Enlightenment, my mother's

Prada purse! So first I had to sell out all our merch. Which gave me a good way to test my post-equinox powers.

While Nick tended to a customer buying two candles, I closed my eyes and whispered, "Let the people at this market choose our stall as their target."

It worked and, in less than a half hour, we had sold out of everything except a few squished tomatoes. Horace started stacking the empty crates into the back of the truck. Duke milled around, sniffing at the ground.

"I'm going over to their stall," I told Nick.

"I want to come with you."

"It will be dangerous for your mother if we let on that we recognize her," I replied. "I plan to pose as interested in the Institute. I'll engage them in conversation. But don't let on that you know her, or they'll shut us down. I have to get inside, so I'll try to get them to invite me to meet Zorn."

When I said that name, Duke growled and lifted his head. It was like the cats at the Contessa's.

Nick looked skeptical. He took my arm and turned me toward him.

"I don't like you going over there alone. This is my problem. It's *my* mother. I can't expect you to take this risk on my account. If you think it's so dangerous, I should go with you. If anything happens, there'll be two of us, and they wouldn't take us both on. Besides, I can yell for Horace."

I wondered, at that point, just how much I should tell Nick about my father—and about me. If I didn't tell him, then that trust he had might just evaporate. But if I did tell him, the same thing might happen. Or he might demand proof or just laugh at me. *Well, this is where the rubber meets the road*, I told myself.

Horace came to stand with us. "Hoi, Miss—Duke and me, we'll keep a watch on you for sure."

"What's going on?" Nick looked at Horace and then at me, obviously suspicious and worried. "Have you told me everything?"

"Let's go sit in the truck." I led him to the truck's cab and we climbed in. I sat in the passenger seat and stared straight ahead. How to begin? This would not be easy. But there was no way I could do what I had to do and still keep what I was a secret. How could he love me once he knew? How could he ever trust me after I told him? He might find it too unfathomable to believe and might think I was a lunatic. But, I figured, sometimes you have to take a leap into what's impossible to predict, so that's what I decided to do.

"Nick," I began tentatively, trying to find a way to start that wouldn't shock him all at once. "This is going to be hard for you to hear and even harder for you to accept."

"Just tell, me, Amanda. Is it about my mother?"

"No and yes. Remember what we went through back in high school, when I was this sort of invisible girl?

"I remember a lot of things. But you weren't invisible to me."

"I know. And that helped pull me out of the shell I'd always been inside, like some turtle hiding from the world. Well, there are things in this world that are hard to believe but that *do* exist. Things that are hidden from view. People who are not what they seem. Or, to be precise, who are much more than they seem."

"Like what?"

"You're a scientist so, for you, I guess, what I have to tell you will be even more difficult to hear, much less accept. All I ask is that you keep your mind open and then try to understand."

He looked skeptical already, but he said, "Okay, I will."

I almost felt guilty for being so sure he'd fight the fact of what I was and all that had happened. But if I had any hope of saving his mother and finding my father and freeing both of them, I had to forge ahead. So I told him. Told him everything that had happened since I first arrived at school. I blurted it out without stopping. I talked and talked, and he never said a word or interrupted me. It was a relief to finally let it all go.

I tried not to look at him and to just keep talking, but I couldn't help it. I had to know how he was taking all this information, all these crazy stories—because that's what they were. Even though I knew everything had happened just the way I was telling it, still, a part of me felt as if I was retelling a movie I'd seen. When I did sneak a glance at him, his eyes were wide and he looked as if he was about to jump out of that truck and run away. But he didn't. When I finally stopped, finally got to the end—to where we were right then and what I had to do—he was silent. So I waited, and hoped, and held my breath for as long as I could.

And finally, *finally*, Nick spoke.

"You know, I've been at Cal Tech for over a year now. I've studied physics and chemistry. I've learned about the solar system and what's beyond it and how to launch rockets and satellites and how black holes operate. And so far, what I've realized is how little we really know about anything. The more we find out, the more mysterious this universe is to us. We have no idea what's beyond our knowledge. We don't know what happens beyond our galaxy or beyond any other galaxy. I mean, how far does space go? Does it curve back in on itself and come back to meet us? Are we anything but specks of dust in a vast, spinning, gaseous soup? I can't imagine that humans are the end of a chain of life. Humans are too flawed to be the ultimate goal of creation—if there *is* an ultimate goal. I wonder about the perfection of the physical laws that govern everything. And I wonder if what we call the universe is but one of an unimaginable boundaryless chasm of spinning gases without end—constantly dying and beginning in a cosmic time warp.

"You tell me you have powers beyond my imagining. And I tell you, there is no 'beyond imagining,' because nothing is beyond possible."

He stopped and I was even more stunned than I can say. We sat there in silence. He never once asked me for proof of what I'd told him. Never once expressed doubt. I guess I had to learn not to prejudge people, especially the ones I loved.

Chapter Twenty-Eight
I Realize My Power

Just before I got out of the truck, my phone buzzed. It obviously wasn't Nick, so I figured it was probably Wispy Clare.

"Oh God," I said when I saw who it was. "Not now."

"What is it?" Nick turned the phone in my hand to see. "Foxy? What does she want?"

"Of all the times to suddenly find her motherly instinct." I shook my head. "What am I going to do?"

"She says she's just finishing at an estate auction in Pasadena and wants to fly up to see you at school after that."

"This is awful. I can't deal with Foxy and all this at the same time."

I'd summoned Emilio that one time, but I'd never made someone disappear. If I tried it, something might go completely haywire and Foxy could end up in Mongolia or somewhere on Mars. I couldn't just hex her memory away so she'd forget me. My mind raced with options, and then Nick took the phone from me.

"What are you doing?"

"The logical thing."

I watched as he poked the forward command and typed in Emilio and then in the text space typed HELP!!! In all caps.

"How did you know I'd have Emilio's number?" It was stunning how he figured things out.

"It's logical."

Then my phone buzzed with Emilio's answer.

What a pleasure this will be. Don't worry. I shall occupy the lovely Foxy...

"I'll bet," I said. "Foxy will be all over him and his Ferrari like whipped cream on a strudel."

I thought it would be hard to get them to invite me to the Institute but, as soon as I stopped at their stall, they swarmed me in seconds—pushing pamphlets at me and telling me all about the miraculous, life-changing enlightenment I would find through the practices and teachings of their founder and leader, Zorn. I acted as if I had come to a crossroad in my life and was looking for a spiritual path, something to follow that would give me peace and security. I made up a story about quitting school and how my parents had tried to bribe me to stay with a new BMW and a trip to Europe. I swear I could almost see dollar signs flashing in their eyes hearing about my rich parents.

Of the four people—minus the two bouncers—at their stall, only three women engaged with me, telling me about their own journeys and how meeting Zorn changed their lives. They were dressed in identical white smocks over some kind of ankle-length gray dresses. Nick's mother never said a word or even looked at me. Nick and I had agreed he would hang back and wait to see what happened. If I went with them, he and Horace would follow at a safe distance since they knew where the Institute was, so I'd left my bag and phone in the truck cab.

Nick's mother kept her head down, but I caught her eye a couple of times and could feel the psychic pain she was suffering, almost as if she wanted to warn me against these people but couldn't. I assumed Zorn's followers were zealous and dangerous. She seemed like a caged animal that had lost its will to break away. Once she reached up and touched the hollow of her throat and I thought I glimpsed a gold chain under the fabric of her dress.

I looked through their books and read a few sample leaflets and then asked a lot of questions. They answered every one with the same party line: "When you come to the Institute, Zorn will tell you everything you need to know."

I kept nodding as if I was ready to accept just about anything they told me, and finally I said I would like to meet Zorn and hear his message.

They told the goons standing around to load up the van and, in no time, we were all piled inside—with me sandwiched between two of the women. The market officially closed at two so, by then, most of the stalls were packing up to leave and all the customers had gone.

No one said a word on the short drive to the Institute. As we crawled up the long entryway, I could see walls surrounding the building. It was built like a fortress. And I sensed, rather than saw, an electric field around the perimeter and noted quite a few video cameras following us toward the entrance, where there was a tall gate with a keypad to open it, plus a speaker. The goon driver gave a password and then punched in a code. The gate slid noiselessly aside to let the van through. It closed immediately and I had the distinct feeling of a prison where, once you passed through, you wouldn't get out.

One of the women told me I had to be properly prepared to meet Zorn. She led me down a series of corridors to a windowless room where there was a cot and a bare light bulb. Laid out on the cot was the exact clothing the three women wore. She told me to undress and change. Then she left and I heard the door lock. Of course, that was no impediment to me. I felt my palm itching where the little iridescent leaf had stuck. To be honest, I couldn't wait to meet this Zorn character. He was in for some fun. And not the kind he was used to perpetrating on others.

I changed and waited for them to retrieve me. Meanwhile, I tried to sense where they might be hiding my father and Nick's mother. I tried to imagine what it would be like to finally meet my father, but it was such a blank that I gave up. I figured this place probably had dozens of well-camouflaged, secure rooms that would be hard to locate. I closed my eyes and concentrated. I saw more corridors, doors, and windowless rooms. I saw a stage and chairs. And I saw a walk-in vault filled with treasure: gold bars, jewels, money—stacks and stacks of it—and a huge bronze box of some kind that had no obvious way to get into it. And guns. Many guns. I thought I would have to neutralize those first and then try to locate my father. As I was imagining a plan, I heard the door unlock and the three women entered and told me to follow them. The smocks they had been wearing at the market had been changed to bright red smocks and black shoes with canvas soles that were silent as they walked. It was all creepy, for sure, but they must be leading me to some initiation ceremony where I'd have to pledge all my wealth—ahem, I had none—and possibly my first-born male child and drink the blood of a wombat, if I was any student of initiation rites, which I wasn't. It may sound like I was taking this all as some gigantic sitcom but, let me assure you, my stomach was doing flippity-flops and my palms felt like I'd just come out of a steam room.

Then, after all the dark corridors and twists and turns, there was light. Bright, white, California, afternoon sunlight flooding a huge open pentagonal plaza with a walkway around its perimeter and doors, lots of doors, leading off the walkway. The entire plaza was made of blazing white marble, which reflected the sunlight like a satellite dish looking for alien life. In the middle was a round reflecting pool with a stacked stone construction over which poured mini fountains of blue water. In the very center of the pool, raised above the water, an eternal flame flickered red with blue at the edges.

Standing there, atop a sort of platform of carved bronze, was the master himself: Zorn. And in the background to all this splendor, eerie music that sounded like distorted pan pipes played in a monotonous loop.

If they weren't all taking themselves so seriously, I would have busted out laughing. This was the guy terrorizing everyone? He was tall, maybe six foot five, and lean. He wore a toga-like thing draped over his shoulders, and sandals like he was some senator in ancient Rome. Or maybe he fancied himself the emperor. It struck me that these guys who had a need to control other people always saw themselves as the center of the universe surrounded by what they considered the trappings of power and wealth. This pentagonal structure was obviously a nod to the Masonic Order, meant to bestow secret powers on its benefactor, the great Zorn. I thought about the Contessa's art collection and what a paltry and pathetic place this was by comparison.

The women led me to the foot of his bronze altar, from which he stared down at me with an intimidating look. He brushed the women aside with a wave of one hand and stooped down to see me more closely. I should have been sizing him up while he was staring down at me but, instead,

I was thinking about how to find the two people I'd come to rescue, while at the same time wondering if Nick and Horace—and Duke—had reached the gate by then. It had certainly been enough time, so I figured they were waiting for some signal from me.

"You have found the Zorn Institute because you wish for a spiritual awakening," his voice boomed.

I could tell he was good at mesmerizing anyone receptive to that sort of thing. But I could not be easily taken in by it. My palm itched as I considered the possible paths to thwart him. But first I had to figure out where Nick's mother and my father were being held.

"Let me lead you to that wondrous place," he went on. "I alone can create for you a new beginning that enriches you beyond your wildest dreams, as I have done for countless others who now kneel at the altar of enlightenment.

"But first," he raised a finger in the air as if making a momentous proclamation, "you must have a new name that suits your spirit. And that name will be ... Pleasing. You will live up to your new name by pleasing me in every way I desire. You may begin by ascending here and taking my hand in yours."

At the same time as this name changing was happening, I noticed not only the two goons who'd stood guard at the market, but four more emerge from behind some of the doors at the edge of the plaza. They moved in closer to the pool and eternal flame. And then, from another door, two more beefy types walked forward, carrying what could only be described as a wedding bed. Festooned with lace and flowers, it was covered in a blood-red satin sheet with multiple pillows of the same color. As they carried this bed, the three women in red smocks joined them in a procession to where I now stood at the base of Zorn's bronze throne.

"Ascend, I say to you, Pleasing," His voice boomed over the monotonous music.

Okay, I thought. *This is where I get off the train. But how?*

I knew that, the minute I hexed even one thing, the whole place would come crashing down—on me. But I had to start somewhere, so I quickly crossed my fingers and whispered ... *May the gate outside this place open like a smiling face.* As soon as I finished, I uncrossed my fingers and hoped for the best—that Nick and Horace and Duke would soon be inside with me.

But then I had other concerns, as the women in red and the muscle-bound goons were approaching me with grim expressions. They looked as if they'd been drugged already and seemed determined to convince me to obey the master. One of them held a rather large syringe, which meant the time had come to begin using my power. At that moment I heard a ruckus beyond the plaza with the fountain. I assumed it was Nick and the others, so I touched my palm and pointed at the syringe.

"May that needle turn blue and its contents turn to glue."

Zorn didn't seem to notice what I was doing. He reached out a hand to me and said, "Ascend, Pleasing, and become one with me here on my throne. Let me show you the way to eternal joy and wealth."

He motioned to the women in red and they moved closer to me, the goons carrying the wedding bed. Then they laid it down in front of the throne and came toward me as Zorn descended, his hand outstretched to take mine.

Remembering I could create things, I raised my right hand and said: *Close the goons like birds in a cage and take them all offstage.*

A cage appeared and clanged shut around them and, poof, they were gone. Then I turned to the women in red. They all stood there, mouths open in amazement, looking to Zorn to tell them what to do.

"What is going on?" Zorn roared. His face contorted and he raised his arms above his head. "Grab this girl," he shouted. "She must be dealt with immediately."

I touched my palm again and pointed at the three women: *Release them from bondage to find safe passage.*

They ran to one of the perimeter doors and disappeared, leaving the door open. I heard Duke bark, so I knew Nick and Horace were now inside.

I turned to Zorn and pointed at him. By then he was screaming commands at everyone, as more people poured through the doorways surrounding the open plaza. And then, I saw more goons run in, waving assault rifles and, in an instant before they could fire, I pointed at one gun and shouted:

Turn guns so hot they cannot be shot.

The goons yowled as the guns turned red hot. Then I pointed to them and said:

Cage them as birds with feathers just like the others.

When they were neutralized, I turned to the others, as Zorn stood on his throne ranting—his eyes blazing red, arms raised, preparing to grab me. I ducked back and ran around the bed, putting it between us. At that moment, Duke ran into the plaza, barking and growling.

All the people left were too stunned to do anything but scatter out of Duke's path.

Take him down from that throne and turn his feet into stone,
I yelled over his voice.

At that moment, Horace burst into the open plaza,
followed by Nick. They stopped when they saw Zorn stuck
on his throne, twisting to get free.

I reached for my locket and held it out to Duke, then
popped it open and said, "See this man? Find him for me,
Duke. Go!"

He looked at the image, sniffed the air, looked at Nick,
and bounded off, with Nick running to keep up.

Zorn waved his arms around furiously trying to break
free of the rocks at his feet.

"I'll kill you when I get my hands on you," he railed at
me.

It was pointless to waste any more time on him, but we
still had to find Nick's mother.

"Where is the other woman? The one from the
market?" I came up right in front of him and demanded.

"So, you need something, do you?" he sneered. "Set me
free and I'll tell you where she is."

The others who had emerged from behind all the doors
milled around mumbling, frightened, and cowering.

"Horace, herd them up and get them out past the gate,"
I said.

"What will happen to these others, Miss?" Horace
pointed to the caged goons.

"I'll take care of them," I told him. "But leave Zorn to
me."

"Aye, Miss," he nodded and began to push the others
out of the plaza to the other side of the compound. They
were all too frightened to disobey him. Besides, they were
used to being told what to do, so they behaved like sheep in
a meadow hounded by a Border Collie.

"You can't," Zorn yelled. "Bring them back here. They belong to me ... to the Institute."

"People don't belong to other people, you big fraud," I told him, hands on my hips. "Now, tell me where she is or I'll take this whole place apart and leave you to rot in your own rubble."

"Set me free and I'll bring her to you."

"I'm not as gullible as those others, you blowhard. I'll give you until the count of three to tell me where she is, or that fire in the fountain will turn into a raging inferno with you standing right here in the middle of it."

He gasped as I pointed my finger at the flame in the middle of the cascading pool.

"Who are you?" he bellowed? "Who sent you to destroy me?"

All I could think about at that moment was something I'd read in senior high history class about despots from the past. Without the encouragement and support of people around them, they are small and powerless. That they derive power from the people who support them, especially those closest to the power center. When that support is stripped away, or abandons them, they fall apart from the inherent weakness they feel inside.

"When I count to three ... through these palms a fire will appear when I say the name—'Jack Wiltshire.'" I looked at him dead in the eye and counted "ONE, TWO ..."

"She's locked in the room next to the vault," he yelled. "Stop counting."

I raised both my hands and recited, *Unlock the door by the vault, and send Nick his mother without fault.*

"And now, Mr. Zorn—or whatever your real name might be—this is your last stand. You will never again imprison people or use them for your own selfish purposes. This is the end of the line for you."

I pointed to the boxed-up goons and said: *Move this crate outside the gate.*

Once it was gone, and that plaza was empty except for Zorn and me, I felt a strange rumbling under my feet. The fountain began to act funny—water running faster and spilling over onto the marble floor. The rumbling got more intense, with a sound like runaway trucks racing downhill and, even though I'd not experienced one since arriving in California, I thought it must be an earthquake. Slabs of marble cracked under my feet, and the stones holding Zorn in place began to loosen their grip on him. It seemed to go on forever, rumbling and cracking and splitting. I didn't know whether to run or stay in place, but the staying in place got more difficult with each second that passed.

I was no Richter scale, but this upheaval seemed to be pretty strong and not something—even with my heightened powers—I could do anything to stop. While the ground beneath me shifted in weird ways and I looked for a place that might be sort of safe, I caught a glimpse of something that made scrambled ground seem like a minor blip. To the right of Zorn's throne thing, emerging from a large fissure between two slabs of marble, I distinctly saw a hand—or at least the bony fingers of one. And in a second, I could plainly see the ulna and radius bones attached to that hand.

But that wasn't the end of it. More bones began to appear—too many to be from just one body—and, as the base of the throne shifted to one side and then wobbled, it looked like it might topple over from its own weight. Even with everything that was happening, it was clear that this earthquake had dislodged a secret burial ground beneath where Zorn performed his rituals. It was just about the most ugh thing I could imagine, but it also became clear to me what had to happen, since it looked like soon he would break free. I knew what I had to do.

I paused just long enough to search my soul and then pointed to the flickering flame that still burned red and blue in the sloshing fountain.

Jack Wiltshire, I yelled to be heard above the rumbling and cracking, *be free of this curse, and find your power be not reversed.*

Beneath my feet, a giant fissure appeared as two slabs of marble collided. I jumped aside just as the flame burst up and spread like an oil spill across the plaza, flames licking at everything in its path—water from the fountain now aglow as flames licked outward and reached Zorn, who screamed and finally broke free of the stones. He tried to run, but the fire caught him and, although he dove for the water, it was also ablaze.

The ground stopped rumbling as abruptly as it had started and I ran, leaving the destruction, the bones, what was left of the building, and Zorn, behind.

Well, as you can imagine, firefighters found the remains of Zorn's work, and the police set about identifying the bodies they discovered. The news was all over it. Gruesome details sell papers, after all. From what I could tell, they couldn't figure out who Zorn actually was. Some people are good at completely burying their beginnings, and no one would have thought to find him in the long-ago history of the Hebrides—and would have looked upon that as folklore anyway.

The converts freed by our invasion would have a hard time facing what they'd been through, but there are professionals who help people in those situations, and the deprogramming would soon begin. How they would rebuild their lives was up to them, but at least they were no longer captives of a dangerous cult.

With Duke again sitting in the passenger seat, Horace drove off in the truck. Nick and I sat in the front seat of his ancient BMW and we helped Nick's mom and Jack Wiltshire into the back, headed for the Contessa's estate. No one talked. I don't think any of us knew where to begin or what to say. As for me, I was trying to figure out how I felt about actually finding my bio dad. I think Nick was in shock about everything. I hadn't even told him yet about the bodies or instigating the fire, and it seemed as if he had no idea what to say to his mom. I could understand that—especially after the way she'd left with no explanation. So he and I were in almost the same situation, and after all that had happened, that was another bond for us.

The Contessa stood outside the open front door when we arrived, hands clasped together in front of her, looking every bit the grand lady, the three cats at her feet, fluffy tails straight up.

"Come in, come in," she waved at us.

We were some raggedy-looking bunch, I have to say. I know I was exhausted and certainly looked a wreck, not even wearing my own clothes. Nick's mom was still wearing her white smock over a prairie dress and kept her head down, seemingly waiting to be told what to do. Poor Nick looked flummoxed and had no idea how to communicate with her. As for Jack Wiltshire, well, I finally had a chance to look him over. I have to say I was not surprised that he was a good-looking, sandy-haired man, with bright blue eyes and an easy manner. He helped Nick's mom out of the car and held her arm to steady her as they walked slowly toward the Contessa. I couldn't tell if he even knew who I was—and I didn't know how he would react when he found out—but I was in no hurry for that.

"Jack Wiltshire," breathed the Contessa, "you haven't changed one bit. Still the country gentleman." She came down the steps to meet them and held out her hand. Jack took it and bowed slightly.

It was a scene from a play, if anything, carefully choreographed—yet the wardrobe mistress must have been drunk when she'd picked out the costumes. Nick in jeans and a Cal Tech T-shirt that had some complicated equation splashed across the chest, and me in what those women had made me change into and sneakers that were all filthy from the earthquake, fire, flooding, and dust from the rubble. Jack Wiltshire seemed to have been outfitted in a hospital ward, wearing something that resembled scrubs and what looked like canvas slip-on shoes, battered and stained.

"Contessa. A pleasure as always. May I introduce this lovely lady, Mrs. Vera Weyland. We've been through quite a lot together." He didn't seem at all fazed by his appearance, which I found odd, but somehow in character.

Well, I thought Nick was about to keel over watching this scene play out in front of us, but he surprised me by approaching the Contessa as she extended her hand to his mother.

"Welcome to my home. Mrs. Weyland. I'm so pleased you could visit," The Contessa smiled graciously as if we'd all been invited to high tea.

Okay, that was not the way I would have handled the situation, but then who would have thought any of us would ever be here together? I caught up with Nick and touched his hand. He jumped as if a rattlesnake had bitten him.

"And you, Niccolò, so happy to see you again. Please, everyone, come in and make yourselves at home."

As I looked back at the driveway, I noticed Emilio's Ferrari was missing, and then I remembered Foxy's text. *Oh right*, I thought. *Emilio with Foxy. I don't have to guess how that's going.*

I hadn't realized how smoothly the Contessa could handle people in distress. I guess that's what they mean by *noblesse oblige.*

I wanted to talk to Nick alone, but that seemed like it wasn't going to happen, and it was clear that neither of us had any idea how to approach our parents—or if they even knew they *were* our parents. Nick's mother looked so beaten down that any abrupt move might just turn her into a pile of sand. And Jack Wiltshire, well, whatever he had suffered in that lunatic cult wasn't obvious, but I was sure he must have some injuries, if only psychic. I wondered if spells could fix those. Or if he had any spells left in him.

The Contessa had thought of everything. From fresh clothes in each guest's room on the second floor to private baths with luxury amenities and even shoes in the correct sizes laid out for us. We followed her directions and, when a maid I'd never seen before knocked on my door, I felt refreshed and altogether like a new person—which surprised me because I'd expected to be totally worn out from my mission.

The Contessa and Aunt Augusta had a really heartwarming reunion. Turned out, they hadn't seen each other in over a hundred years. I expected to hear: "But darling, have you had work done? You haven't changed a bit." But, no, that didn't happen. They hugged and chattered and sent me to the kitchen to show everybody what I'd learned so far at culinary college. Even Tessa was there to help, although I was afraid she might turn the main course into a bucket of pig slops. Still, she had on a crisp white uniform, and her hair, for once, stayed up on the middle of her head. I suspected super glue.

I created prawns in chunky guacamole, with cherry tomatoes and chives paired with a Vermentino from Italy, a grapefruit sorbet palate cleanser, snapper with shallots and oyster mushrooms en papillote with a side of garlic-roasted new potatoes paired with a Mediterranean Picpoul de Pinet, mixed baby greens salad with gorgonzola and pecans, and, for dessert, I reproduced my winning croquembouche from class. Finally, a dry Sauterne and then coffee accompanied by a giant bowl of whipped cream.

This dinner proved to me that well-prepared food served in the right atmosphere can be a restorative experience. It showed me once again why I loved to cook and how great it feels when people enjoy what you make.

When Tessa served the appetizer of prawns, Jack Wiltshire and Aunt Augusta seemed to be toasting their reunion. Nick, sitting next to his mom, looked absolutely shocked when, as she was served, his mom leaned over and I heard her say, "I saw you at the market. I wanted to say hello but I couldn't then. I hope you can forgive me someday.

And thank you for helping me." Well, Nick's face went from shock to surprise, to confusion all in about two seconds.

The Contessa stood with her wine glass in hand. "Thank you all for being here. And I toast all the people who have found freedom and each other."

The meal continued, and the more wine we drank, the merrier we became. Before dessert was served, Jack Wiltshire stood up, wine glass raised, and we stopped chattering to let him speak.

"I am, perhaps, the luckiest person at this table tonight. Well, maybe one of the luckiest. Being held captive robs you of more than freedom. It robs you of human dignity, which all of us deserve. But, and I hope this good lady doesn't mind me saying this, it is a double indignity to be used as a pawn to coerce another person into bondage. So I am lucky to be free, and we are both eternally grateful to all these people for coming to our rescue. But I am lucky in one other even more important sense.

"Amanda," he raised his glass to me, "I did not know you when you came into this world. And now, to find you here—the courageous, beautiful, indomitable young woman you are—fills me with such richness of spirit that it is impossible to describe. I hope we can spend time together, get to know each other, and come to understand what it means to find a family you never knew you had. If it is true that healing can result through the efforts of others, then you have truly healed my soul."

It turned out I had been way off about Jack Wiltshire.

After he sat down, leaving me completely speechless, Nick's mother spoke. Still seated, but with her head raised so we could all hear her.

"I have a lot to make up for. Lost time. Lost experiences. Lost opportunities." She looked at Nick. "But I want you, Nick, to know that I never stopped thinking about you. The one thing from my previous life that I kept during these years was this."

She reached under the blouse she was now wearing and pulled up a gold chain with a locket. She slid the chain over her head to take it off and held the locket in the palm of her hand. It looked eerily like the locket Bauble had left in my own hand.

"Please," she said to Nick, "open it."

Nick took it from her and, when he clicked it open to look inside, he stared in stunned silence.

"It's me when I was just a kid," he said softly. I remember when this was taken. I'd just learned how to ride my bike."

I could see tears building at the edges of his eyes. He tried to hold them back. Tried mightily. I wanted to hug him so bad. But I knew then that healing would be possible for Nick and his mom. And that I would get to know Jack Wiltshire. Maybe his powers would be restored, too. It was all going to be all right. Or at least as all right as anything ever is.

It was hard to realize only two short weeks had passed since I'd landed in San Francisco to start a new life. That left the rest of the school year for Nick and me. Even if that meant weekends and vacations, it would be enough. And no one could say how long we would be together or how far our journey would take us.

Chapter Twenty-Nine
I Define Family

Nick bought me a plane ticket to get back to school. It was an easy flight. I wasn't even in the air long enough to think through everything that had happened. Jack Wiltshire and Nick's mom stayed at the Contessa's. She said it would be good for her to have some company until they got their lives sorted out. I decided it would be too dangerous all around to tell Foxy about any of it, and I hoped Emilio had steered her far off course.

On the way to LAX, Nick was quiet until he asked, "What do you think 'family' means?"

I wasn't at all sure how to answer.

"I mean," he went on, "is family what you're born into? Or is it a feeling you have?"

Finally, I said, "Families aren't neat and tidy. We don't live in a candy-box world. You can't taste every piece and discard the ones you don't like. You just have to take it all and make the best of it. Sometimes, that's more than enough."

Maybe things would change in the future. For me, at that point, maybe life was not what I'd always hoped for but, like I told him, it was enough. Finally being part of a family felt right, and Nick had a family now, too. I hoped it would be enough for him.

I ran into Emilio as I walked back to feed Quetzal after class on Monday.

"Ah, cara mia, I am sorry to have missed the reunion with your father and Nick's mother, but your lovely mother and I enjoyed a fabulous dinner in San Diego at Addison."

"Am I supposed to know what that is?"

"As you progress in your culinary pursuits, it will be important to know the great restaurants of the world. And one day, perhaps, you will be able to sample them all."

"What happened to Foxy?"

"You know she is not the kind of woman to pass up a chance meeting. I arranged for us to sit next to a well-known and recently divorced billionaire. I believe his yacht sailed from San Diego for Puerto Vallarta on Sunday morning. I am told there was a beautiful lady aboard with him."

So Foxy had no plans to visit after all. I wondered how much shopping she could get done from a yacht.

After that, I happened to scroll past a headline about the Institute on my cel feed. It detailed the fire and that it looked as if an earthquake had hit the building, but that no earthquake had struck the rest of the area that day. The story said it was a mystery what had happened but that the local police had been looking into The Zorn Institute for more than a year. One thing it noted was that an enormous sealed bronze vault had been recovered, but so far no one—not even expert safe-crackers—had been able to find a way to open it. It had been carted off to a warehouse until forensic experts could figure out what it was.

Maybe one day I would pose as a forensic expert and get that thing to reveal its secrets.

One day ...

About The Author

L B Gschwandtner is the multiple award-winning author of eight books under her own name and two books under her pen name, Bea Alexander. Her novel, *The Other New Girl*, was a USA Best Book Awards winner and received an honorable mention from Reader Views Literary Awards. You can see all her books at lbgschwandtner.com.

Website: Lbgschwandtner.com
Bluesky: @lbgwriter.bsky.social
Facebook: www.facebook.com/LBGschwandtner
        & Bea Alexander Author
https://www.facebook.com/profile.php?id=61571339319956

Books By Bea Alexander (pen name)

Escape To Zendara (dystopian love story with multiple plot twists set against the backdrop of a corrupt city)

Books by LB Gschwandtner

The Other New Girl (Teenagers in trouble at a Quaker boarding school)

The Wish Granters series: They'll grant a woman one wish; the rest is up to her.
Shelly's Second Chance (The Wish Granters, Book One)
Carla's Secret (The Wish Granters, Book Two)
Emma's New Love (The Wish Granters, Book Three – Coming Soon)

The Naked Gardener (a woman gardens naked then goes on a wild canoe trip with gal pals)

Page Truly and The Journey To Nearandfar (a fantasy for middle graders who love adventure and imagining what might be)

Maybelle's Revenge (short stories with a twist)

Foxy's Tale (mother/daughter angst with vampires)
    Coauthored with Karen Cantwell